Praise for the Hebrew Edition

"*The Prophet of Tenth Street* could serve as a basis for a Woody Allen movie: introspective characters, a New York arena, Jews and gentiles, occasional quotes of selected excerpts from the literary canon . . . Many readers will identify with Keller's characters."

— Yaakov Yoseph, *Yedioth Ahronot*

"Marcus Weiss, the protagonist of *The Prophet of Tenth Street*, is a man obsessed with books, and 'his' authors. His girlfriend, Gina, constantly tries to bring him down to earth and show him what real life is all about . . . His interior world is rich, and his literary knowledge and respect for the written word are admirable . . . One enjoys the richness of Keller's language, her descriptive powers, and the complex shaping of her characters."

— Osnat Blayer, *Ma'ariv*

"Keller's cinematographic descriptions bring to mind Bergman, Antonioni, and even Andy Warhol . . . Marcus Weiss is an intellectual, with an acute self-awareness . . . Marcus longs for a simple, primal human contact . . . His girlfriend, Gina, radiating her femininity, her libido, attempts to get him to live the everyday, the here and now in Manhattan, the most exciting and stimulating cultural center of the modern age . . . *I think, therefore I am*, seems to be his motto."

— Reuven Miran, *Haaretz*

The Prophet of
Tenth Street

The Prophet of Tenth Street

— A Novel —

TSIPI KELLER

excelsior editions

State University of New York Press
Albany, New York

Cover Image: Michael Falco
Published by
State University of New York Press, Albany

© 2012 Tsipi Keller

For information, contact State University of New York Press, Albany, NY
www.sunypress.edu

Excelsior Editions is an imprint of State University of New York Press

Production by Eileen Meehan
Marketing by Fran Keneston

Library of Congress Cataloging-in-Publication Data

Keller, Tsipi.
    The prophet of Tenth Street : a novel / Tsipi Keller.
        p. cm.
    ISBN 978-1-4384-4208-2 (pbk. : alk. paper)
    1. Jewish men—Fiction. 2. Interior monologue—Fiction. 3. Life
cycle, Human—Fiction.   4. Psychological fiction.   5. Jewish fiction.
I. Title.

    PS3611.E43P76 2012
    813'.6—dc22   2011025876

10 9 8 7 6 5 4 3 2 1

Grateful acknowledgment is made to the following for copyrighted material: Excerpt from *Juan the Landless*, by Juan Goytisolo, translated by Helen R. Lane, published by Serpent's Tail (1990), and reprinted by permission. Excerpt from *The Piano Teacher*, by Elfriede Jelinek, translated by Joachim Neugroschel, published by Serpent's Tail (1991), and reprinted by permission. Excerpt from "Response to a Request," from *Walk*, by Robert Walser, translated by Christopher Middleton, published by Serpent's Tail (1993), and reprinted by permission. Excerpt from *Mr. Palomar*, by Italo Calvino, translated by William Weaver, published by Houghton Mifflin Harcourt (1983), and reprinted by permission. Excerpt from *Madam Bovary*, by Gustave Flaubert, translated by Eleanor Marx Aveling, published by Wordsworth Editions Ltd (1994), and reprinted by permission. Dan Pagis's poem, "Written in Pencil in the Sealed Boxcar," is translated by Tsipi Keller, with the permission of Ada Pagis.

WRITTEN IN PENCIL IN THE SEALED BOXCAR

here in this transport
i eve
with abel my son
if you see my firstborn
cain son of man
tell him that i

—Dan Pagis

Where books are burned, people will be burned.

—Heinrich Heine

One

Where should he begin? With anti-Semites? A subject locked in his heart? His veins?

He could open with the champion of civil liberties, the guardian of animal and human rights, the illustrious man renowned and admired the world over as a strict humanitarian.

From the pile of books on his desk, Marcus Weiss picks *Down and Out in Paris and London* and again goes over the hateful passages he has marked with a pencil.

It gets to him every time. The impeccable righteousness, the snub-nosed indignation of the young, well-bred Englishman. The nasal, clipped staccato, the distaste, the haughty aversion to everything Jewish: "The shopman was a red-haired Jew, an extraordinary disagreeable man. . . . It would have been a pleasure to flatten the Jew's nose."

The Jew. The perennial Jew. The infamously famous, the infamously culpable nose. The Jew, like a pest, is not to be rid of. A shifty, nasty lowlife who unscrupulously swindles the jolly, unsuspecting citizens about him. Just look at his eyes, his bulging Jew-eyes, his dark eyeballs, how they dart in their holes. Is it any wonder one thinks of rats when confronted with a Jew, his bushy eyebrows? One can tell, instantly, the Jew is up to something, cooking some unholy, yet kosher, scheme.

With two fingers, his heart filled with contempt, Marcus lifts the paperback by the edge of its cover and holds it over the wastebasket. How easy it would be to just drop it—a profanity of sorts, but how else can he settle accounts with Mr. Orwell? Mr. Orwell who had been his idol.

How painful the shock, the disbelief, when he first came across these passages.

He aches to dump the book, but knows he won't. He tells himself he might need it later on, for further quotes, but the truth is he could never bring himself to destroy a book. Not even a *Mein Kampf.*

He puts Orwell back in the pile.

These are words. Words on pages bound by a cover.

Dangerous words. Words that incite and legitimize hatred.

How he detests them, those who detest him. He regrets not believing in hell. If he believed in hell, he could wish Orwell to burn there, with the rest of them, for all eternity.

He is not a fanatic; he is just seeking justice. The Jews specialize in seeking justice.

Marcus takes off his reading glasses and rubs his eyes, the bridge of his nose. What is it about the nose that irritates them so? His own nose isn't large; it's aristocratically aquiline, as a matter of fact, if on the long side.

He likes his nose. Gina likes his nose. She has said, after cunnilingus, that she finally understands why Jews are so endowed, why they were chosen at Mount Sinai.

Gina is a Jewess who likes Jews, particularly the males, if only because they're good in bed, and are circumcised. She says Jews, born responsible, are reliable lovers, punctual in their needs and desires.

Aesthetically speaking, and she is qualified to speak—aesthetics is her business—a circumcised penis is more pleasing to the eye. In her opinion, this must be the naked truth behind the ritual. It was probably a woman, Gina is convinced, who had come up with the idea to cut away the excess skin—a swift and practical solution. And man saw that it was good, but later clothed the truth in verbiage.

When Gina talks about Jews, everything she says is like succor to his soul; it calms him.

Succor, he thinks, is such a Yiddish word.

Because of their special history, Marcus says, Jews have developed a talent for *mitleid,* compassion. From an early age he himself has taken on his shoulders the suffering and injustice inflicted on his people, and has carried in his heart their pain, their afflictions. They call to him from the grave: they want to reclaim their unfinished lives, the lives of their children.

He tells Gina: "We Jews don't love ourselves enough. We're insecure. We could never be successful enough. No matter how hard we try, we'll never be *them.* And we want so much to be them, although we don't want to. When it comes to PR we fall behind, we can't be bothered. Our martyrs do not acquire the status of saints—imagine all the saints we could have had! Millions of them. Those who died for *kiddush hashem,* and those who died because born into the wrong faith. But we do excel when it comes to holidays. Festive holidays, filled with songs that defy the goyim: 'In every generation they stand up to destroy us, and God saves us from their hand.' In our homes, our synagogues, how we love to sing these songs. Such harsh words, such catchy tunes. We remember them from our youth, when we learned to shout them at the top of our lungs."

"Look at our parents," Gina says. "The humiliations they suffered. And still, they counted themselves lucky. For the Jews in Europe, the word *lucky* took on a special meaning. My parents, you know, fled Romania on foot. You and I," she accuses, "never knew our grandparents. A whole generation deprived of its cushion, its security blanket. For a sense of self, parents are not enough. When I was little, my most fervent wish was to know whether or not my grandmother had been pretty, whether or not she had painted her nails red. My mother would say, Yes, of course she was pretty. Yes, of course she had painted her nails red.

"Our parents," Gina says, "were not the Wandering Jews; they were the running Jews."

Shoes, Marcus thinks. Jews and shoes. His parents, too, had to flee, with him, still a baby, in a satchel. They fled Germany, and never again, not even once, repeated a word in their mother tongue.

At his desk, Marcus looks up the term, the Wandering Jew.

According to a medieval legend, the Jew had insulted Jesus and was therefore condemned—conveniently, one might add—to wander the earth until Judgment Day.

Who was it that said that trees have roots, Jews have legs.

He dials the New York Public Library; he needs to find out when and where the term *anti-Semitism* originated. He wonders how it happened that such a fancy term is applied to something so base. What's wrong with the simple and direct, anti-Jewish?

The line is busy. Marcus tries again—it's still busy. Of course, he reasons, anti-Jewish is too overt and, in modern times, one needs to camouflage and elevate his hate. It feels more respectable, even authentic, to be called an anti-Semite; it sounds progressive, scientific. What's more: it is cleansed of the mention of the Jew.

Marcus pushes the redial button. A sleepy male voice comes on the line, and Marcus, in the gentlest of tones, inquires about anti-Semitism. He thinks he detects a quick intake of breath on the other end, but knows he might be mistaken, it could be his overworked imagination; he is overly touchy, sensitized, always on the alert. When he reads, his trained eye spots, involuntarily, all the capital J's on the page. The word *jewel,* invariably, gives him a fright, and he has to stare at it for a while before he lets go. Only when he knows the author is Jewish, he relaxes his guard. Mostly he feels proud that a Jew writes about Jews—openly, without excuses. And even when he disagrees with the content, at least he doesn't feel he's been abused or violated.

Gina says he is not a true American, he takes most things too much to heart. He hasn't learned, she says, to ignore, with equanimity, the inevitable shortcomings of others. He tortures himself with questions, he doesn't know when to stop.

"Hold the line, please," says the librarian, and Marcus thinks: If he lets me hang on for an inordinate length of time, then I'll know for sure . . .

He gazes out of the window at the stark branches of the trees in the courtyard below. In the building across the way, all the windows are shut and draped. A shudder, a chill, runs through his body, as if to corroborate the information just processed in his brain: it is cold outside. It is warm and cozy in his study; it feels like a womb.

He is still holding. He puts the call on the speakerphone, to let the man know he hasn't been sitting there, like a schmuck, holding an empty receiver to his ear.

He wonders about librarians—what makes them tick.

He drums his fingers on the desk. During the summer, the windows he faces are friendlier: the drapes are pulled aside, and he gets to see a chair, a table, an elaborate lamp. He may reach for his binoculars and scan the windows for movement. He himself is on the twelfth floor, which affords him a full view of about forty windows. He doesn't expect much, just a stranger in a room, moving about, watering a plant or straightening up. When he catches someone in his lenses, he remains with them until they leave; then he waits for them to return, reflecting how oddly empty, deserted, a room seems after one has left it.

"Hullo?" his speakerphone interrupts his musings, and Marcus, suddenly remembering who he called and why, grabs the receiver, thankful that the librarian has come back on the line without disconnecting him.

The librarian is very helpful. The term, Marcus learns, first appeared in 1879, in an anti-Jewish pamphlet written by a German, an apostate half-Jew.

So there, he thinks. That's where he might begin.

Two

Marcus Weiss. Fifty-two years old, and still in good shape. He is five feet ten inches tall, and of slender build. Same as a girl's, Gina insists, especially around the pelvic area. One evening, as he comes out of the shower into the bedroom, she approaches him, staring intently at his pubic hair, as if confronted with something she's never seen before. Not now Gina, he thinks. We have to be uptown in half an hour. But she takes him by the hand and positions him in front of the full-length mirror, covers his sex with her hand and looks in the mirror. Something is still displeasing to her, something is still not right. She moves his penis to this side, then that, as if his maleness were in the way. He observes in the mirror how she handles his flesh. He notes the matter-of-fact efficiency of her long, cool fingers, and reflects, I love this woman, this dark-haired woman. Even if, or because, she fingers my sex as if it were a piece of tenderized meat she's about to toss in the oven. "Gina," he asks, forbearingly, "what are you doing?" "I want to show you something," she says, tucks his penis between his legs, peers at the result in the mirror. "Forget for a moment," she says in an absent-minded tone, a tone, he imagines, she employs with her clients who come for a fitting. "Forget for a moment what you've got down there and concentrate right here on the surrounding area. You can see for yourself how it is immediately apparent that the overall shape of your triangle is exactly the same as a woman's. It inspires a tenderness, a girlish tenderness."

"I don't know about that," he says, although he does begin to see the resemblance she is talking about.

"It does, it does," she says and releases him, resumes getting dressed. "It's perfectly normal," she continues, informing him that there's a neuter period during which all human embryos are female, and only later become male when male hormones are introduced. "Are you sure?" he asks. "Positive," she says. "It's called the undifferentiated or indifferent period." "I thought," he says, "it was the male chromosome." She regards him a moment, considering. She then regroups and says, "Perhaps, but not in your case." In his case, she knows for fact, some crucial combination was interjected just in the nick of time. Another minute or so and he would have remained a girl forever, bereft of his superior male credentials.

But his hands, his hands, she loves his hands. "They're definitely masculine," Gina says, "and very sexy." On this he agrees. He contemplates his hands, turns them over. Yes, they're good hands, expressive. And the network of veins, very blue and prominent, suggests an artist's, an otherworldly, sensitivity. His fingers are long and square-tipped; his nails are strong, blessed with a natural shine. Gina, who tends to bite her nails when tense or excited, envies him his nails.

But what he likes best is when she tells him she loves his voice. She says she hears his love for her in his voice, especially when they speak on the telephone.

To better remember what came first and what happened later, Marcus divides his life into befores and afters: the before and after Paris; the before and after he married Myra; the before and after he joined his father's business; the before and after their daughter, Rosina, was born; the before and after his divorce; the before and after his parents died; the before and after he sold his business and began working on his dictionary; the before and after he met Gina.

The before and after Paris—Marcus recalls with affection. His golden years as a foreign student in the City of Light. It was pure luck that landed him in the *quartier,* on the *rive gauche,* with all the students and artists. He was twice lucky for having a faucet, all to himself, in the privacy of his room, and triple lucky for having hot water as well. He shaved every morning in front of the small mirror, brushed his teeth, moved a wet cloth over his skin. Once or twice a week, he went to the public baths, for a real shower, or even a bath. He felt grateful for every moment, and often, walking the streets, he'd suddenly remember that he was actually in Paris and he'd marvel at himself, at his good fortune. He walked the same streets, frequented the same cafés as his famous expatriates; he lived on a street named Dante.

On the sixth and last floor of 7, rue Dante, life was shared and equal. Tomas, the German, was the indisputable leader. And for good reason: he had been there the longest, had the largest room on the floor, as well as a kitchenette. But most of all, he had a woman living with him, his own, twenty-four-hour woman, a tall, soft, honey-haired Yugoslav named Johanna, whose wide mouth caused traffic jams in Marcus's mind, especially when she smiled. He thought he would need at least two pairs of lips just to engulf her lower lip. She was motherly and sexy at the same time, and she moved so slowly, so nonchalantly, it tore at his heart. He thought she was a goddess, and observing her the way he did convinced him he was destined to be an artist. He noted her smallest gesture, noted the elegance, the tension, in her stretched fingers as she held a cigarette, between puffs, away from her face. Every day he hoped to get invited into Tomas's room, watch Johanna prepare a meal. For Tomas was generous that way, inviting friends to sumptuous, late-night snacks, the ingredients for which were mostly stolen.

Under Tomas's tutelage, they all became expert thieves. Tomas reiterated the rules: Never get caught in the same store twice: first offenders are let go by the store detectives without calling in the cops. Know your rights: If they catch you stealing and search your bag, they cannot confiscate goods you've stolen elsewhere; those belong to you, tags and all.

They shoplifted everything: food, clothes, books, records. When Marcus got good at it, he joined Tomas on thieving expeditions, often filling orders for friends who needed this or that. They were very near the top of the world: they attended classes at the Sorbonne. A student in Paris was king, the Latin Quarter his kingdom. Education was free, medical care was free, movies and transportation were discounted. But the best deal of all were the subsidized student cafeterias—the breeding ground for animated discussion and revolutionary talk. The cafeterias were spacious and clean, and the French matrons behind the counters were tidy, severe, but dispensed the tasty, five-course meal with a motherly mien. Marcus marveled at the generosity of the French who had taken him in, him and the thousands other foreign students. Tomas said that Marcus was naive, sentimental. The French had taken them in to extol the grandeur of French civilization, French thought. Their aim, in short, was propaganda: brainwash the foreign student in the French way. Feeling grateful, Tomas warned, was provincial, petit-bourgeois, traits Marcus had better get rid of fast. It's not a matter of gratitude, Marcus argued. It's a matter of reciprocity, of paying respect to the country that hosts you, that tolerates your thieving so long as you don't get caught in the same store twice.

They were choosy. For their late-night snacks they stole pâtés, caviars, exotic rice from the Orient; anything that came in packages or fancy jars. They took the stuff and brought it to Tomas's where the loot was assembled on the double bed for Johanna to feast her eyes and to decide the night's fare.

Day and night they roamed the streets, not only in the *quartier* and its environs, but everywhere, all the quarters, the plush ones and the seedy ones, in a mad and wild pursuit of their freedom. They got to know the city well, all its secrets, its ancient passages, its very narrow streets and alleyways. They got drunk on Montmartre, sang bawdy songs in one of the small cafés. They got drunk with the *clochards* down by the Seine under Pont Neuf, explored the wonders of rue Mouffetard. But most of all, he loved the sound of wheels on cobblestones. He loved to listen to the cars rumbling down the wide boulevards, along Les Champs Élysées, coming around Place de la Concorde, or La Place de l'Opéra. He couldn't believe such beauty, and he didn't care if Tomas was right about the French: he himself was sold on the French, on the way they crushed their R's, on the way they played *Flipper* in the corner bistro, swearing, *La vache!* The way they puffed their cheeks, threw their arms in the air, to indicate that some things in life were absurd and couldn't be helped. He loved their baguettes, their salad dressing, their rich milk. He loved their *boursin à l'ail,* and he devoured kilograms of their *céleri rémoulade.* He loved their ham, their *crêpes,* their *croque-monsieur* and *croque-madame;* and when he woke up early he'd go down to the café and have his *croissant sans beurre,* a hard-boiled egg, and a *demi-tasse.*

In time, except for his accent, he became French: he puffed his cheeks, threw his arms in the air, yet in his heart he knew he'd never achieve the fluency of mere kids; would never come close to the tough old men in the square, scarved and bereted, a stub of a cigarette dangling from their lips, feeding pigeons or playing *boules.*

Together with Tomas, he worked nights for a while at Les Halles, not only for the money, but for the "experience," hauling produce crates off trucks. For two weeks in the summer, he lived in a village near Bordeaux, picking grapes with the peasants and gypsies. He sneaked into the empty château of the local baron who owned the grapes, the village, and everything in it, and lost his virginity on the marble floor.

He learned a lot in France, he felt inundated. In his sixth-floor garret he wrote assiduously, in French, a little play about two clocks at a repair shop, discussing their lives and the lives of their owners. He leaned against his window and gazed dreamily at the slanting rooftops, the windows, the expanse of the sky, and breathed in the solemn serenity of a still life. He bought an easel and watercolors and tried to lift the landscape onto his canvas. But his hand, holding the brush, felt awkward, uncertain, inadequate, and the harmonious composition he saw out there and envisioned in his mind as the final drawing never materialized on the canvas. He thought he might write and direct movies, for he did, didn't he, always carry images in his head. And every so often, he did remark to himself, didn't he, that this or that image would make a good opening scene for a feature film. And when he witnessed something funny or sad on the street, he did, didn't he, instantly freeze the picture, enclosing it within the dark frame of a camera lens.

At other, less auspicious moments, it occurred to him that his artistic aspirations brought him too close for comfort to Frédéric Moreau, Flaubert's idle dreamer from *Éducation Sentimentale.* Life was enchanting, but once in a while he got a glimpse of what he thought must be the dark side of Paris when, on a gray morning, he and others watched, with great solemnity, as the police pulled out from the thick, murky waters of the Seine the drowned body of a young woman, wrapped her in plastic, and drove away. Unrequited love was his awesome assumption.

After three years in Paris he went back to New York and joined his father's business. He got married, had a child, became a successful businessman.

Years later, he returned to Paris for a visit and looked for his past. He had forgotten most of his French, but insisted on speaking it, errors and all. The old Latin Quarter seemed more crowded and, to his bitter astonishment, except for a few remnant patches, the cobblestones were gone, replaced by the smooth, uniform paving of asphalt. He walked around as if in a daze: how could they have done such a thing? Le Boul' Mich and Boulevard St. Germain had lost their charm. At the hotel, at cafés, he inquired of the French: Why? Why? And they looked at him, surprised at his question, then shrugged, smiled, said, *Mais c'est mieux, non?* It's much better for the cars. The cobblestones were very bad, *n'est-ce pas,* for tires, for drivers. Drivers prefer asphalt. But the beauty, he said, the beauty of Paris. They puffed their cheeks, threw their arms in the air; at least in that they hadn't changed.

He revisited the old haunts; incredibly, they were all there, untouched, except for Café Flore, which had revamped its toilets, installing shiny mirrors and brass. After digesting his disappointment over the cobblestones, he fell in love with Paris all over again, walking from morning to evening, noting with pleasure the lyrical eccentricity the French displayed when naming their streets: rue des Mauvais Garçons; rue des Bons Enfants; rue des Manteaux Blancs. For lunch he devoured a ham sandwich *avec crudités,* sipped a glass of beer, savored *le tabac brun* of filterless Gauloises. And every morning, at the hotel, as he woke up and lay in bed, listening to the soft, intimating voice of the radio announcer, he felt again the soft, gray melancholy of Paris tug at his heart. He reflected on how morning radio shows captured, and revealed, a country's, a people's, mood, its character. Especially so the French whose soft and musical tones stirred the soul of the foreign listener who years before, in his youth, felt he belonged, felt he was home.

Marcus sighs, reminiscing. During the three years after Myra and before Gina, he spent a lot of time with Oscar, his dear and old friend. He smoked and drank, was up at all hours, went out when he wanted to, shut himself up if he felt like it, without having to explain or report to duty.

In those, now distant, days he was happy to conclude that it was easy to get along with men, and that women only brought stress into your life. After twenty years of marriage, it was normal for him to assume that he knew something about women, but, as he began dating, he very quickly realized that what he had become accustomed to were Myra's idiosyncrasies. And those very same idiosyncrasies now made him suspicious of all other women, of their peculiar, often annoying, mannerisms.

Then Gina came and, like the good fairy in a story, changed everything. He eats healthy foods now, drinks in moderation, and when he craves a cigarette he sticks a plastic straw between his teeth. He sleeps regular hours, does yoga, and never misses his annual checkups. He never has heartburn. His bowel movements come easy, and he has learned from Gina to delight in them as the obvious and reassuring sign that all essential organs in his body are in top form. Yet every so often, when he lies on his back on the living room carpet, his legs drawn up to his chest in a strenuous stretch, the blood pounding in his face, he begins to talk to himself, saying things like, Get off the floor, you jerk. Who needs this? You'll get a heart attack.

At such moments he wonders how Gina has managed where Myra had failed. Was it Myra's wrongheaded approach, or is it simply the fact that he, like most men, has finally succumbed and placed himself in a woman's caring hands?

That's the key, he thinks. Caring. Myra endeavored to change him, not for his sake but hers.

When Gina is in a special mood, she stretches out on the couch and coaxes pleasant reminiscences; she invokes the past and distorts it a bit. A favorite with her is the night they first met at that awful New Year's party in SoHo four years ago. She says Marcus fell in love the minute he heard they were neighbors. She says he somehow sensed that she would insist on keeping her own apartment. And he, already well-rehearsed, says, No, *au contraire*. In those distant days, when he celebrated his freedom every night of the week, he would slowly retreat the minute he learned that the woman he'd been speaking with lived within a forty-block radius of his refuge on Tenth Street. No, he says. What attracted him to her was the yellow sofa.

"Oh, yes." Gina laughs as if she's hearing this for the first time. "The yellow sofa."

He first saw her thighs, one long, sheer-stockinged thigh crossed over the other under the black mini-dress. She sat on a bright yellow sofa, more on her side than on her behind, her body twisted to face the man she talked with.

Marcus had installed himself in a chair and gulped down his whisky, hoping to get drunk before midnight. Sadly he noted that, excepting Oscar, he knew no one in the huge loft; that he, the only guest who understood nothing and cared only peripherally about fashion or design, would have little to say to whomever he might engage in conversation. He scrutinized the men who, both in style and fabric, were as extravagantly clad as the women. No wonder, he consoled himself, that he felt out of place in his old-fashioned wool trousers and dark pullover.

And then he saw her—first her legs, then her face. By that time, he now thinks, he was pretty far gone. He muttered, soundlessly, "It takes guts to sit on such a yellow sofa." He considered getting up to look for Oscar and ask to be introduced to Long Legs, but then questioned the wisdom of such a move, telling himself he'd never get his chair back, it would be snatched as soon as he stood up. But he stood up all the same and went to her directly, like a somnambulist, the floor dancing before his eyes. And just as he was making his way to her, all around him the countdown chant to midnight began, and he, his ears ringing, still concentrating on her thighs as his final destination, stepped on her foot, and she looked up, her face contorted in anger and pain, and he, stepping backward, lost his footing and reached for support, while she, instinctively, reached up and held him, and he remembers thinking, God, she is strong.

Then they all kissed and hugged, and he stood there, an island of confusion, and watched Long Legs kiss the man on the sofa. She kissed him on the cheek, he noted, not on the lips. Then she stood up from the sofa and kissed him too, and as he felt the imprint of her full lips on his cheek near the temple, he thought, She's as tall as I. This will take some adjusting to.

As it turns out, Oscar, who writes about fashion, had known Gina for quite some time. "How come you never introduced her to me?" Marcus asks one night and Oscar shrugs. "I'm not in the matchmaking business. Besides, she and I aren't close, we just move in the same circles." A few nights later, lying in bed after their first lovemaking, Gina suddenly turns to him and says, "Oscar is gay, right?" "I don't know," Marcus says, a bit annoyed at the question. "What do you mean you don't know? I thought you were best friends." "We are," Marcus says, "but we've never talked about it." "Why not?" Gina asks. "Because," Marcus says. "If he'd wanted to talk about it, he would have." "But," Gina pushes on. "Aren't you curious? Don't you want to know?" "No." Marcus's irritation level rises. "I don't care. End of discussion, all right?" "All right, no need to get so uptight," Gina says and jabs him in the ribs.

Looking back, he is amazed that he'd allowed himself to employ such a raw, heated tone with her. Now, tamed and domesticated, he'd never dare.

Gina. Gina Bloch. Her sorrowful mouth. Her long, slender figure. The short hair, parted in the middle and falling to her ears. A face, he thinks, that is easy to draw, lending itself perfectly to the lines of a box: the straight line of the forehead, the short line to the cheekbone, the slightly angular line of the jaw, the square chin.

The round head he likes to cap in his hand, the long delicate throat. The very mobile dark eyes.

Here she comes. He hears the key turn in the lock. Even with locks, he reflects, Gina is uncompromising. As if a key, once held in her hand, should open all doors. He goes into the bedroom where, he knows, Gina will be changing into a T-shirt and sweat pants, but, to his surprise, Gina is spread-eagled on the bed, fully clothed. He admires the plethora of multilayered fabrics and soft hues, conceived and designed by the one and only Gina Bloch. He admires in particular the long velvety scarf, dark on the outside, bluish on the inside.

"Well, well," he says, bending down to kiss her.

"Unlace my shoes, please. I can't move."

"Of course."

"I work too hard." Gina stretches and yawns. "Five new orders came in today."

"Good."

"I don't know," she says. "I'll have to expand, hire another seamstress." She smiles contentedly. "Will you run my bath and make dinner? I stopped at the butcher's, you'll find lamb chops on the counter."

He has taken off her shoes, and is now unbuttoning her wool pants, anticipating the exhilarating sight of her white tummy, her white thighs. "Anything else?"

Gina laughs. "Yes. You can pour me a brandy and bring it in while I bathe."

Three

Most nights Gina sleeps over. In the morning, after she's run out, around seven-thirty, and quiet is restored, he gets out of bed, showers, and shaves. By eight o'clock he is at his desk with his first cup of coffee. He may, or may not, have a piece of toast with cream cheese and jam, but come eleven o'clock his stomach calls, and he goes into the kitchen to prepare a snack, what the British would call his elevenses. Around one or two in the afternoon, he'll have a bowl of soup, tuna salad, or whatever leftovers he finds in the refrigerator. Around five in the afternoon, he leaves his study and goes into the living room where he'll read or relax in front of the TV, while waiting for Gina. At any point during the day he may, or may not, go out for a walk.

Some mornings he is quick on his feet, eager to get started, eager to get past the chore of shave-and-shower, a wasted half-hour that contributes nothing, except perhaps an occasional, straying thought. But other mornings, a heaviness weighs on him, an apprehension, and for the first half-hour he is groggy, even miserable, feeling his life has no purpose, no direction, that he walks in it, in his life, as a minor guest who's allowed little or no say. He often wonders who and what controls his mood swings, and helpfully concludes it must be the food he ate the night before, which affected his digestion, which affected his dreams, which affected his sleep, and which affected his waking. At times, not too often, thankfully, he must enter Gina into the equation; Gina who had decided to disrupt his peace of mind and pick a fight.

This morning, after his elevenses of Quaker Oats, he gets his coat and goes out. Coming down in the elevator, he already feels like a freed man. He salutes the doorman and walks out to the street in a resolute step. It is almost noon. He imagines the lunch crowds in midtown and feels a sudden promise, a sudden uplifting. He wants to join them, mingle among them, even as an outsider.

He takes the uptown bus and gets off at Forty-sixth Street and Madison. He walks west one block and turns onto Fifth Avenue.

His heart expands. It is the season. The sidewalk is jammed with tourists, with Christmas shoppers. Women in furs and men in long overcoats carry large, glossy paper bags, containing wrapped packages.

He walks among them and feels for them. He imagines their anguish as they hunt and shop for the perfect gift. He himself is hopeless when it comes to gifts. In the four years with Gina, he has bought her a ring, which she wore for a while, then dropped in her jewelry box, not to be seen again. Myra made him go with her to her favorite stores, where she would point to what she wanted and he would take out his wallet.

So he feels for them. He thinks Christians try too hard.

Christians try too hard. Tomorrow night, he'll run this one by Oscar when he comes to dinner. After dinner, Oscar and Gina will plan the party Gina and Marcus are to give on New Year's Eve. They gave one last year and the year before that, and therefore, Gina says, it is now a tradition they must honor. Anything Gina does more than once, immediately acquires the venerable status of tradition.

Her parties, invariably, are a success. She calls them gems.

He is walking uptown, toward Fifty-seventh Street. Right ahead of him, he spots a family of four, strolling leisurely. Tourists, he thinks, out-of-towners. He walks in step with them, glimpsing their profiles. The man and woman are in their forties, their son and daughter in their early teens. All four are impeccably dressed, especially the girl in her sky-blue, bell-shaped coat, her black, patent leather pumps. The woman holds her daughter's hand, the father and son walk a little farther ahead. Together they present such a perfect package, Marcus feels a pang of sorrow: they seem so serene, noble, vulnerable. It is obvious to the observer that if life touched them, disturbed their fragile constellation, they'd be shattered.

He remembers his own Rosina and resolves to call her as soon as he gets home. Every time he calls, he gets the impression she can't wait to get off, to get back to her life. She is at Berkeley, but he knows better than to ask about her grades. She has told him, firmly, she has enough pressure as it is, without having to worry about pleasing mom and dad. She wants to change her name because Weiss is too Germanic and Rosina too precious; it is painfully apparent, Rosina says, that her parents tried too hard when picking a name for her.

Marcus listens, tells her he misses her. After a moment's silence, she says, I miss you too, and they hang up.

The family of four has gone into the Pierre Hotel, and Marcus turns back and goes down the avenue.

In his heart, he blames Myra for the way Rosina has turned against him. It's a complaint he can't voice because Myra, recently remarried, has been very civil, and he wishes to maintain, for as long as possible, a semblance of peace and normalcy. Myra has confided that with her, too, Rosina has been difficult; a phase, Myra believes, they'll have to endure. Berkeley, she reminds him, was his idea.

He goes into St. Patrick's Cathedral, advances toward the altar and sits down in a pew. Years ago, he stood in line with the others and received communion here. In those days, when he had his business on Forty-seventh Street, the church had been his refuge on hard, hectic days. He loved the dimness, the hushed, respectful silence. There were always people in the pews, kneeling, praying. He loved to watch them, some obviously engaged in urgent pleas, an urgency he surmised from the way they bowed their heads, clasped their hands. Once, as he sat through the service, he decided he must try it: stand in line and receive communion. See what the wafer tastes like. He had a vague idea he was doing something wrong, that only Christians who confessed may receive communion—not that it mattered much in his case. He considered stepping out of the line and walking out, but he didn't. And as his turn approached, his heart began to pound, as one who, at any moment, may be found out. He noticed that some opened their mouths for the wafer, others took it in their hands. He decided that he, too, would take it in his hand.

And then it was over. Before he knew it, his daring act was over. The thin wafer was bland; it very quickly disintegrated on his tongue. And being so absorbed in the unorthodoxy of his act robbed him, in fact, of the actual experience, for he forgot to pay attention to what he was feeling.

Emerging from St. Patrick's, blinking against the sudden, bright light, he decides to take the rest of the day off, treat himself to a small, well-deserved holiday, to a leisurely lunch of a bacon cheeseburger, French fries, and a glass of wine. After lunch, he'll walk home, to walk off the damage of such forbidden foods. On a side street off the avenue, he finds an Irish bar-restaurant and seats himself at a table in the bar section. He orders his burger medium rare, asks the waitress to forgo ketchup and get him mayo instead, as well as raw onions on the side, and a glass of red wine. He hasn't had a burger, or bacon, for so long, he has forgotten how to miss it. In the evening, he'll have to suppress an urge to tell Gina, the regulator of his diet, about this lunch, this transgression of red meat and saturated fat.

When the food is brought to him on a heavy, white plate, he breathes in the wonderful aroma of the fries, dips a long one in mayo and bites it in half.

It is good, he think, that man enjoys his food.

He smiles. A few days ago, describing a meal in his novel, he became hungry describing it.

He tells himself to take his time, prolong his pleasure. He chews slowly, observing the lunch crowd along the bar, mostly the wide backs and behinds of men in dark suits. They're in groups of two or three, talking, laughing, having a great time. For a short spell, they have been let out of their stuffy, overheated offices where they must obey corporate rules and etiquette. But here, with a drink before them, they can relax, shed the rigid corporate mantle and order a drink, a brisket or corned beef sandwich. This is the best hour of the day: one orders the food one likes, one slows down, taking time out.

Their gaiety is contagious, and soon Marcus thinks himself as happy as they. In the dimness of the bar, they seem to have no worry, and for a moment he wishes he were like them, so carefree and easy and jovial. And yet—he is quick to remind himself—he knows nothing about these men, about their lives: they may be laughing, chatting, having the time of day, but in their hearts, for all he doesn't know and could never hope to know, there lingers a burden, a sense of futility and foreboding, much like his own.

He notices that the waitress who serves him, a young woman in her twenties, on the plump side, with soft Irish features, has a slight limp, and he feels for her, rushing as she must back and forth from kitchen to tables, maneuvering trays and heavy plates in the crowded, noisy bar. He decides to tip her generously, even though Gina would argue that when he overtips a waiter or a cabbie, he's actually insulting them, confusing tips with charity. Gina says that for all his worldliness, when it comes to service people, he becomes overly delicate, one could even say, intimidated. Why can't he, like other normal people, call out to a waiter, Waiter!, and Driver! to a driver? Because, he replies, it is demeaning to call a man by what he does for a living, by the narrow demarcations of his occupation. Therefore, it is more appropriate to use, Sir! Miss! Gina, of course, disagrees. Such delicacies of spirit, she says, point to a guilty conscience.

He has finished his burger, his glass of wine. He feels heavy with food, sleepy. He remembers the promise he's made to himself to walk off his lunch, but now begins to doubt his resolve. He'll probably cab it home, take off his clothes, and crawl into bed for a quick nap. When he gets up, at around four, he may do some work for an hour or so, or read his book until Gina arrives.

His bill comes to sixteen dollars, and he aches to leave the waitress a five-dollar tip. But taking Gina's words into account, he leaves only four.

Outside, revived by the cool air, he stands a moment, debating whether to cab it or walk home. Two women in business suits and fashionable coats walk past him, and he listens to the clicking music of their heels, when one of them says, "We should do this more often." And the other woman says, "Oh, yes, definitely." He turns and walks toward Fifth Avenue, guessing at the meaning of the woman's words. Did she mean: do lunch more often, or get away from the office more frequently and lunch outside? Mature women, he thinks, wearing business suits and high heels, can command the world. Turn men into tail-wagging poodles at their feet.

Women like Gina: well-dressed, resolute, and outspoken. No one, not even brutes, will dare stand in their way.

He reaches the avenue, puts on his gloves, raises the collar of his coat. He decides to walk it, after all.

Back at his desk, Marcus looks at his watch. It's four o'clock in the afternoon. Some days drag, some zoom by; but always in the evening he is filled with wonder and apprehension, realizing that once again another day has slipped by, and who knows how many more are left him. Even under the best of circumstances, the significant numbers in a man's life are ridiculously small, appallingly absurd. One would do well to adapt the attitude of Diderot's Jacques, in *Jacques Le Fataliste*. For, if one is lucky and gets to live seventy-five years (seventy-five years of good health and prosperity); years in which one hasn't missed even one meal (due to illness, fasting, and so on); even then, one may expect to consume only eighty-one thousand meals, including the bad ones, the ones that have caused the heartburns, the constipations. He himself has already consumed most of the meals allotted him. Unless he lives to be a hundred and four.

Seventy-five years may sound impressive, even substantial, and yet it's only an illusion. Closer to the pulse and the truth is the counting of days: twenty-seven thousand in all. Twenty-seven thousand! Less than one's annual salary on minimum wage. Maybe that's why yogis measure life in heartbeats—three billion of them in an average lifetime.

Marcus massages his right shoulder, rotates his head; it feels good just to hear his joints crack, right where his neck and spine join. He stands up, moves from the desk and bends at the waist, lets his head pull him downward, lets his arms dangle. He hangs this way for a couple of minutes, blessing the quiet, the flow of blood to his head. He wishes he could rest like this for a couple of hours, remain where nothing exists but this good feeling. Slowly he straightens up, stands a moment, then goes into the living room to wait for Gina, when the phone rings. Gina says she's tired. She wants to be alone tonight, she's going straight home. "All right," he says. "I'll see you tomorrow." "Yes, tomorrow," Gina says. "It's wonderful, you know, that we have this freedom." "This freedom?" He laughs. "You have this freedom. I'm always here, ready for you."

All right, he thinks, going to the kitchen. He's a free man tonight. After dinner, he'll go back to his desk, put in a couple of hours of work.

He looks in the refrigerator and decides on rye bread, Swiss cheese, a tomato, hard green olives. He prepares a sandwich, thanking the Earl of Sandwich, for whom the sandwich is named. The earl is a man after his own heart: he loved to eat, yet couldn't tear himself away from the card table. Ingenious that he was, he had his servants serve him sliced beef between two slices of bread. Perhaps, Marcus thinks, the day will come, and they will name something after him. But what will it be?

He could include this earl and his sandwich in his novel. He could include everything in his novel, have a smorgasbord.

His budding novel. The bud of a novel he carries in his head.

He sits down to eat. He opens the book he is reading and places a heavy knife across the pages to keep them in place. Currently, it is Juan Goytisolo's *Juan the Landless*. Goytisolo delights him: ". . . to wield the pen . . . allow its filiform liquor to trickle over the whiteness of the blank pages, to attain the delicate perfection of the soloist, to prolong with subtle artifice the tumulary rigor, to postpone the climax indefinitely . . . to do away with the stubborn avarice of the real order of things . . .

". . . to eliminate from the corpus of the novelistic work the last vestiges of theatricality: to transform it into a discourse without a trace of a plot: to explode the inveterate notion of the character of flesh and blood: replacing the progressio dramatica of events with the conjuncture of textual clusters obeying a single centripetal force: the nucleus that determines writing itself, the genesic fountain pen that is the source of the textual process: improvising the architecture of the literary object, making of it not a tissue of logico-temporal relations, but rather an ars combinatoria of elements . . . rivaling painting and poetry on a purely spatial plane . . ."

Marcus chews his food energetically. With each bite his appetite grows. Again he thinks: it is good that man enjoys his food. It would have been too humiliating if food were consumed only to subsist. It wouldn't surprise him to learn that some of the people who contemplate suicide, resent, in fact, their being chained to the kitchen table, reminded, with each bite, of the uncompromising decree that faces them: Take it or leave it, it's in your hands.

The will to live dictates that one must swallow his pride and go on. In the words of Schopenhauer, which he copied into his notebook only the day before: "How shall a man be proud, when his conception is a crime, his birth a penalty, his life a labor, and death a necessity?" Man is an object of pity; he must be handled with supreme care. Man, in the face of death, refines his cuisine. Like a squirrel, he stands on his hind legs, energetically rubs his paws, planning his meals.

Marcus shuts the book and smacks his lips. The sandwich was good, it hit the spot. He pours himself another cup of coffee and returns to his desk. He feels a surge of renewed energy, renewed hope. It is delicate, though, flimsy; so flimsy, in fact, he sits still, afraid it will dissipate with his slightest move.

He assembles his characters. He knows who they are: he sees them, hears them—they stand like phantoms. Like actors on a dim stage, they wait for his word.

He knows them, the full contour of them—it's magical. All he has to do is get them on the page.

Out of nowhere, an old man joins them: an intruder. Marcus is amazed to see him there. Who is he, this stranger? What does he want? He could be, Marcus reflects, the older self of one of the characters. But, Marcus asks. Does he want him there? An old man? What possible use does he have for an old man?

The old man steps forward; he asserts himself.

Marcus is charmed, he relents. If the old man, for whatever reason, feels so strongly about joining them, he must let him. For now, at least. He'll try him out, let him compete.

Four

Under Gina's supervision, he prepares jasmine rice, cooked to perfection, and rinses in the sink leaves of three lettuce varieties—red leaf, green leaf, Boston—and a few leaves of arugula. After he washes the leaves and shakes out the water, delicately, without squeezing, he tears the lettuce with his fingers, one leaf at a time, into a large glass bowl. Gina is in charge of the veal cutlets, and she will also prepare the salad dressing, for there are duties in the kitchen she will not entrust to his hands or to anybody else's. And it is she who is in charge of tearing the leaves from the bunch, for only she can estimate precisely how many leaves are required to make a salad for two, three, or however many guests they have over for dinner. Every so often, as they work together shoulder to shoulder at the counter, she glances at him, at his hands, making sure he follows her instructions exactly. Sometimes she praises him, sometimes she chides him.

He, too, glances her way, but merely to admire her swiftness, a swiftness he associates with the practiced exactitude of the long-limbed. But mostly, in the kitchen, he drifts in his mind until Gina interrupts with a new command, or a refinement, a modification, of one already given.

He doesn't mind her intrusions; as a matter of fact, he welcomes them. Her tyranny in the kitchen amuses him, for he knows she revels in the power she holds over him, he knows she likes it that he obeys her without question. But what he finds most affecting is the similarity he sees, and which he keeps to himself, between her fanaticism in the kitchen and her relentless pursuit of multiple orgasms, a pursuit he is only too happy, even eager, to indulge and help her fulfill.

Usually, after dinner, when they don't expect company, they go into the living room to read and relax. Gina reads her trade magazines, he reads a book. Gina takes the couch, he takes his chair. They sit and read, quietly, once in a while remarking to the other about something just read, something funny or interesting, or about a suddenly remembered urgent business they—namely Gina—must discuss on the spot.

It may happen that, as he reads, he suddenly remembers where he is, and he glances up, looking for Gina who has been so quiet, and who should be, he knows, sprawled on the couch, reading a magazine; and yet he finds her sitting up, cross-legged, her hands tucked under her crotch, as if to keep warm. But what's most startling to him is that instead of reading she is staring at him, a distant, yet intent, look in her eyes.

During that one fraction of a second when their eyes meet and register the other's reaction, and before either of them says a word, a few thoughts run parallel in his head: In her still, impossibly erect posture, she resembles a panther squatting on its haunches. Why is she staring at him like this? Note the intensity of the human gaze. Is she trying to reconstruct, rearrange the scattered pieces of his personality into preexisting molds she has fixed in her brain?

"What is it?" he asks.

Innocently she smiles, shrugs her shoulders, shakes her head. "Nothing. I was just thinking."

"About?"

"This article." She taps the page of the open magazine at her side.

"But you were staring at me."

"I wasn't staring at you. I was thinking, and my eyes, you might say, got stuck, or caught, on you. That's all. As usual, you're reading too much into just about anything."

"Look," he says. "I don't mind your staring. I'd actually welcome it. You don't look at me enough."

"I look at you plenty, trust me."

Tonight they have a dinner guest, and when Oscar arrives they sit down to eat. Marcus, answering their questions, talks about the progress he's been making. He is past the stage of taking notes, of devising a sort of outline for his novel, for its characters, and has now begun the actual writing, has gone through the first couple of chapters, though he cannot guarantee, not at this point, that these preliminary chapters will indeed constitute the beginning, or even, he says with a wave of his hand, be included in the final version. "You never know these things," he says, sounding too important, even pretentious, in his own ears. "Not at this early stage."

As he talks, conflicting emotions run through him. He wants to tell them everything, he wants to tell them the Truth. He wants to impress on them his difficulties, yet without appearing to be soliciting their sympathy, although he does crave it. He wants them to appreciate that what he does is special, and yet without his having to spell it out.

From memory, he quotes Katherine Mansfield, who told her diary she wanted "to keep a kind of *minute notebook,* to be published some day. That's all. No novels, no problem stories, nothing that is not simple, open."

He then mentions the old man who seems to have appeared, at the last moment, as if from nowhere, an orphan of sorts.

"An old man," Gina says. "How odd."

He looks at her. "Why odd?"

"From what you've told me so far, I don't see where he fits."

"Well." He lets frustration sneak into his voice. "As I said, he appeared from nowhere, but he seemed determined. I had to leave him in. As I told you already, it is too early at this point to tell what might happen."

"He could be an older version of you," Oscar suggests. "How old is he?"

"Old. About eighty."

"Or," Gina says, "you could be him."

"How do you mean?"

All at once, Gina seems confused, as if unable to connect with what she just said.

"It's the same thing, no?" Marcus persists. "What you said is what Oscar said, only in the reverse?"

"I know," Gina says, and now she sounds frustrated. "But a moment ago it was clear to me that what Oscar had said was different, in perspective, from what I was saying. And now I think I've lost it. I hate it when this happens."

"This is very important to me," Marcus, suddenly alert, says. "Let's start from the beginning. Oscar said that the old man could be me—thirty years from now. Then you said, No."

"I said, Or—"

"All right, or. You said that I could be him. How is it different from what Oscar said?"

"Well," Gina begins, slowly at first, but then, triumphantly, gaining momentum. "I guess the difference is that Oscar says that you write the old man, imagining yourself thirty years from now, and I say the old man, who might be you thirty years from now, is looking back and writing this present moment, as you lived it with me and Oscar." She looks at him, smiling, proud of herself. "What do you think? I mean, do you see what I mean?"

"Yes I do, of course," he says slowly, digesting. This double, superimposed vision of past and future has touched a nerve; he shudders.

"What's the matter?" Gina asks.

"I saw my ghost," Marcus says, and Gina and Oscar exchange a quick look.

"What about the dictionary you've been working on?" Oscar asks, putting down his wine glass. "All the work's gone to waste."

"Not really," Marcus says. "I read the books I wanted and needed to read, so the benefit is all there, even if I don't complete the dictionary. Besides, I haven't abandoned it, I'm still adding to it."

"I liked the conceit, the idea of such a dictionary, and the title you chose for it." Oscar, to indicate pomp, raises his hand in the air.

" 'The Human Gesture in Western Literature.' It's pretty grandiose. What I mean to say, the title itself is a kind of gesture. I remember when you read to us, from Nabokov, I think, about a boy and his mother coming out of the house. And I took to heart what you said, that only writers take the time to describe, to grasp, the minutest movement . . ."

"I don't remember that passage," Gina says, furrowing her brows.

"And not only the movement," Marcus picks up where Oscar has left off, "but the whole delicate constellation of the relationship, the delicate constellation of the personalities involved."

"But whatever you do," Gina says, rising to clear the dishes, "you must make your characters attractive, especially the women. Make them pretty and smart. Loveable. Although, I don't see how you, of all people, could achieve that." She laughs. "Just kidding. Come, help me clean up. Then let's go into the living room and plan my party."

In the living room, Marcus reads his book, while Gina and Oscar consult over the list of hors-d'oeuvres, the cheeses, the breads and salads, and, of course, the desserts. Occasionally, Marcus interrupts his reading and gazes at them, marveling at the absolute and serious attention they devote to a party. It is only a party, he once ventured to remark, and Gina, instantly, turned on him, saying how dare he demean her work? He, the hypocrite, who would happily reap the benefits of a successful party and claim center stage of the willing, well-cared-for participants, but who would all the same choose to remain oblivious of—or worse, dare slight—the planning behind it. "You take too many things for granted," Gina added with an aplomb he thought totally absurd and much too overblown for the occasion. Unprepared for the attack, he just stood there at first, amused more than upset or hurt, but as she went on and on about his ingratitude, he felt a righteous anger rise in him, an anger he decided not to suppress. "What's the matter with you? All I tried to tell you is that it pains me to see you waste so much time on something as trivial as a party." "Well," Gina yelled. "Look for your pain elsewhere. I enjoy this. Got it?" "Got it."

Gina and Oscar are the two people with whom he feels the most at ease, and even though, by now, he is aware of how important it is to them to produce a gem, he is still tempted to call out, if only in jest, and say: Hey, life is passing you by. As you sit there, planning a party that will come and go, life is passing you by.

Yeah!—he hopes they will shout back, in imitation of him. Read a book instead!

But he doesn't take any chances; right this minute they don't seem to be in a joking mood. Together they have named him The Prophet of Tenth Street, and, when in company, and when the spirit so moves them, they begin their habitual spiel, with Oscar gradually retreating, leaving the field for Gina, who then shines alone, sparkles at the dinner table, or party, as she explains Marcus, his peculiarities, to those gathered in the room. She especially shines when there are newcomers who are meeting Marcus for the first time. She tells them she has named him The Prophet of Tenth Street because he can't bear the idea that others, friends in particular, are not exactly like him. He cannot understand why they don't do as he does when it is so obviously, don't you know—and here she pauses, significantly, the hint of a smile on her lips, in her eyes—for their own damn good!

And yet, she says, she is willing to concede that the prophet is sincere. As he himself would point out, and rightly so, where is his gain in all of this? All the aggravations he endures, the precious time he invests in trying to educate the masses? And it is not as if he is easily seduced, or impressed, by his own ego, his power to sway; such concerns are beneath him, he is absolutely selfless: he truly feels for humankind, truly holds their common good in his heart. The only problem is, he doesn't have the courage to go out and relieve himself, in public, of his message. And yet, Gina continues, she can just picture him, out on the streets, his arms outstretched, trying to stop all of them, those herds and herds of consumers who flock to the stores because they don't know any better. He would plead with them: You don't need all that stuff, it only clutters your life. Your videos, your VCRs, your electronic gadgets. It's all a distraction, a diversion designed to blind you, steer you off track. Why don't you—and here Oscar will join her, the two of them already convulsed with held-back laughter, to chorus the punch line—read a book instead?

The guests' laughter is Gina's prize. Marcus shrugs, smiles, looks into his glass. Yes, he'll admit. He feels a great affinity with those biblical bards who roamed the barren hills of Judea and Samaria, calling, in vain, for the people to mend their ways.

"Imagine," he says. "A whole life spent on delivering a message no one cares to hear."

"He walks in our midst," Gina says. "He behaves, but he doesn't really fit."

One of the guests might say, "None of us really fits," but faithful Gina stands guard: she won't allow that her Marcus be lumped together with mere mortals. "No, no," she says, "Marcus is different. Marcus is your true purist, and not because I say so. The first thing he does when he comes into my house, and without wasting any time, is go straight to the videos!"

"Ha! Ha! Ha!" The guests laugh, slap their thighs, and Marcus raises his hand, affably, as if to say he is not one to spoil their fun. He says he has never denied that if it's there he'll use it, he is not against progress, he is against frenzy, against technological gluttony. If they want he'll read Maimonides to them, it will only take a minute. "Not now," Gina might say, depending on the mood she senses in the room. But if she says nothing, Marcus goes into his study and returns with his notebook, and in no time he sits there, quoting from Maimonides's *Guide for the Perplexed:*

"The soul when accustomed to superfluous things, acquires a strong habit of desiring things which are neither necessary for the preservation of the individual, nor for that of the species. This desire is without limit, whilst things which are necessary are few in number and restricted within certain limits. . . . Observe how Nature proves the correctness of this assertion. The more necessary a thing is for living beings, the more easily it is found and cheaper it is, the less necessary it is, the rarer and dearest it is. E.g., air, water and food are indispensable to man: air is most necessary . . . water is more necessary than food."

And, if Maimonides is too remote, here's Adam Smith: "What pleases these lovers of toys? How many people ruin themselves by laying out money on trinkets of frivolous utility?" "You see," he says. "All I'm calling for is moderation."

Moderation. They smile at him forgivingly. A modern-day saint.

Modern-day saint.

He prefers to think of himself as a modern-day Tevye the dairyman who, like his neighbors in the shtetl, quotes and misquotes the Bible, the Sages. He, Marcus, uses quotes, too; he may quote from the Sages or the prayer book, but mostly he quotes from his writers, and, at appropriate moments, reads selected passages to his friends. He compares himself to a guide in a museum who leads the spectators from exhibit to exhibit, pointing out the obvious and less obvious merits.

And if Gina and Oscar do not always seem to appreciate his efforts, he doesn't give up. He thinks that with time, patience, and persistence, on his and their part, they will come to see the wisdom of his advice, of his repeated warning that one must not take reading for granted; one has to learn how to read.

They listen to him, impassively, he thinks, as he cites himself as the obvious example. "Take me," he says. "I apprenticed myself for seven years before I could even read a writer like Fichte, or a book like *The Waves*."

"For seven years," he repeats with a rueful smile. "The number of years biblical Jacob had to work for Rachel, only Jacob was cheated and got Leah instead, and had to work for seven years more. In those enlightened days," he adds wistfully, "you could have as many wives as you could support."

"You can hardly handle me," Gina sees fit to announce in public.

"Natural atrophy," he says, then continues: "Think of the cows in Pharaoh's dream, the seven fat cows devoured by the seven skinny ones."

"Cows!" Gina and Oscar are seized with laughter.

"Think of it this way," he says, unperturbed. "A musician, a composer, who listens to a complex symphony, his enjoyment is richer, and more demanding, because he knows what he is listening to, he knows what it takes to make music."

"Fine," they say in unison, "we're not musicians."

He has tried different tactics. He has pushed many books into their hands. Books that have given him ecstatic joy, books they have returned with a resigned, tired look, saying they could not get through. For one reason or another they've lost interest in Joyce, Nabokov, Broch, Woolf, Faulkner. He has read Perec (relative of the Yiddish author I. L. Peretz! he adds with excitement) and Sarraute to them, and they've begged mercy; he's read Musil to them, and they've nodded, as if to say, "All right, it's good, what do you expect us to do? Jump for joy? We're not as overwhelmed as you are, that's all."

"But look here," he says. "Watch how Calvino dissects a lawn. See how a man, a Mr. Palomar, and his wife, seated in their garden, react to a pair of blackbirds. All that is said and is left unsaid. It's genius," Marcus offers, looks at them encouragingly. "Let me read this to you."

"No, not now. Some other time."

"Just this one paragraph."

So he reads to them, just one small paragraph, then looks up at them and says again, "This is genius, you see."

"Yes, maybe," they agree, but they don't seem overly impressed; they seem to take such beauty for granted. They seem to be saying that as readers it is their right, their elemental right to expect beauty, or whatever other terms he chooses to throw at them.

He looks at them, thinking that perhaps they do appreciate it as much as he does, but are not necessarily as demonstrative as he. It then occurs to him that perhaps he is an anachronism, even a clown. He is the one who displays, who overreacts. It is possible that while he prods and digs their ribs, trying to make them "see," they see something that he fails to see, namely himself.

He doesn't like such thoughts, but he has to admit them. He has to allow the possibility that his eager proselytizing is a form of self-aggrandizing. He parades his love, he revels in it; he wishes the whole world to witness it. What is it with him? Why must he meddle in other people's lives? Why does he have to bring them over to his side? Why does he care? Does he truly believe that if people all over the world were more involved with literature, the world would be a different place?

Well yes, he does, as a matter of fact. It may be his failing—so be it. He never claimed he was perfect, and yet he aims there. Each day he aims toward perfection. Each day he gets closer to eternity.

Five

There's so far yet to explore, the infinite planes and vistas his brain opens up to.

The old man boils water for his afternoon tea. He dislikes kettles and is therefore boiling water in a small, round pot. He stands by the stove, drawing from its warmth, and watches the circle of water in the pot. At the edges, just below the surface, the water begins to agitate, then to rise and swell, forming mountains of waves that finally collapse onto themselves, breaking into a multitude of furious, white bubbles.

He lets the water boil for a while, mesmerized by the seemingly futile rage of the bubbles. If he chooses to let it boil, the water would boil itself out of existence; it would disappear, evaporate in the air.

We learn so many lessons, he reflects with affection. We're bound so intimately to the physical world.

The old man is gaunt and there's an uncompromising toughness in his long, linear features. It is hard to tell the color of his eyes, sunk so deep in their sockets; they could be gray. Every morning he makes it his point to shower and shave, put on a clean shirt and trousers. He thinks he owes it to himself to look the best he can, even on cold winter days when the longest trip ahead of him is twelve flights in the elevator down to the lobby where he picks up his mail.

It is strange, he thinks, how the human psyche works, for although he doesn't really expect or look forward to meeting anyone in the elevators or down in the lobby, he feels an emptiness, a disappointment, when he goes down and up again without having had occasion to smile at a face, say hello, perhaps exchange a word about the bitter weather. On such days, he doesn't even see the doorman who must be cooped up in his tiny office near the entrance.

He's an old man, he tells himself. He must accept loneliness. Going back upstairs in the elevator, the thought crosses his mind that he won't last this winter. He fights the thought away, telling himself that as long as he is breathing, as long as his brain is alive and engaged, death will have to wait. Absently, he looks over his mail, remembering that usually, as soon as he walks into his apartment and goes into his study, something switches in his mind, and he becomes again the private, single man, preoccupied with questions of enormous interest.

Right this minute, he appreciates the fact of adaptability. He wishes he remembered every fact of his life, every face he's ever seen. He reflects: With every step, we lose something, although we gain in distance. With every step we get closer to eternity. In the meantime we learn, instinctively; we internalize, personalize the physical world. Take a hard-boiled egg. You know—either from experience, or you've been told by your mother—that in order for the shell to come right off, all you need do is let the egg cool in cold water, or under a running faucet. Then you crack the shell against the counter, *et voilà*, it peels right off. You assume that the shell and its membrane, shocked by the cold, harden against, and separate from, the still trembling white of the egg. What you know for certain is that man, or more probably woman, has learned this simple physical fact by the mere impossibility of holding and peeling a hard-boiled egg when the shell is still too hot to the touch.

New studies, the old man reflects, will have to be conducted to find the definite link between the everyday, practical discoveries of housewives throughout the centuries and the great scientific explosions.

In his case, he knows for sure, it was from his mother that he had first learned about the egg. Every Friday afternoon, preparing the Sabbath meal, she boiled several eggs and prepared one of his favorite dishes: *tzibale-mit-iy*, literally, onion with egg. She boiled the eggs, let them cool in water, peeled and chopped them, chopped a large onion, mixed in salt, pepper, and mayonnaise, sprinkled parsley on top.

While this was going on, her famous chicken soup and homemade noodles stood ready on the stove, and the large, bright kitchen was filled with the aromas and anticipation particular to Friday afternoons. With the sun setting, his mother lit the candles to welcome the Queen, the Sabbath. She moved her hands above the flame in circular motions, then covered her face and said a silent prayer; and he, the five- or six-year-old boy, knew he was not to interrupt, for at that private moment his mother communed not only with God, but also with her mother, her father, her brothers and sisters, all lost in the Holocaust, and of whom she had only a few photographs left.

Watching his mother disappear behind her hands, he always feared that she would not come back, that she would cut herself off from him and become another person with a new face. But always she returned, emerging, after a few moments, from behind her hands, cheerful, laughing, hurrying to finish up the rest of her chores, and he could again look forward to the moment when his father returned from synagogue and the three of them would sit down to the evening meal, his father blessing the Sabbath, the wine. He particularly liked their mute procession to the sink to ceremoniously, ritually, wash their hands, filling the special cup with water, pouring the water first on this fist, then the other, and returning to the table, still maintaining their silence, as is ordained, until his father blessed the bread, tore a piece of challah for each of them. Only after they bit into it were they allowed to talk, all of them, by then, usually bursting with something to say. Then dinner began, his mother serving the first course, the delicious, pale yellow *tzibale-mit-iy,* spread evenly on the round, first-course china plates, garnished with thin slices of tomatoes, cucumbers, and radishes.

The old man turns off the water and pours it into his cup. Young children, he reflects, having no concept of the future or the past, cling to the moment.

He goes back to his desk for another hour or so of work. Around five o'clock, as is his custom, he seals his workday with a word or two he finds at random in the dictionary and copies into his notebook. A word perhaps forgotten, a word he likes the sound of, a word he wants to resurrect. He has observed many times that new words, once learned, have a way of turning up, unexpectedly, as new and eager acquaintances, grateful for the opportunity to meet again. Often, upon encountering, in his reading, or when browsing in the dictionary, a word recently acquired, it seems to him that the word winks from the page as if to say, Here we are, the two of us, meeting again.

He reaches for the Webster's on his desk and after a short search copies two new words into his notebook:

colporteur \n [F, alter. of ME *comporteur*, fr. *comporter* to bear, peddle] (1796): a peddler of religious books.

fardel \n [ME, fr. MF, prob. fr. Ar. *fardah*](14c) 1: a bundle. 2: a burden.

Six

Gina has been true to her word. She promised she'd keep the party small, and she did.

There will be only the nine of them:

Lottie and John Fisher

Becky and Howard Novack

Oscar Ross

The hosts, Gina Bloch and Marcus Weiss

And two newcomers: Assya Adler, a recent acquaintance of Gina's, and a male friend she'll bring along.

"Assya," Gina tells him enthusiastically, "is beautiful. She teaches art history at Hunter College."

Lottie, Oscar's mother, and John, her most recent husband—her fourth—will be the first to arrive. They always are. Lottie likes to say that John is the best yet among her husbands, so good, in fact, that she doesn't mind having had to wait seventy-five years before she found him. John repays in kind, saying it took him seventy-eight years to find her.

Lottie will wear a black narrow dress, high heels, and sheer black stockings; John will don a tuxedo, a white *foulard*, which, he says, complements his silver-white mustache.

The mustache, thick and yet silky (each individual hair bristling with self-assured dignity), could easily be cause for manly envy, as well as the chiseled face that carries it.

Becky and Howard will arrive next. Neither he nor Gina can tolerate Howard, but Becky is his only cousin, his only family in the city, and when she stands in the doorway, in her slightly plump figure, her red wavy hair, her wide smile, Howard is diminished; he disappears.

He loves Becky. He hugs and kisses her. She brings back memories, she has known his parents. "Hello stranger," she whispers in his ear. "I love you too, even if we meet only once a year." "We should meet more often." "Yes, we should." "I'm serious." "So am I."

Oscar arrives, wearing a colorful vest they all admire. It's from Kashmir, he tells them. Handmade. Marcus remarks that the green thread, ingeniously interwoven among the other, stronger colors of the vest, is the same color as the eyes of the wearer.

"It's not green, it's turquoise," Gina says.

"You can't argue about colors," Marcus says. "I see green."

They drink champagne. They help themselves to the artfully arranged, bite-sized delicacies.

John, seated in one of the deep, velvet armchairs, moves his hands back and forth along the armrests, saying, "I've always liked this room; it's large, but it has atmosphere."

"It's the fireplace," says Becky.

"No," says Lottie, "it's the spirit of the man who lives here. A toast to our host."

"I live here, too." Gina feigns a pout. "If only at night."

"Sorry, dear, of course you do. We toast you, too. Before you came along, this man"—Lottie points at Marcus—"was a wreck. Look at him now. So calm and collected, a real mensch."

"He works very hard." Gina takes the side arm of Marcus's chair, and leans into him. "His novel."

"So Oscar tells me. Are we in it, dear?"

"You, definitely." Marcus smiles.

"It is so hard, I imagine," Lottie says. "To push things around. To know what comes before what, and how, and when, and most of all, why." Lottie uncrosses then recrosses her legs, and Marcus admires her still youthful look, her sharp mind. Women like her, he thinks, who have lived in the city their entire lives, are the true landmarks of the city: someone should write a book about them.

"He kicks me in his sleep," Gina says. "I don't sleep anymore."

"I never sleep on my stomach," John announces, wiping his mustache with a napkin. "Only on my back or my side. But Lottie here, she sleeps on her stomach. I can't put my arm around her. I think this is her way of rejecting me."

"I don't sleep on my stomach," Lottie objects. "I may turn in my sleep, but I don't sleep on my stomach. People who sleep on their stomachs are hiding something. I have nothing to hide."

"What do you mean, hiding something?" Howard asks from the settee where he sits alone, his arms folded across his chest.

There is a short, awkward pause, as if no one expected Howard to speak.

"That's what they say, Howard," Lottie says dryly. "People with an unclean conscience sleep on their stomachs."

"I've never heard such a thing."

Lottie shrugs, inspects her nails; Marcus thinks she harbors a smile. "All the same," she says.

"Howard is worried," Becky says, "because he sleeps on his stomach, although not exclusively, not all the time."

Marcus looks at Howard. Not a bad-looking man, but sour-faced and unpleasant. Such things, Marcus reflects, are determined in childhood. Having to do perhaps with repressive or overprotective parents who somehow arrest their child's normal development. And then, of course, there's the inevitable matter of heredity and genes.

John stands up, and Marcus, looking at him, notes with admiration that a man in a tuxedo reflects the best in Western culture.

"Who else is coming?" Becky asks.

"Assya Adler and Nick White," Gina says. "She teaches art, he's an anthropologist."

"An anthropologist," Lottie says, and her intonation makes them all laugh. "Why are they late?"

"It's not late." Gina consults her wristwatch. "It's only nine."

"I'm going to the john," John says.

"Go ahead, dear."

Marcus laughs. "You've got him well-trained, Lottie. He goes nowhere without your permission."

(Later, in bed, Gina chides him for having made such a tactless remark. "Don't you see," she says, "that it's a sign of his age, his confusion?"

"What is?" he asks.

"His slowness. His announcing his steps. Don't you see he seeks reassurance?"

"No, I don't," he says, and instantly realizes that she is right.

"Oh you," she says and turns her back on him. "You see nothing."

"I see your back," he says. "And I dislike your tone of voice."

"I dislike it too," she says after a silence. "But you make me."

"I make you?" he says, knowing, from the tickle in her voice, she's no longer upset.

"Yes, you make me.")

Assya and Nick arrive and suddenly it seems as though the party has expanded, as though the room has filled up with many people, with talk, with laughter. They all stand up for the introductions.

Indeed, he thinks, Assya is striking. She's not a beauty, as Gina has so enthusiastically advanced, but there's something about her, that same something that Howard is lacking. Whatever Howard lacks, Assya has in abundance, and she radiates it.

They shake hands, and he feels pleasantly warm; happily, he drowns in her very fair skin, her small blue eyes. Her front tooth is crooked, her nose is hooked, but the way her upper lip flattens, stretches across her teeth when she smiles, turns these small imperfections into assets.

"Assya," he repeats, "Assya Adler. You know, I spent my childhood years looking for a girl whose initials were identical. I was actually looking for a B. B.—for a Brigitte Bardot—but I never found you, her, I mean."

She continues to smile, but says nothing, not committing herself. He wonders what goes on behind the wide forehead, the small blue eyes. He releases her hand.

Now her smile broadens. "I've heard so much about you, about your work."

He nods, smiles. Her voice, too, is surprisingly pleasant. The even, measured voice of a teacher, a lecturer. He imagines she must be that rare type who knows more than she lets on. The type who speaks dispassionately, as if passion in speech connotes a weak argument. She shares her knowledge without trying to show off, or to get people on her side. Calmly, unhurriedly, she presents her thoughts, occasionally allowing a pleasant smile to light up her features. She never has to raise her voice; when she speaks, a respectful hush falls in the room as all eyes are drawn to her.

She is still waiting, smiling. He thinks what he should say next. He asks, "Can I get you a glass of champagne?"

In the living room, Marcus observes his guests. He feels responsible, fatherly, he wants them to have a good time. The women, in their makeup and jewelry, are at their elegant best, the brilliance of each reflects the brilliance of the other. The men, in their assigned role of protective companions, are more somber and reserved; they serve as backdrop against which the women glow.

Assya and Nick take the other settee, to the right of Marcus's chair, and Marcus, observing the way they sit, side by side, tries to determine the level of intimacy between them. From Nick's somewhat rigid posture, and Assya's leaning more toward the side arm of the settee, Marcus concludes that Assya and Nick are not physical intimates; they appear to avoid casual contact. He hopes that Assya, in the course of the evening, will shed her dark jacket and remain in her beige, silk shirt. He imagines licking her nipple—not sexually, but in the delicate, small manner of a cat's pink tongue lapping milk from a bowl. She is wearing black silk slacks, and something tells him that the shirt is sleeveless, and that the arms are as creamy as the face and throat. In his opinion, the bare skin, the soft flesh of a woman's upper arm is often more than a man can bear, for the upper arm is excruciatingly suggestive, especially when the rest of the woman is covered and clothed. What is it, he wonders, that makes it so suggestive? The proximity of the breast? The secrecy of the armpit?

He stands up, adds a log to the fire and stokes it, viewing himself as the ever-benevolent country gentleman in his flannel trousers and cashmere cardigan.

His guests are relieved that Christmas is over, with Lottie confessing that she vows every year she'll never shop again for gifts, but every year she finds herself drawn to the stores, willingly swept away by the general frenzy.

"You Christians," Marcus, returning to his seat, says with a smile, "try so hard. Every year, around Christmas, I am filled with compassion for your exuberance, your boundless cheer and hope."

"What do you mean?" Nick asks. "About our trying hard?"

"Just that," says Marcus. "The shopping for gifts, the expectations, the inevitable letdowns. I think it takes a lot of courage."

"Courage has nothing to do with it," Nick says, shifting in his seat, causing Assya to shift, too. With the back of her index finger she wipes her upper lip. She is warm, Marcus notes. "Don't Jews engage in exchanging gifts?"

"To some extent we do." Marcus leans forward in his chair, reaching with his hand toward Nick and Assya as a man communicating not only his opinion but his goodwill as well. "But the idea behind gifts has always been to give to the poor who cannot afford the traditional foods of the holidays and, more importantly, the Sabbath. You give to the poor, so that they, too, may participate in the celebration of God, His Sabbath, His holidays. To this day, every religious community takes care of its poor. You won't find a Hasid on state welfare."

"That's good," Nick says. "The less on welfare, the better."

Marcus nods. Assya has taken off her jacket, and now folds it over the side of the settee. On her left wrist, a thin gold chain shines—a detail that he has not anticipated—but her upper arms are just as he imagined them. Casually, as if meditatively, he leans his head in his palm and contrives to see whether or not she shaves under the arms. He thinks he sees one or two strands of pale, soft hair sprouting from her armpit.

Assya shifts in her seat, and Marcus, too, shifts, scratching his head. Now very deliberately she crosses her legs, leans her elbow on her knee, offers her face, openly. Her hair, streaked with various shades of dark and light ash-blond, falls to her shoulders in light waves.

From his corner chair, Oscar says, "Nick, you should know that our host is a well-meaning male, if a bit lopsided."

Surprised, they all laugh, Marcus included.

Gina, pleased, picks up the thread. "It's true, Nick. In some arguments, he's quite predictable, and yet, occasionally, he can show himself to be open-minded, even intelligent. He's gracious, too, wants nothing better than the well-being of his guests. He follows with his eyes their every move; he needs to know they are comfortable. He tries to memorize their every word, every muscle twitch. Right this minute he watches my mouth, marvels at the sounds that issue from it, wonders how my thoughts, unpremeditated, unthought by me only a fraction of a second ago, arrange themselves, syntactically, into sentences, simultaneously, it seems, as I think and speak them. He notes the way I hold my head, move my hands expressively. He notes how you listen to my every word, how he himself listens and observes. He may use it in his work."

Smiling, Marcus turns to Assya and Nick: "Gina likes to discuss me in the third person: this is her cameo performance of which I am the chief beneficiary."

Nick whispers in Assya's ear, and Assya laughs. It stings Marcus; he wants to know what Nick said and why Assya laughed.

"Marcus is lucky to have you, Gina dear," Lottie says.

Becky, sitting on the couch between Lottie and Gina, says, "Men are lucky, period. First, they are born of a woman, an alien being, and are, therefore, conditionally blessed into a life of wonderment. They can soar, nothing holds them down. Second, as they grow up, they learn to look at women, and what a treat! Such variety of form and feature, of psychic depths. Each hairdo, each getup, a mystery. But when we, women, look at men, what do we see? No great variety— you get muscle and bone: men are a simpler life form. Some may be handsomer than others, but on the whole they present a certain uniformity of thought and behavior. With most men, you get what you've bargained for, although you hope for more. With a man, you see pretty much what you get, you get pretty much what you see."

As Becky speaks, Marcus notices that her crossed leg jerks convulsively back and forth. He wants to go over to her, place a calming hand on the nervous leg, the restless knee.

"You're very eloquent tonight," Howard says sardonically.

"I'm glad you've noticed," says Becky.

"Now, now," Oscar calls, "it's New Year's Eve."

"Easy for you to say," Becky says, "you're not married to Howard."

There's a momentary pause; then Lottie laughs, inviting the others to join.

"Not a word." Bracelets jingling, Lottie warns Howard, raising her hand, her ringed index finger pointed at him. "Not a word. Let Becky have the last word."

Let Becky have the last word, Marcus reflects, watching Lottie and Howard. Flaubert comes to his mind, Flaubert's anguished preoccupation with the minutest detail of each scene he envisioned for his novels. Marcus wonders what kind of meticulous details Flaubert would have lavished on the set of characters now seated in his living room. They are nine men and women who, at this moment, are very much alive, engaged in the little drama between Becky and Howard, while each, it is possible, in the back of his or her mind, recalls similar quibbles they've had to endure in their own lives. This unexpected, small disruption has fractured the moment to allow the participants to glimpse the red central vein, usually hidden from view.

People socialize, he muses, to forget the moment, postpone the thought of their very last and inevitable scene. No one has ever died while engaged in conversation; a moment later, maybe, but not in midsentence, he doesn't think.

Now, as host, he must break the silence. He thinks of an appropriate opening. He could say to his guests: Think of sacred invocations—speech has the power to keep death at bay.

Or, he could start by saying it was amazing how people in a group always found a subject they could all discuss.

"You know," the words suddenly leave Marcus's mouth, "last night, still half awake but already drifting into sleep, I suddenly felt as if the hairs on my head were electrified, were electrical conduits. I felt as though a threatening electrical halo was buzzing around my head. And this morning, upon waking, I thought about all that goes on in our heads, in our bodies. Sometimes I experience a strange, metallic taste in my mouth, and I wonder whether it has to do with all the electrical appliances that have become a matter of course in our lives. How are we to know for sure what affects us and how?"

"It could have been toxins," Assya says. "In your system. Toxins released in your sleep."

"Could be," Marcus says. He notes that she sits closer to Nick and he thinks that perhaps they are involved after all. Women sometimes are generous; Assya seems generous, perhaps too trusting. You can never know, Gina has said, what appeals to a woman in a man. It could be a twinkle in his eye, a twinkle no one sees but she. Take me, for instance. There are those who probably wonder what I see in you. Frankly, he admitted, I often wonder about this myself. I still don't know what gave me the chutzpah to approach you that first night, but looking back I know it was pure whisky courage. Whisky courage, Gina repeated dreamily. It was your eyes, your Jewish eyes that caught my attention. Ah, Marcus said. Anyway, Gina went on. You're not especially handsome, you're not especially bright, but when you lie on top of me, your features change, taking on an ominous darkness that only I know and which appeals to me, a darkness that reminds me you're a stranger, a momentary, if welcome, invader of my body.

Marcus clears his throat and continues, "But, it is a mystery, isn't it? Don't we, all mammals and other living creatures, share in the fact of our senses, our orifices, our digestive systems? We have nipples, genitals, backsides. We smell, we taste, we listen. We're all suspicious, jealously desirous of our breaths. I have to admit, when I think of all this, the idea of a God indomitably presents itself."

"I'll tell you when I believe in God," John says in a booming voice. "When I look at Lottie's delicate earlobe, I believe in God. Don't laugh, please. When I consider the finishing touches, I think of God. Look at our women. Women, especially, were designed with love. Some women, you can't deny it, are simply works of art—do not touch! Such exquisite, refined lines. Like the arch of a silky eyebrow, the delicate curve of the cheek, a nostril. God must be a hell of a craftsman, breathing life into such thoroughbreds."

"This is what got us in trouble in the first place," Howard says. "The overglorification and mystification of women."

"To each his own," John says.

"I agree with you there, John," Howard says, and his voice, Marcus thinks, trembles a bit.

"Come, come," Oscar says. He leaves his chair and sits down next to Howard on the settee. "Out with the chocolate truffles, Gina. We're ready for dessert."

But it seems that Howard is bent on remaining the evening's pariah. He states that for most people, life is experienced at the very basic level of holding down a job, that the U.S. has successfully developed a nation of employees, a mentality of employees. The blame, according to Howard, is to be found in the female consumer. And here all of them begin to talk at once.

"I resent that," Lottie says.

"You're confusing Japan with the United States," John says.

As if to save the situation, Marcus stands up and says there's something he's going to read to them, something they'd all find most interesting.

"Read what?" Gina asks, her eyes narrowing.

But Marcus won't be stopped. Heading for the door, he says, "From one of Hitler's letters."

"Hitler! On New Year's Eve. Not tonight, Marcus, you promised. Give us a break!"

But Marcus is already in his study and soon returns with a notebook under his arm. "This will only take a minute," he promises. "It's very pertinent, I assure you. It's from a letter Hitler wrote to Ernst Hanfstangl. I think Howard should hear it."

"Leave me out of this," Howard barks.

"Please, just be patient," Marcus says and begins to read: " 'Someone who does not understand the intrinsically feminine character of the masses, will never be an effective speaker. . . . Like a woman, the masses fluctuate between extremes . . . the crowd is not only like a woman, but women constitute the most important element in an audience. The women usually lead, then follow the children and at last . . . follow the fathers.' "

At this point, Howard explodes. "Thanks for the comparison, pal. When my wife gives a speech about the dysfunctional, retarded male, everyone is happy. Then I say two words about the female consumer, and our scholar here runs into his study and comes back with Hitler, no less. You want to know my opinion? I think he is right. We hate to admit this, don't we, but like he says, the crowd, the mob, in character, is female."

Becky runs out of the room and locks herself in the bathroom. "Thanks a lot," Gina shoots in Marcus's direction as she runs after Becky. She knocks on the bathroom door, but Becky refuses to come out, unless Howard and Marcus apologize to her through the closed door. Marcus, willingly, is led to the bathroom door and apologizes. Then Howard, somehow, also agrees to come to the door and apologize, and the two men apologize to each other—another miracle compromise Gina has pulled off.

Back in the living room, Gina says, "I don't mean to start it all up again, Howard, but since we are on the subject. Throughout our history, you'd have to admit, man did his damnedest best to attribute all that's lewd and smelly and sinful to the female. Even today, among us sophisticates, when you say female, a funny odor attaches to it. But when you say male—what open vistas, what vigor. Until quite recently the word *woman* was to be avoided in polite society. Man has pulled off the worst possible smear campaign. So effective, in fact, he got woman to believe it, too. We should all sue you for libel. And while giving us females a bad name, man, at the same time, has constructed for himself the solid image of a credible, rational being. He is so noble and tolerant, he is even willing to put up with this lesser creature God has thrust upon him."

As Gina speaks, Marcus observes her, admiring her artistry, steering the conversation and Howard. He could use someone like Gina in his novel.

"Obviously," Howard says, mollified, totally devoid of anger, "we all carry our grievances. Blaming one another doesn't help."

At midnight they kiss and hug. "God." Lottie sighs deeply. "We need so much. I'm so happy we're all here together. Let's drink to the new year. Let's drink to meeting here again next New Year's."

"Amen!"

They begin to sing old romantic songs, and Gina, secretly, wipes a tear: another gem she has saved from ruin, a gem she can now wrap in soft tissue paper and place securely with all the others.

The next morning, Marcus wakes early; it is the first day of the year and he wants to begin with a disciplined mindset. He leans onto his elbow and, for a moment, watches Gina sleep. She sleeps on her back, both hands clasped on her chest on top of the covers. As he watches her, he is suddenly overwhelmed by the fact of her, by all five feet six inches of her, a physical fact that is alive and breathing right next to him. God, he thinks, the breathing flesh and blood of a human being, the awesome all-ness of one human being, with a mind all her own, her needs and wants.

Marcus rolls over and gets out of bed, quietly shuts the door behind him. He feels surprisingly alert, fully awake, and he congratulates himself for being up so early when in all fairness he could have given himself a break and stayed in bed.

He pours his coffee and goes into the study. Slowly he sips the hot, bitter coffee and gazes at the windows across the way. Behind the curtains, in hushed, darkened rooms, humans on their backs, on their sides, alone or in pairs, sleep off excess. He imagines a cat walking through the rooms, screwing its nose at the sour smell of wine and whisky and champagne left over in glasses or sheer plastic cups. A cigarette butt, a piece of bread, float in brown liquid. Last night, while cleaning up, he and Assya were alone in the kitchen, and as he bent down and held the garbage bag open for her to scrape the remains of food off the plates, he said something to the effect that he specialized in housework. Then she, in response, said something that now, for the life of him, he cannot recall, and he said, "Are you always this candid?" And she said, "Only when I want to be," smiling at him, a smile he thought to be lingering mysteriously, challenging him, and he asked himself, Is she flirting with me?

Fantasy won't do him any harm, he reflects and allows himself a flash of an image where Assya's face is very close to his. They kiss, their lips, at first, barely touching, but then, as their passion rises and the nearness of the other is so palpable, not only through touch but also through the delicate, yet audible, quickening of their breaths, they go at each other with mounting force.

He's got an erection in his hand: it feels good, but what is he going to do with it?

Put it in your novel, Gina would say, although she and Oscar have complained to him about male authors who, it appears, cannot help themselves and must refer in their books to their genitals, to what happens to them under their pants. They seem to love the word "erection" or "big" or "hard." Gina especially resents those authors who refer, coyly in her estimation, to their member as being limp and pale. "I can just picture him," she says, "your average white male author, sitting at his desk, cultivating an image of himself as the harmless, brainy author, the author who, nonetheless, is sexy to the ladies, because this pale, limp thing can easily, gigantically, be transformed.

"You too," she says with sudden inspiration. "Who knows what you're doing there, when you sit at your desk. I won't be surprised to learn that when the fancy strikes you, you take him out and look at him; it would take no effort." "But I don't," he says, although he has to admit that every once in while as he sits at his desk, he suddenly becomes aware of his physical existence, the physical space his body occupies in the room. At such moments he remembers his penis, unimportant right then, curled over his balls in the fit of his underwear. When this happens, Gina may or may not come to his mind, lazily, with no urgency. Gina on her back, her legs around his sides, her knees digging in his ribs as if she were the rider and he the horse.

At other times, coming out of the shower, he squats to the floor, tucks his head between his knees and observes his dangling manhood.

"I wonder," Gina says, "whether female authors feel a certain envy, even animosity, vis-à-vis their male counterparts. I know I would. Females don't have such a tool at their disposal. They don't have a sex they can pull out at will and do things with, shake and weigh it in their hands, watch it grow and be a thing in the world. When a woman gets aroused, she gets aroused; there's no attendant feeling of accomplishment and pride."

Enough. Marcus turns to his folders, his notes, his manuscript; it's time to get to work.

If only it were possible, he reflects wistfully, to spill it all onto the page in one, huge, perfectly chaotic, perfectly coherent, outpouring.

Seven

His system works like clockwork. At times he thinks he himself is clockwork. He writes out his life, his thoughts, on bits of paper he tears from 4" x 6" pads he keeps around the apartment. So as not to be wasteful, he determines beforehand the approximate size, space, he will need, and tears off a scrap of paper, assessing the length of the thought standing at the ready at the gate of his consciousness, a thought that only a moment ago did not exist, or perhaps, who knows, loitered with all the others until it surfaced and he grabbed it, hooked it, and froze it to allow him time to reach for one of his strategically placed pads.

But often, as he writes down the thought, he realizes he has made a judgment error, he should have torn a larger piece of paper, for the thought, now free to move, expands and evolves as he writes it down, as if to say: Look, there's more of me. And he, like the eager treasure seeker who can't believe his luck, speeds up his writing, realizing now he will need more space. So he tears off another small scrap, a sliver, thinking that this time, for sure, he is almost done writing out the thought. But soon, again he realizes that he has underestimated the length, and in the end he ends up with three or four small notes marked I, II, etc., instead of one, large, neat page.

But he'd rather err on the side of caution than have a sentence or two written out on a whole sheet of paper.

He has also developed a sort of affection for the torn, oddly shaped pieces of paper bearing his notes; they seem to confirm him, they suit his personality. The notes record the thoughts that have broken through, randomly, it seems—unless the thoughts, as thoughts, have their own agenda and govern their own priorities—from the general reverberating silence in his head.

When the notes accumulate, he copies them into one of his notebooks for possible future use and reference.

He is in the kitchen, making coffee. While waiting for the water to boil, he leans against the window and looks out. It is a gray Monday morning in mid-January. It snowed all weekend and the sky still hangs low with white clouds. He thinks of Gina schlepping through the cold, icy streets, on her way to work. He said to her, "Take the day off, stay home, it's miserable out." And she, instead of saying, gratefully, "You're right, it's the only thing to do," fixed him with her gaze, saying, "You have your work, I have mine," and strode off to the door. "Huff-huff," he barked to make her laugh, and she turned to look at him, considering her options; then, voting yes, she laughed, opened the door, and left.

Earlier, the two of them still in bed, Gina sits up, excited: she's had the most extraordinary dream, she must tell it to him. And he, accustomed to such introductions, waits. Gina believes her dreams are special, and often they are. She likes to tell them to him, sometimes confusing the terms *dreams* and *films,* for indeed her dreams have the quality of a film, an ethereal, delicate film.

Usually her dreams are long and busy: she meets people, she goes here, there. But this morning it's a short one. She goes to visit her father and finds him in the backyard, working in his garden. When he sees her, he comes toward her, takes her in his arms and holds her, and a great peace, Gina says in wonderment, descends on her. Such a great tranquility; everything else is washed away, all tensions, all fears; she becomes light.

Gina is doubly happy about this dream, as well as mystified. Since his death, more than six years ago, this is the first time her father has made an appearance in a dream. And this wonderful feeling of peace and tranquility is something she has never experienced before. It's not possible, she says, to experience such light in life, and therefore she feels privileged to have experienced it in her sleep. She says, "If this light is death, then death leaves you with a good feeling, although it might be boring if this is all that death is." Marcus nods. He says he is jealous. He says he wishes he knew exactly what it felt like, this light she is describing.

"It's really impossible to explain," Gina says. "Think of yourself as awash in light. Your head, your entire being, opens up, you become fluid. You know what I think? I think the mystery of dreams is what prompted humankind to investigate itself."

Tonight is Gina's night off: she'll stay home, just around the corner, on Ninth Street. She says it is good for them to spend time apart, usually one or two nights a week. It is good for the psyche; one has room to spread, flex the muscles of one's brain, one's spirit. Couples who don't have this break, this breathing space from one another, suffer for it. Whether they admit it or not, Gina says, they secretly resent it, resent the existence of someone else so constantly near, resent their having to put up with it, and, naturally, resent feeling resentful and feel guilty for it. Then they resent their sense of guilt, resent the person who's brought guilt into their lives. They begin to resent their life, then life in general. They resent the world, society, their neighbors. Soon, their resentments feed off each other's and harden like tumors.

He turns from the window. His heavy winter gloves are on the counter. They seem alive, as if his hands were still inside of them. One black glove is placed palm down. The fingers are half raised, as if tapping the counter with the fingertips. The other glove is laid on its side, thumb folded in, four fingers open in a delicate, perhaps supplicating, gesture.

What happens to my characters when I take a break? Marcus wonders. When I go to sleep and no longer think of them? Or do I, when I sleep, think of them?

What happens to a character when I leave him somewhere in his chapter, and go on to another character in a new chapter? What does he do while he waits? What happens to him, in his life, in his thoughts, as he remains frozen in limbo at that particular moment of his existence? Does he resent having to wait for the author to return and shine his spotlight and so revive him?

He himself, for instance, goes on with his life, although no one thinks him, thinks of him, or follows him. His characters, just like him, may be having their morning coffee, or, like Gina, may be on their way to work.

And what happens to a character while the reader turns the page? They're suspended together, reader and character, as if in the air, until the reader connects again with the print on the next page.

Indeed, Marcus thinks, there are two kinds of turning of the page. There's the arbitrary one where the writer ended a chapter and the printer left the rest of the page blank. And there's the turning of the page where the page simply ends.

Both turnings of the page involve two different mental processes: in one, the reader, complying with the author, mentally prepares for the short pause, as if taking a new breath for the new chapter; in the other, the reader hurries on to the following page, holding the last word in his mind until it connects with the first one on the new page.

And when the reader, at night, shuts the book on its marker and turns off the light, they sleep side by side, reader and character.

The water is boiling. He pours it into the cup and goes into his study.

Eight

The old man takes his tea into the living room, carefully sets it on the table, and sits down. He leans forward, puts his palms around the cup. It's nice and warm, even hot. Presently his skin cannot take the heat, and he removes his hands, picks up the cup by the handle and sips the tea. Good, good. He's had a good day's work. And his daughter called, and his very new great-grandson babbled in his ear, and he laughed from deep in his heart. It's been a while since he's heard himself laugh like that. As soon as winter was over, his daughter promised, they'd all come to New York for a visit. Oh, he said in earnest, let winter end already.

He sighs, puts on his glasses, and reads the notes he has just copied into his journal: "I think I found it, the connective, cohesive tone that will act as agent, as invisible membrane between the parts, making them parts of the same whole. The tone that will allow me to digress, to leap out of sequence, ignore the strict rigidity of temporality. A unifying tone that will liberate me from the confining dictates of logic and plot.

"To touch on all basic assumptions, retrace and isolate each stage in the progression of the Given.

"To penetrate through the tissue, puncture the sturdy, yet fragile, texture of life, of human endurance and appetite; touch at the stuff life has turned into a mind, and vice versa: touch the stuff of a mind converted into tangibles we call life; achieve virtual reality in the novel, in the life.

"Draw the writer and reader into the pulsating life of the novel, its serous fluid.

"To reach the optimal intimate distance between oneself and the work.

"Adopt a seriousness, a sober matter-of-factness, a committed understanding.

"Know that you repeat yourself, and why.

"Where there's motion, there's no present. Only the dead exist in the present; the past, as Faulkner said, is never dead; it's not even past.

"Does one write a novel so one can finish it?"

His notes give him pleasure. This is the reliable pleasure to be had at his age. And the loving preparation of good basic foods like toast and cheese, an egg, soup. Tonight, though, he'll indulge and order in. Maybe Chinese. Or, on second thought, maybe rice and beans and some vegetable dish. And coconut ice cream for dessert.

Nine

In the evening, Gina arrives and flops on the couch in the living room. "I'm exhausted," she says, while he pours a swirl of Napoleon into a deep snifter and hands it to her.

She says, "Thanks, you're an angel," and he looks at her. "Angel?" he asks, and she shakes her head, "I'm sorry, I'm still in the office." She takes a sip of the cognac and slumps against the cushions, balancing the glass on her stomach. "I met Assya for lunch."

"Assya," he says slowly, as if trying to recall who she is. "Assya," he repeats. "How is she?"

"She's fine."

"I meant to ask . . . she and that guy?"

"Nick?"

"Yes, Nick, are they . . . ?"

"No, they're not, they're just friends."

He considers this a moment, then says, "I love the way women, with a flip of tongue and finger, dismiss friendship, or certain relationships."

"I'm not dismissing friendship." Gina smiles.

"Besides, they could be just friends and still do it."

"But they don't, I tell you. She told me."

"Maybe she's not telling you the whole truth."

Gina eyes him. "Why wouldn't she tell me the whole truth? And what's the whole truth anyway?"

"I'm not saying that she doesn't. I'm just suggesting it's a possibility. She strikes me as one who keeps things to herself. How come she never married?"

"Just like me, *Marling*," Gina stresses, shaking her head, making a point. "She's never found the right man."

"The right man." Marcus pours himself another whisky. He likes the way she calls him Marling, the way her voice rises and falls. She presented Marling—a combination of Marcus and darling—as a gift to him on their first anniversary. "The right man. It sounds too complicated for words."

"You're right." Gina laughs. "It's an oxymoron."

He laughs with her. "I mean, she's good looking and all, Assya is. She probably didn't want it, a relationship."

"She's had relationships, long-term relationships, and they ended, like all good things."

"Then she did find the right man, several of them."

"No, not the absolutely right man. They were substitutes, temporary help."

"What am I, then? Right now I seem to be the right man, but in a year or two it may turn out that I, too, was just a substitute."

Gina thinks a moment. "True. I try not to think about the future."

Later, after a light dinner of soup and salad, he tells Gina: "Yesterday, I imagined you going home from work. I saw you get off the bus and cross Fifth Avenue in your long, sure stride. I saw you lean into the wind as you crossed the avenue diagonally. Since you stubbornly, fashionably, won't button your coat, you need your hands to do the job. One gloved hand hugs your waist, holding the flap of the coat in place, while the other reaches up toward your throat, holding up the collar and seeking extra warmth in the silk folds of your scarf. I know you so well."

Gina smiles. "I took a cab home last night. It let me off right in front of my building."

"It doesn't matter," Marcus continues. "You cross the avenue, a tall, slender figure whose long skirt, whipped by the wind, gets between her legs, hindering her steps. You reach your building and Jack, your doorman, leaps to open the door for you. No wonder—you're one of his favorite residents. You're not only a good-looking chick, but you're nice, and also generous when it counts."

"Thank you, Marling."

"When you get upstairs, you drop your bags and paper . . . No, wait. First you pick up your mail. Your keys are already in your coat pocket, and as you enter the building, you bring the bunch out and head for the mailbox. You feel mildly important, if a bit tired, entering the pleasant foyer of your building, your *domicile,* after a day's work, carrying your briefcase, your shoulder bag. The heels of your shoes click pleasantly on the glossy marble floor. Other neighbors come and go. They cross the lobby, some arriving, some leaving, some taking their dogs out for a walk. You exchange smiles, greetings. You're all politely aware of your good fortunes. You may take it for granted that those who live under the same communal roof as you belong in the same civilized, urbane group.

"Your box is full. You bend a little to better collect all the folded magazines, the envelopes, the occasional postcard. You lock the box and go to the elevator, leafing through the envelopes, looking for a special one, perhaps a letter, perhaps some unexpected good news. As you're looking over your mail, you're aware of your neighbors, waiting for the elevator with you; they, too, are looking over their mail. It is very possible that you and they sneak a glance to check how many envelopes the others hold in their hands. The more mail you receive—real mail in first-class envelopes—the more respect you command. You're a well-connected member of society, and many seek you out.

"The elevator arrives and all of you file in, leisurely, still leafing through your mail, perhaps for the second or third time. In order to save time when you get upstairs, but also to show your neighbors you don't attach much importance to the mail thing—namely, that you don't mind if they see that most of your mail is indeed junk and bills—you begin to separate out the envelopes, placing the real ones in your bag, and holding the others in your hand to be tossed, as soon as you enter your apartment, into the recycling paper basket."

"You're very thorough," Gina says.

"You're finally upstairs. Home. You drop your things by the round table in the vestibule and go straight to your bedroom. You undress, planning your steps for maximum efficiency. The more efficient you are, the sooner you'll be in your bath, then your kitchen, and finally on your couch, eating your dinner, watching the evening news. Bliss. A night alone. A night without Marcus."

Gina smiles.

"You're naked now. I forgot to mention that you've let your bath run. As a matter of fact, as soon as you came into the bedroom, you switched on the light and went into the bathroom to let the water run. You sprinkle your bath with relaxing herbs and return to the bedroom to undress. As you unzip your skirt and let it drop to the floor, you get out of your shoes. You unbutton your shirt, unhook your wonderful bra, then sit on the bed and peel off your stockings, your panties.

"Now you go into the bathroom, wipe the steam off the mirror and peer at your face. You look a bit tired. You imagine that this is the face you offer to strangers on the street; like them, you've become anonymous, drawn into yourself, your face blank and drained of expression.

"You remind yourself that anonymity is one step closer to death.

"So you smile at yourself, to relax the rigidity of your expression. Winter, especially, exacts its toll on us. You test the temperature of the water with your toe. You're very proud of your toes because they descend, from the big toe to the small one, in a beautifully proportioned line.

"In the water, you relax. You lean back and close your eyes with a sigh. After a while, you begin, very lightly, to soap yourself, maybe humming a little tune. Now you reach for your pumice stone, rub the soles of your feet.

"When you come out of the water, you pat your skin dry with a large, engulfing towel, then rub onto your skin a fragrant body lotion, paying special attention to your feet, ankles, knees, and elbows, those areas most susceptible to dryness.

"And in all this time, dear," Marcus says, "you haven't given even one little thought to yours truly."

"That's not true," Gina says, but not forcefully.

"Come sit in my lap."

Gina cozies up in his lap. "Is this for your novel? This description of me?"

"Maybe," Marcus says. "I still know very little, but I'm compiling details, small, everyday things. I think my life in sentences."

"With commas and periods and question marks?" Gina laughs. "We're so good when we're alone, just you and I."

"Most couples, I think, are best when alone."

"I've given you my best lines when we're alone."

"When we're in bed," Marcus corrects. "Like you said, you have respect for me only when I'm erect."

Gina laughs gaily.

"And you've named my penis, 'The Great Redeemer.' You're a handful," he says, pushing his hands under her, shifting her weight on his thighs. "I think you'd better go back to the couch."

Ten

Diligently, he copies into his notebook:

He has decided to employ the present tense, a present tense, he hopes, that will be fraught with the past. He borrows these words from a critic whose name he has forgotten, but who said that Katherine Anne Porter's "Flowering Judas" was written in a present tense fraught with the past.

He has apprenticed himself by reading. One book leads to another in a long succession, a long, unbroken chain. He reads everything, philosophy, religion, science, but in the past couple of years, for the sake of his dictionary and his novel, he's been concentrating more and more on works of fiction. He can safely assert that he's read all the important Western authors, as well as some Chinese, Japanese, and African authors.

There's a steady stream of books in his apartment, and he's very meticulous about their organization. There are stacks of books in nearly every room, placed according to subject matter and his level of eagerness to get to a certain book or author. His friends know they are not to disturb the arranged order of the books, unless they ask his permission first and promise to return the book to its exact place in the stack.

The most urgent stack is in his study, and that's where he places most of the books when they arrive from the store. The less urgent ones are placed near his bed and in the living room. It may also happen that an urgent book becomes less so after he's read a few pages; such a book is placed on a special stack, also in the study, of books begun but not yet finished.

A few months ago, he placed an order with Serpent's Tail to send him all the books in their catalog.

When he is done with a book, he looks up, stares for a while into the distance, then gets up, places the book on the shelf, and proceeds to one of the stacks. He picks up the next in line and takes it, a weighty promise, to his chair.

At times, reviewing his stacks of books, he experiences a quickening of the breath, overwhelmed by all the work still ahead.

He has dedicated himself to his dictionary, a dictionary through which he would transmit to the public the absolute importance of literature, the utter pleasure to be found in its treasures. He'll point out the painstaking, intuitive genius the author engages when immersed in his work, an immersion he'll later require of his reader. Indeed, quite often, reading a novel, a reader will suddenly catch himself, remember himself as a being in the world; he'll raise his eyes from the book, perhaps gaze out of the window or straight ahead, and reflect how crafty the author is, leading him, the transformed reader, through the various layers of narration, plunging him deeper and deeper into that area in his brain where he and the words are one; the area in his brain where he and the author are engaged in a duel from which they'll both emerge the winners, as twin Olympians.

For, as Nabokov has said, the author does battle with the reader.

He has titled his dictionary *Dictionary of the Human Gesture in Western Literature*. Diligently, he copied into his notebooks those select paragraphs where his authors take the time and pain to break a gesture down to its minutest quiver, finding the words to paint it for themselves and, ultimately, for the reader, all the while avoiding the pitfalls of preciousness. Those same gestures that cannot be conveyed in one verb. Those involuntary gestures and twitches common to all.

Those we may look for in others as telltale signs of dishonesty and dissimulation. Those that betray our hidden emotions, and which we try to conceal from others.

Such concentrated reading, he believes, perforce makes a reader human.

Marcus leans back in his chair. There's room in his mind for the whole universe; his mind, in fact, contains the universe.

After an hour of concentrated work—an hour, one might say, that never existed, an hour that zoomed by while he was bent over his desk—Marcus feels he's under a spell. He could materialize in a thousand places all at once: he feels alert, invigorated.

In his mind, he sees a man seated at his desk, both hands gripping the desk. The man sits forward in his chair in a state of readiness. He's ready to spring, but where to, what for? It's very cold out, a cold February morning. If he did go out, he wouldn't walk far.

At least it's not raining, and it's not very windy. If he dresses properly, he could go for a short, brisk walk, fill his lungs with air. The cold air will condense his thoughts, refocus his mind. The vein he's been exploring and probing this morning has been exhausted, drained.

Two months already into the new year! Soon it will be three and four, then it will be summer, his favorite time of the year, and before he knows it, this new year will be over. And again they'll celebrate the new year, as if they hadn't grown older, as if their muscles hadn't got slacker, their bones more brittle. They'll eat, laugh, and joke as if undaunted by the immutable fact that another year has gone by, never to return.

He picks up the pocket calendar Oscar has given him and flips through the pages. Oscar gives him a new calendar every year. And every year, upon receiving it, Marcus squeezes and twists the calendar to squeeze out its newness and make it pliant. Every year, as he squeezes the calendar, he reflects how wonderful it would be if man could knead his days to suit his needs, work the days and hours into malleable matter.

It is a quality, leather-bound pocket calendar, the kind he and his past business associates, year in, year out, pulled out from their breast pockets, together with their Pelicans, their Mont Blancs, their Watermans, to mark off a date, a future commitment. A subtle, and yet not so subtle, status statement came with these accessories, and he always felt a bit self-conscious when participating in this ritual, aware that the businessman across the desk or lunch table, seemingly oblivious of Marcus's pen, had definitely noticed the make, the model, just as Marcus, also seemingly oblivious, noted his colleague's.

He felt self-conscious, but he played along, caught between the obvious silliness of the situation and its obvious trapping seductiveness. Silliness because one could not resist the tickle of self-importance, a tickle countered by the immediate recognition that this feeling of self-importance was in fact based on very little. And obvious seductiveness because there was a genuine pleasure to be had in owning and handling such exquisitely made objects, works of art in themselves.

Again, Marcus leafs through the crisp, gilt-edged pages. The paper crackles pleasantly between his fingers. Such quality paper invites writing, intimating that across its smooth and shiny surface, the tip of a pen might perform miracles; the nib or the ballpoint alike would glide without a hitch, would form beautiful and vigorous letters on the page. On such paper, one's handwriting would acquire a new vitality, a new authority. As a matter of fact, to this day, he is fascinated by the movement of pen on paper. He likes to watch how others hold their pens, between what fingers, and with what intensity; he likes to watch how letters rapidly form under a pen. At times he thinks he can actually see the inky words hang from the tip of the pen; at times he thinks that the words on the page chase the tip of the pen.

He examines the azimuthal equidistant projection map, centered on Washington, and its six points of distance. He lingers over the colorful map of the globe—such a tiny, accurate-looking map. He remembers from his school days that each color stands for something: for mountains, rivers, borders. He remembers how he labored over his geography assignments, copying out such maps into his notebooks.

He remembers how he wished that his notebooks would acquire the same busy, yet neat, look of those proud notebooks belonging to some of his classmates, usually girls, those extraordinary notebooks inflated with drawings and pertinent clippings.

Such memories fill him with nostalgia, the same tender nostalgia he was filled with a few years back when he happened to pick up one of Rosina's textbooks, her geometry textbook, and the distant, yet familiar, pages of triangles and definitions contracted his heart, filling him with a sweetness, like condensed milk. He tried to solve a simple problem, and when he succeeded he relived the ecstasy of the hard-won accomplishment he had felt as a boy when a certain definition, a certain problem, suddenly opened up and revealed its logic: it was as if two opposite pulses clashed in his brain, clicked off a new connection, and in a flash he understood that in a parallelogram, if side AB is equal to the sum of AC and BD, and since AB is equal to CD, CD is equal to the sum of AC and BD.

The illusory premise of his school days, he now reflects. The misleading, simplified message: the world makes sense.

He puts on his coat, hat, and scarf and walks out the door, turns, and locks it. He first locks the top lock, then the bottom. As he performs these motions, his hand on automatic pilot, the quiet in the hallway echoes the quiet in his mind. He asks himself whether he has forgotten something, and since he can't think of what it might be, he goes to the elevator and pushes the down button, aware of how annoyed he gets when people press both the up and down buttons, several times, as if this futile action will bring the elevator faster to them.

Downstairs, one of the handymen shampoos the long rug that leads to the mailboxes, and the superintendent, his arms folded on his chest, stands nearby and observes him. Leave the guy alone, Marcus wants to tell the super. How can he do his job properly if you stand there and watch him with your hawk eyes? He dislikes the super, for the super reminds him of a German butcher with his wide, square skull, his fat, chicken-white face, his small eyes, his short, thick fingers.

He doesn't like the way the super stands, his elephant legs apart, his stomach thrust forward, as he watches the young Hispanic shampoo the rug. But as soon as the super notices Marcus approach, he brings his feet together, unfolds his arms, and courteously greets him. Marcus returns the greeting, feeling uncomfortable both for himself and the super, who doubtless can sense Marcus's dislike and unease. But who is he to judge? It may very well be that the super is a good and generous man. And he sure does the work, for the building is run smoothly and efficiently, and Marcus, as a resident, benefits.

Out on the street, he puts on his gloves, looking left, then right, as yet undecided where and how far he wants to go. A decision of which he is vaguely aware is reached in his mind and he turns right and walks west, thinking he might walk all the way to the river. In his mind, he draws a quick map of the streets he'll take to get there. It's not as cold as he thought, and it's been a while since he's gone that way.

He walks up to Sixth Avenue, crosses Sheridan Square, and turns into Christopher Street. He taps his pockets and realizes that he's forgotten to bring along a pad and a pencil. If a thought comes to him, he'll have to go into a coffee shop, ask to borrow a pen, use a napkin.

This won't be necessary, he thinks. If a good idea or thought comes to him, he'll repeat it in his mind until it sticks; so that when he gets home he'll be able to retrieve it and write it down. Besides, most valid ideas have a way of coming back, of popping up and presenting themselves—whole, proud, smugly coquettish, aware of the eagerness with which they were sought after.

It is ten o'clock in the morning; it is very unusual for him to be out at this early hour, breathing the morning air. It seems to him that the streets, under the gray sky, are in hibernation. There are very few people out, mostly young, carrying books, and something in the air—the narrow streets, the square, the stark trees—reminds Marcus of Paris, of his carefree days as a student. In those days, he'd be walking down the street and would be suddenly reminded that he was in Paris, Paris! and a sudden elation would overtake him, an elation that told him that he had managed it, managed to arrive and live in Paris—how privileged he was, how fortunate. But together with the feeling of elation, another feeling slipped in as well, a feeling of a terrible and oppressive sadness, a sadness whose source he could not find in himself, and yet he knew it came from him. It had to do, he speculated, with the all-too-powerful, the all-too-historical beauty of the city. It was as if all the people who'd ever lived in it had not only left their mark, but were still there, ghost-like, refusing to leave.

He reaches the river and leans his foot on the low stone wall and watches the dark, gray water flow south. His thoughts, too, run south, floating on the water.

"If it isn't Marcus Weiss!" someone calls at his side, and it happens so fast, he doesn't even have time to be startled. A stranger in a long, gray overcoat, a gray fedora, smiles broadly at him. A handsome, pleasant face. Bernie! Myra's younger brother. Bernie. He used to like Bernie.

"Bernie," he exclaims. "Bernie Katz. What in hell—"

The two men hug, pat each other on the back.

"I thought you got lost somewhere in Australia. Myra said you got married there."

"And divorced. I'm back. Good as new. In my soul"—Bernie Katz laughs—"I'm a poet. I go crazy when things around me are too neat and orderly. Let's go for coffee."

"No, not now," Marcus says, then hastily adds, "I have to get back. But come over to the house. Come tonight. Come whenever you like."

"I will, I will." Bernie pokes the pavement with the tip of his shoe. "How are things with you?"

"All right. As well as can be expected."

"Good, good."

"And you?"

"Fine, can't complain, although I could if I wanted to."

"Yeah." Marcus nods. "But please come, I mean it. I want you to promise."

"You bet." Bernie puts his arm around Marcus's shoulders. "I plan to become a fixture in your house. You're the only friend I've got in the city. So what's your hurry? Why can't we stop for coffee and a friendly chat?"

"I've only come out for a few minutes, to air my thoughts. I'm working, you see, on a novel."

"A novel." Bernie grins. "You? A novelist?"

Marcus shrugs, a bit embarrassed to admit that yes, indeed, if not a novelist yet, at least an aspiring one.

"Well, congratulations. You always seemed a bit detached, off in your own world, so I guess it fits. What's it about?"

"Oh." Marcus mulls over the "detached" attribute. "I'm not sure yet. A compilation of sorts, I think."

Bernie gives him a look. "You guys are not to be trusted. You kidnap us, unsuspecting souls, and sacrifice us at the altar."

"Nothing for you to worry about, Bernie. You're not in my plans."

"You never know, though, do you?" Bernie laughs, a twinkle in his eyes. And, sure enough, a few days later events are lifted from Marcus's hands, for as soon as Gina meets Bernie and approves of him, and as soon as she receives Assya's consent, she sets a dinner date, a dinner she and Marcus will host, so that Bernie meets Assya, and Assya meets Bernie.

Eleven

Gina is excited; such matters, Marcus reflects, occupy her to the fullest. "Why not?" she counters when he comments on her matchmaking efforts. "Why not put together two human beings who may be looking for the same thing, who may each offer what the other wants. It's a simple, everyday transaction."

In the morning, at his desk, he repeats her name, Assya, Assya, testing the hypnotic duration of the syllables, marveling at the reluctance with which he lets go of the sound when he finally parts his teeth and lets the *s*'s swim out into the vowel.

Before Gina interfered, he had worked out a plan where Assya was incorporated into his life, his novel. In his mind, he envisioned a schedule, a kind of coexistence where the three of them, Gina, Assya, and himself, were bound together with no real complications. He played around with different scenarios: in some, Assya and Gina were aware of, and accepted, the role the other played in his life; in others, Gina had to remain in the dark. But even in those, where he had to lie to Gina at times, he allowed only one serious difficulty: the fact of the women's consecutive periods. Twice a month, he imagined, he was confronted with the emotional tidal wave, released by menstrual bleeding, and with the unmistakable, primitive odor that placed his women on the plane of legendary Amazons, and that reminded him, very pungently, of his status as mere worshipper.

Their periods. He projects onto Assya Gina's belief that a woman's menstruation is a rest period for her cunt.

Before Gina interfered, Assya appeared so vividly before him, he could actually pick her scent; Assya, who gives herself freely, expecting the same absolute commitment from her partner.

"How old is Assya?" he asks Gina as he helps her in the kitchen. Tonight their guests are due, and Gina, who believes that a good meal is conducive to romance, is at her imaginative best, marinating four tuna steaks in soy sauce, crushed ginger and garlic, a drop of extra virgin olive oil, and black pepper she grinds over the steaks. At her side, he washes out the lettuce, red peppers, and scallions, his mouth watering as he breathes in the aroma of soy sauce and garlic, as he watches Gina's glistening fingers turn over the tuna, making sure each steak is equally saturated on both sides.

"Why do you ask? Forty-four," Gina says.

Later they arrive, first Bernie, dashing in a profusion of soft, varying shades of gray—his favorite color, he tells them—then Assya is at the door, so happy and glowing, so soon, in fact, after Bernie's arrival, that Marcus suspects that the two, too eager to wait, have taken matters into their own hands and have met already, perhaps even intimately. All at once he feels old and clumsy, superfluous. He resolves to keep an eye on them.

He follows them into the living room, offering drinks. Assya sits down in the armchair to the right, while Bernie goes around the coffee table and takes the couch. They both seem a bit ill at ease, even timid; indeed, as two who have never met before, but who, at a first, furtive glance have found the other attractive. But, Marcus considers, they may be playacting. As soon as his back is turned . . .

He hands Assya her sherry, Bernie his scotch, then sits in the chair next to Assya's.

Slowly, they thaw.

Bernie says something about small talk, and Assya replies that a thread of inner logic runs through conversations, even if it is not always apparent.

Soon, Gina joins them and sits next to Bernie on the couch. Here we are, Marcus muses. Two couples. Two men and two women, spending an evening together.

He wonders if Assya finds him, Marcus, attractive. He knows that Gina finds Bernie attractive; she's made it her point to tell him that.

He sneaks a glance at Assya, then Bernie. There's something glamorous, he thinks, about a new, fresh, as yet unattached couple. Whereas he and Gina are almost ancient, these two, Bernie and Assya, seem alive in comparison, alert, full of adventure; there's so much promise ahead of them, between them.

But why should he care? Why must he constantly compare this to that? Do the others, now seated in his living room, bother their heads with such questions? As they nod and smile, just as he nods and smiles, what are they really thinking? If only he could ask them to reveal the background commentary running through their heads, ask them to talk to him heart to heart and tell him everything.

But are we ever capable of telling the truth? The whole truth, and nothing but the truth, so help us God?

How can one tell the truth? On the witness stand, one should be sworn not to tell a lie. How can one be expected to translate the whole truth into words?

What was the name of that German linguist who wished for a language where a lie, automatically, would stipulate a syntactical deviation?

"Marcus prepared the salad," Gina says. "He's very good with salads."

"She lets me rinse the lettuce," Marcus says, modestly, and Assya laughs. Her laughter is contagious, liberating in fact, for now they all laugh. Pleased and encouraged, he continues. "I'm allowed minor, menial tasks. This is not a joke. You should see Gina in the kitchen. A real despot. She doesn't trust me as far as she can throw me. Once in a while, I offer to take some responsibilities off her hands, but there's no way she'll relinquish any to me. Least of all, shopping for produce. Only she knows exactly which tomato to pick.

She's good friends with the potatoes and onions, and has a special affinity with eggplants."

In her measured voice, Assya says, "I don't trust men, either. And when it comes to shopping, not even women." She laughs, looking at Gina. "I think it's in our genes, women's genes. We've seen our mothers pick and choose and smell and squeeze, and we think, like them, that only we know best."

"If I were a woman," Bernie says, "I wouldn't trust men. It's a miracle, I think, that women trust us as much as they do."

"How do you mean?" Marcus asks.

"That they allow us to come near them. I mean, with one blow a man could—"

"But we love and respect them," Marcus says. "In emergencies, for instance, or any kind of catastrophe, women and children are rescued first."

"It appeals," Bernie says, "to the male's valiant ego."

"True. But, like you just said, it is in our nature to be valiant. To pull together and defend our women."

"We need to breed. And," Bernie adds, "men kill women every day."

"Can we please change the subject?" Gina says. "It's time for dessert."

For dessert Gina serves coffee and cheese strudel; a strudel, Assya says, that practically melts in one's mouth. Bernie asks if strudel is German or Austrian, and Gina says she believes it's Austrian; the Germans are only famous for sausage and beer. And all things mechanical, Bernie says. Marcus tells them that he happens to be reading a great German writer, Hubert Fichte, a writer he recommends they all read.

Gina lets out a delicate, warning cough, but then Assya says she's read Fichte, and Marcus is delighted. He tells her that many of his favorite authors hail from postwar Germany and Austria. Hail, Heil, Bernie says and laughs, adding that it's not funny, but the way Marcus said hail and Germany in one breath, reminded him of a few hateful *h*'s, like Heil Hitler and Hep! Hep!, the anti-Jewish movement in Germany in the early 1800s.

"But more to the point," Bernie adds. "I have little patience for books, novels, that is, but I'll read several newspapers cover to cover. I'm a news addict, I guess. It runs like blood in my veins. I have to have it in the morning."

Here Gina turns to Bernie and cautions him that it kills Marcus to hear such talk. Reading the paper, after all, is a definite waste of time, while death, don't we know, gets nearer all the time.

"Well, yes," Marcus admits. "It kills me that millions and millions just go through the motions. They buy the paper because their parents bought it, their neighbors buy it. It's the automatic, reflexive thing to do every morning and every weekend. I want people to change their habits, those habits they have never stopped to question."

"But why should they?" Bernie asks. "Why should they question something that gives them pleasure, something they enjoy?"

"Because papers deceive them. And I don't mean in the usual sense that newspapers lie, but in the deeper sense that they get us to believe that what they sell is important, truthful. The amount of paper they heap on us. All those articles and critics and specialists and experts, the new gurus. We're gullible, desperate for direction in questions of style, health, and the rest of it. We're so busy looking for experts, we forget to listen to our own voice; we forget that we, too, count."

"It takes me ten minutes to read the paper," Assya says. "I read the paper to get the news, to know what's going on."

"What news?" Marcus waves his hand dismissively. "The headlines? Journalism today, for the most part, is nothing but gossip on a grand scale."

"He reads *The New Republic*," Gina says. "He thinks it makes him better. Smarter."

"My point is," Marcus explains, patiently. "People should take their lives into their own hands. They should read books rather than—"

"All right, all right." Gina gives Assya and Bernie a meaningful look. "We'll read. We swear." She laughs and the others join her.

Assya, in her merriment, leans over and strikes Gina on the knee, and Marcus, in spite of himself, smiles.

When they calm down, Gina says, "And that's what I have to live with. Believe me, it can be painful. The thing, though: it truly bugs him. Sometimes I feel for him. I feel his frustration with the way we choose to live our lives, with things human. But he likes strudel."

Again they laugh, and Marcus relaxes; he begins to enjoy himself. At least, if indirectly, he made them laugh. "It's really none of my business," he offers, but in his heart of hearts he rebels against the sentiment of his words, for it is his business—people should assist one another. Didn't Unamuno already say that men must strive to impose themselves upon one another? Must give their spirits to one another? "But I'll say one more thing. If all of us devoted more time to books and to each other, we'd be living in a far better world."

"Maybe. But people, you know, they do have other worries, other priorities," Bernie says. "They have families to support. They hold down jobs. You don't expect them to read Dostoevsky when they get home after a day's work."

"I do. Two or three pages before they go to bed. Try it. A few quiet moments to settle your mind before falling asleep. Your sleep, I guarantee, will be deep, and you won't need a sleeping pill."

"It seems to me," Bernie says, "that your frustration, as Gina puts it, probably originates elsewhere. I don't see why you should care what Joe Schmo reads."

"Don't waste your breath," Gina says. "He wants everyone to be like him."

"Not true," Marcus says, suddenly animated. "I want people to . . . oh, never mind. Let me just remind you that families, before we had this TV machine, used to sit together and read aloud from a book, and then talk about it." To his surprise, his heart is pounding, hard.

"All right," Assya says, "I volunteer." She leans her elbows on her thighs and clasps her hands. "Before I leave tonight, give me a list of authors you recommend that I read."

"I'll be happy to." Marcus takes a deep breath.

"Are you all right, Marling?"

"Yes, I'm fine." He reaches for his glass of water. "Just a bit thirsty."

"And I want to hear more about your dictionary," Assya continues. "The idea of the gesture as being so central."

Pleased, Marcus says, "It's the first thing we learn, don't we? Movement. The baby in the womb flexes its muscles. Later, it's a question of refinement, of how we move, what we wish to convey. From childhood on, we adopt the mannerism that we find so charming and attractive in others. We go through phases, adopting this gesture, dropping that one. But essentially, although we all draw from the same pool, we have our own set of gestures, those gestures that define us, those gestures that, for the most part, we're unaware of. One day, soon I hope, you'll let me read for you from my excerpts."

Gina pours cherry brandy from a crystal decanter into glasses she's brought to the table. "He specializes in notebooks," she says. "That's where he lives, happily. Between the pages of his notebooks. Sometimes he looks at me and I can see him deciding in which notebook he wants to place me. It's beyond funny. He has a notebook for quotes, a notebook for his novel, a notebook for facts, a notebook for his dictionary, a notebook for his journal, and one that he keeps for general data that won't fit in any of the above. And." She raises her hand. "He keeps a separate notebook where he lists the books he's read."

Marcus watches Gina. Her thin arms seem whiter, longer, thinner against the black, sleeveless stretch-cotton dress. There's a very fine line she has never crossed before, not in company at least, the line between poking gentle fun for fun's sake, and letting real feelings or resentment show. She hasn't crossed it, not yet, and, hopefully, never will, but he guards against it, awaits it nonetheless, feigning good-natured insouciance while listening intently for that one note, that one nuance that will tell him she has finally crossed over to the other side.

Marcus shakes his head. "You don't know what you're missing. We think we remember a lot more than we actually do. A few years from now, you won't even remember that we met here, that we sat and talked, that we had a good time. Assya and Bernie may remember tonight as the night when they first met, they may remember a few words they exchanged. But for Gina, my good Gina, tonight will blend in a blur of many other similar nights, a night spent with friends, poking fun at Marcus. Whereas I, a few years from now, may open my journal and remember the authors I have yet to recommend to Assya. I'll remember where each of you sat, what you said . . ."

"I'm not poking fun," Gina says.

"I am," Marcus continues. "If you look at it from my angle, I have the upper hand, but I offer it to you. I want you to have it."

They look at him.

Bernie stands up, shakes out his legs, and sits down again. "But," he says. "Think about the chunk of time you take out every day to record your life. Imagine what you could have accomplished during that lost chunk of time. You could have lived your life instead of writing it."

"Don't worry," Marcus says. "I live it doubly. When I live it and when I write it. The rest is *gogul-mogul.*"

"Gogul-mogul?"

Marcus smiles. "Something my mother used to make. A glassful of heaven. I say glass and not cup, because that's what we drank from when I was growing up. Take the raw yolk of an egg and mix it with honey and very hot milk. It's a Jewish mother's preemptive strike against colds, against the evil eye and other misfortunes, God forbid, that may befall her child. I loved the stuff, even prayed to get sick so she would make it for me. It was sweet and thick, like nectar for the soul and body."

In a sudden show of affection, Gina deserts her seat and lands in Marcus's lap. "To tell the honest truth," she tells Assya and Bernie, "I like his lectures. Sometimes, when I tune in, I actually learn something, if not always what he intends for me to learn."

Assya laughs. "You look so nice together, the two of you."

"Thank you, Assya," Gina says. "You and Bernie don't look so bad yourselves."

"Success!" Gina declares after their guests leave. Now she's all business, efficient and quick, directing him in the task of putting away the clean dishes and glasses.

"What is?" Marcus asks.

"Bernie and Assya."

"How do you know?"

"I know. I can tell. The way they looked at each other, the fleeting, casual touch."

"I didn't see it." Marcus, genuinely surprised, a clean, sparkling glass in his hand, turns to Gina.

"You don't look." Gina takes the glass from his hand. "That's why."

"Well," he says. "Since you see everything, what do you think they're doing right now?"

"Hmm. Maybe having a nightcap somewhere."

"Where? At Assya's?"

"Probably." Gina smiles at him. "Why?"

"Do you think they'll do it? Tonight?"

Gina gives him a look, then laughs. "God, you're such a child. And why the alarm? Why be so stingy? So grudging?"

"I'm not stingy," he defends himself. "I just—"

"Well, *obviously*, I don't know for sure, but I don't see why not. They may test the water. They're two adults. They may do as they like, even if you don't approve."

Twelve

Marcus copies into his novel notebook:

He reminds himself he must endear his characters to the reader. Love, he has learned, is the best means. Through his love for another, be it a child, a parent, a lover, a character reveals himself. Someone capable of love draws the reader close. Often, just a nickname will do the trick, a nickname the character comes up with for the person he loves. A well-chosen nickname will work on two fronts: it will reveal the character as tender, affectionate, and inventive, while also shedding light on the person loved, on the one who has inspired such affection, such a funny, loving, endearing nickname.

Love propels one to act. Love changes one, colors one's thinking. And many other, valiant aspects are appended to love, and are subsumed: risk taking and courage in the face of doom (for love, in most cases, is doomed), nobility, loyalty, as well as remorse, defiance, and a foreboding sense of loss.

But, he muses. As he endeavors to endear his characters to the reader, who is there to endear him? Endear his own character, his personality? Who is there to speak up for him when he himself can't speak? Who is there to care about him? Sing his praises?

Absorbed, he looks out the window. He becomes aware of his breathing, of his heartbeat. He allows everything in him to lapse, to become suspended. He envisions his characters, moving in slow motion, in long, deliberate strides. They're ghost-like, willful and stubborn. They're clad in long trench coats, the color of clay or ash. A menacing quality emanates from them as they advance toward him, somber, unsmiling, messengers from the underworld. He wishes they were a bit less aloof, a bit friendlier, more forthcoming.

As he copies out his notes, one after the other—reaching for the pile, copying out the note, discarding it and reaching for another—he sees himself as an old, small-town chemist who, at the end of the day, records in the log all the filled orders and prescriptions.

Affectionately, he refers to his notes as "prompter" notes, notes he jots down in one of his pads. He may be in the hall, on the way from the kitchen to his study, or on his way to the bathroom; he may be in the living room, the bedroom, when he'll think of something, a sentence fully formulated, or still formulating itself in his head; and he, so as not to interrupt the workings of his mind, will keep himself focused, concentrated, turn and walk to the nearest pad, a man under a spell.

For the most part, these notes indeed serve as prompters, as reminders of issues he might want to develop in the future. But it also happens that he begins to elaborate on the idea right there and then, jotting it down on a piece of paper he's torn from the pad; and as he runs out of space, having underestimated the potential length of his thought, he makes his letters smaller and smaller, to fit the ever-shrinking space still left him; and a warning begins to flash in his mind that a few days hence, when he sits down to copy the note into his notebook, he won't be able to decipher what he has written. Then the warning turns to advice, and he tells himself he'd better continue on a fresh sheet of paper where he will have all the space he needs to complete his evolving thought. But he knows from experience that he always, in the end, deciphers his notes and, being economical, he's in love with an order he himself has imposed. And so, not wishing to interrupt his flow for the duration of time it will take to tear another sheet off the pad, he continues to maneuver on the same piece of paper, taking pride in the fact that indeed he's managed to get it all to fit on that one single sheet; that indeed he's managed to fit the last words in the very last available space by turning the page sideways, then over, writing along the edges, his letters by now no longer letters but dots, twigs, and hooks, resembling the coiled, spineless forms of worms that may, at any moment, wiggle off the page.

But, at times, all his maneuvering is for naught and he has to reach for another sheet, sometimes aggravatingly so, because of just one word.

Having copied it out, he discards the note, with some reluctance, for he would have liked to preserve these notes, crammed as they are with his words, and whose meaning is held together by arrows in the margins pointing the way along the progression of thought.

He likes to tell his friends he's a compiler of notes, a collector of odds and ends.

It occurs to him that he thinks his life in sentences. With periods and commas. Dashes. Question marks and exclamation points. These last two, he remembers, were taught on the blackboard together, walking hand in hand in textbooks. He thinks he remembers himself, during the first year at school, as an obedient, attentive child, looking up at the teacher, aware of the seriousness of the enterprise, aware that he was there to learn. He can't remember now for sure, but it is likely that his immigrant parents must have coached him, telling him what his role at school would be. And he, once there, along with all the other pupils, seated at a desk for the first time, took his parents' preparatory instructions to heart, aware that his mind was on the alert in a new way, adjusting to a new mode of learning: the deliberate and methodical accumulation of knowledge.

There isn't much variety in his life, and he doesn't seek it. Some people claim he is detached, and even though he accepts their judgment, he doesn't really feel detached. He thinks of all the people who share the continent with him, the round globe, the steamy earth. It seems that each man waits for life to begin. At some rare and sparkling moments, the waiting stops and life arrives, meets up with the waiting, briefly, in a moment of fusion and sudden clarity.

Would man, ever, overcome moodiness, nastiness, pettiness? Would there, one day, be a new human being, a being so abstracted and distanced from the pulse of life that time and waiting would lose their meaning, their urgency?

Since human beings—caught up as they are in their own flesh, manacled as they are to their own history, to the unique compendium of their genes and idiosyncratic cells—are not, as yet, equipped to penetrate, but only to infer, another's experience, he, too, has to accept the order of things and conclude that no matter how hard and long he persists in trying to break down each component of human behavior, he can never distill the human experience into a simple formula, even if he wants to believe that each human being, fundamentally, is a walking/behaving problem, acting according to a certain set of decipherable mathematical formulae. The day may come when a powerful computing machine will be given the task to sort out and compress the myriad pieces of human data fed into it—data that will include every human convention, every known behavior—and to arrive at the exact formula for each individual, translating his messy traits into neat codes, and effectively break the lock to the human enigma.

Marcus takes off his glasses and rubs his eyes. He leans back in his chair and hoists his feet up on the desk. At certain points in his book, he wishes that the reader, as if digesting, will stop reading, gaze into the distance and then flip back the pages to find the exact spot where the author veered off, made an unscheduled detour.

Thirteen

It's a done deed. Just as Gina has predicted, Assya and Bernie are in fact a great success. They won't leave one another's side; one wonders how they ever managed to live before. From now on, when one refers to Assya, automatically the image, if not the name, of Bernie will appear in one's mind; and vice versa. From now on, when an evening or a party is being planned, Assya and Bernie, side by side, will be placed on the list. Perhaps even at the top of the list: a brand-new, exuberant couple. Even he has to admit that the eye is pleased, and the mind is at peace, when one looks at Bernie and Assya. Together they impart a certain tranquility, serenity. Assya, especially. A new fluidity accompanies her movements, and Marcus observes, mutely, how Assya leans toward Bernie, whispers something in his ear. He watches how she flicks Bernie's earlobe with her tongue, and then continues with the tongue down Bernie's neck. Does she know I'm watching? Marcus wonders.

At the breakfast, or elevenses, table he draws comfort from his writers. He measures himself against them, stores in his mind those instances where he and they share the same sensibility, the same understanding. This morning it's Cocteau who courageously stands up for the seemingly petty and trivial. "If someone asks me," Cocteau declares, " 'What did you eat?' and I made a mistake in my answer, I will rectify it the next day even if I'm taken for mad, for I believe that exactitude, even in trifles, is the basis of all greatness."

Yes, yes, Marcus thinks, wishing this to be uncontestable truth. For he, too often, catches himself meddling with and worrying about what seem to be trifles, and he chides himself for it, derides himself vehemently, horrified by the thought that if his mind can be bothered with such unimportant nonsense, such insignificant details, it is definite proof that he is not worthy of the lofty vocation he has set for himself. His pointillistic insistence on exactitudes, his excessive obsession, his tortured preoccupation with Truth, with who said what and when and why, sometimes arouse his suspicion that he is, fundamentally, a pedantic and tiresome character, that his potentially wonderful mind is, in effect, of a minor, mediocre caliber, if only because he obsesses so. A mind thus preoccupied with the petty cannot possibly soar to the higher reaches of abstraction. But here comes Cocteau and in a few simple words restores the faith he wishes to have in himself, reinforces and confirms him in his ways.

Of course, if he chose to, he could now start worrying—and he does for a moment—that perhaps the trifles and exactitudes Cocteau refers to are not the trifles and exactitudes that endlessly assault him. But quickly Marcus rejects this inkling of a thought as being precisely the kind of thought, the kind of worry, the kind of back and forth haggling and petty accounting he wants to avoid.

Marcus sets Cocteau aside and pours another cup of coffee. It is March already. The days are getting longer; season-wise, his life and his novel coincide. He wonders how important the question of the weather is to authors when they choose the time of year in which their novel will begin. He asks himself whether or not it happens to coincide with the actual weather outside their window. For him, like night and day, one follows the other, his life and his novel. In both forms—the writing and the living—his life unfolds in a relay race where one picks up when the other leaves off, while he, the author, as a sort of referee, removed from the action but totally involved, looks on. Yet, he also feels that his life and his novel run parallel, like two lanes that start from him and optically converge into one in the far distance.

When Gina or Oscar ask him if he writes about events that have actually happened, he tells them that as soon as he imagines it, the thing imagined actually happens.

Back at his desk, he considers the fate of his characters, tries to perceive their world, their patch of sky, those parts that inevitably must remain in the dark. For he, unlike God, cannot be everywhere at once. He cannot witness and report all of his characters' small, everyday actions and concerns: the neighbor they dislike and encounter, too often, in the elevator. The stranger they observe on the street, a stranger who asks directions of them, and they, only too happy to help (for, indeed, most people like to be helpful in small ways; like to point a stranger, perhaps a tourist, in the right direction, put a friendly face on the streets of their city), and even volunteer to accompany the stranger some of the way. The polite words they exchange with the superintendent, the postman, the clerk at the dry cleaners' around the corner. The quality of light in their kitchens and bedrooms, and how it changes with the seasons. Are they generous? Are they good tippers? How do they see themselves? Does the principle of justice burn in their hearts, or do they become involved only when the injustice concerns them directly?

Actually, thinks Marcus, since I do have to worry about such matters for the sake of my characters, it is good that my brain is practiced in the trivial and petty.

He asks: Do they sleep naked, or do they insist on pajamas? When alone, do they let down their guard? Do they pick their noses? Scratch their genitals then sniff their fingers? Sniff their armpits?

An author, perforce, is as finicky and fussy as a housewife, petty and inquisitive as a lawyer, an accountant.

Marcus feels for his characters. There's so much he wants to do for them, with them. He tells himself he must think more deeply, develop a more accepting, forgiving nature. Especially toward those around him. It is easy to be cordial to a stranger on the street, show him your best, most gregarious self for a few minutes. He should give more of himself to Gina and Oscar, just as they give of themselves to him. He's been so busy waving books in their faces, he has neglected to simply listen to them, learn from them. He's been so intent on haranguing them about their seemingly narrow concerns, he's failed to notice and read their faces, the subtle nuances of what they say and mean. From now on, he resolves, he'll pay more attention. He'll tell them what they must know already, but perhaps don't think much about: that when alone, or when in company, there's so much we remain ignorant of. It is us, the body we carry around with us, that we remain ignorant of. The expression we carry, its physical manifestation, is not for us to see, only to guess at. When engaged in conversation, we can never catch and hold and verbalize even one of the many hints and intricacies that flash through our mind as we watch and listen, digest and process, aware that the person facing us cannot see himself, and we, at that moment, the ultimate judge, take in the whole picture, decide the face ugly or pretty, truthful or lying, intelligent or ludicrous. But then it is our turn to speak, and we, aware of the thoughts that just ran through our mind, now expose ourselves to the other's, possibly cruel, scrutiny.

They'll shrug, smile, they'll say, So, what do you expect? That's the way things are. That's the air we breathe but can't touch, the words we hear but don't see.

It has turned nasty outside. The skies have opened and a hard, sudden downpour strikes at his windows. Rain makes him hungry. For his elevenses, he has had two slices of rye toast, rubbed, on both sides, with garlic, and sprinkled with vinegar and olive oil. Now he feels like having two more slices, but decides to wait for lunch. With the tip of his tongue, he searches his mouth for crumbs, then sips the last of his coffee. He rubs his hands together and pushes them between his thighs. The rain, now mixed with sleet, falls in thick, blinding sheets, knocking hard against the glass. He often wonders how windows withstand such violent power. He watches how small puddles, small pockets of rain, form on the pane before the wind twirls them upward on the glass where they mix with the new falling drops and again stream downward to form new pockets to be twirled upward by the wind.

A bolt of lightning zigzags across the sky, claiming it. Behind the horizon, thunder begins to roll, gaining a rumbling momentum.

Watching the storm, Marcus feels an emptying out. Good writers, he thinks, must be great humanists. Through his characters, he thinks, he, too, has a chance.

He gets up from his desk and goes into the living room. He lies down on the couch, rolls onto his side, throws his arm over the back, pushes his face against the upholstery, and lies still. He takes a deep breath and shuts his eyes. It feels so good just to stretch, to disappear into the fabric.

Later that night, after a dinner out, Gina takes a bath, and he settles in his chair with Diderot's *Le Neveu de Rameau*. Gina comes out of the bathroom, humming a tune, and he listens as she goes into the kitchen, then back into the bedroom, and the thought of Gina moving about in his rooms—a separate, independent being—fills him with a peculiar sense of relief. He imagines Gina in the kitchen, Gina in the bedroom, Gina in the living room. It occurs to him that Gina gives his life substance, a roundness it would otherwise lack. She is his helpmeet, his helpmate, his counterpart.

Well, he thinks. She definitely adds a dimension to my life, if only for her physical, carnal presence; it is the simple fact of another living out her life in these very rooms, breathing the same air, stepping on the same soft carpets.

Diderot speaks to him through the mouth of the nephew: "Though I had convinced myself that I had genius, at the end of the first line I am informed that I'm a fool, a fool, a fool."

Marcus smiles, his head bobbing. Like the teenagers on TV, he wants to shout, YES!

Wrapped in her white terrycloth robe, her hair wet and shiny and combed back, Gina comes into the room and settles on the couch. She stretches out her long legs and rotates her socked feet, exercising her ankles. She asks him to be a sweetheart and get her a drink, a lingering shot of brandy.

"My pleasure," he says and shuts his book.

"You look," says Gina, "like the cat who's got hold of a secret bowl full of cream."

"Diderot," he says, and points at the book. He goes to the bar, pours brandy into two glasses, and returns to his chair.

Gina is shaking her head. "It's wonderful how books affect you," she says, and an agreeable, childlike warmth spreads in him. "I heard from Assya," Gina continues, "and it looks like dinner next week."

"Good," says Marcus.

"In case you wondered," Gina says, a teasing gleam in her eyes, "he is well hung." Gina laughs, pointing at the surprised expression on his face.

"So that's what she told you," he says, and Gina nods. "Then you must have reciprocated and told her, too." Again Gina nods. "What did you tell her?"

"The truth."

"Which is?"

"You're well hung too."

"Well." Marcus wants to but cannot contain his smile. "So long as you girls keep yourselves busy. Now you tell me. How am I supposed to look her in the eye, knowing that she knows I'm well hung?"

"Just as," Gina says, "Bernie will look me in the eye. I told you, and she told him."

"You can't be sure."

"I am. She tells him everything. She told me she does. She said she'd never had such an open relationship with a man before."

"Hmm," Marcus says. "So now we all know that we know we know because we've been told."

"Yes." Gina laughs. "Why don't you read your book?"

"I'm watching you instead."

"That's a first."

"That's not true."

Gina brings a hand to her mouth and yawns. She examines her fingernails. "It's been a week," she tells Marcus. "I haven't chewed them in a week. Remember when you said that people adopt other people's mannerisms, gestures? That's me, a hundred percent. I remember distinctly, from very early on, I was maybe nine or ten, becoming aware of what I'd now call style, and began to very deliberately construct my image. First, I remember, it was my posture. We had this beautiful blonde for a neighbor, and one day I suddenly noticed how she walked, with so much pride, her head up, her shoulders pulled back, and I was so impressed, even stunned, I immediately, desperately, became her, began walking like her." Gina shakes her head. "I can just see myself, trying so pathetically hard to be transformed, to become as accomplished as she obviously was, at least in my mind. Then there came the matter of my hands, my fingers. One day I noticed the beautiful fingertips of my friend. They were delicately long and narrow, the fingertips, I imagined, of a pianist. And the nails seemed strong, healthy and pink, with a small, white crescent up here near the flesh. I then looked at my own fingertips and discovered, to my horror, they were pudgy, formless, with flat, lifeless nails sunk in a heap of flesh. I immediately set to work, pressing down the flesh to make the nail more prominent, push the flesh into shape. I still do it, to this day." She extends her hands and shows him her nails. "And biting them—this, too, I learned from a girl in class. She was absolutely striking, and she bit her nails so pensively, so affectingly, I had to, immediately, do the same. I thought it fit my image."

Marcus listens. He loves it when she talks. When she tells about her past.

"But at least," she adds, "I don't bite them down to the flesh." She clasps her hands on her chest. "I wonder if other girls took something from me." She yawns again, turns to peer at him. "Are you staying up much longer?"

He glances at his watch. "It's only ten. A little while, yes."

"Then take me to bed. Undress me."

"You only have to slip off your robe."

"Still." She moans and stretches.

He rises from his chair, helps her up, and leads her to the bedroom. It is one of their rituals. Normally, she'd be wearing her sweatpants and shirt. She'd collapse on the bed, and he would pull off her socks, briefly massage her toes, sometimes leaning over and kissing them. He'd pull off her pants, her panties, and bury his face in her pubic hair. He'd pull up her shirt and, with her face still covered, he'd bend over and take each nipple in his mouth. And she, naked as a baby, content and giggly, would get under the covers, and he'd tuck her in.

But tonight, with the robe, there's not much to do; she's not even wearing panties. But she throws herself on the bed, stretches out her legs against his chest, and he pulls off her socks, first the one, then the other.

"Thank you, daddy," she says.

"You're welcome."

"You know . . . something I've never told you?"

"Yes?"

"When we make love, and you push my legs back and up over my head, exposing my tush, my sweet vulva, an image flashes in my mind of myself as a baby being diapered. You do it so well."

"Do what?"

"Undress me."

Fourteen

With a pang he remembers his mother's Passover china set—the only valuable item she refused to leave behind when fleeing the Nazis. When he thinks about all that was left behind by Jews running away, or worse, relocated to ghettos and camps, he is filled with rage. Not only rage, but also disgust. Disgust when he pictures fine china and lace in the callous hands of ruffians and rabble. It's our houses they wanted, our chandeliers, his mother repeated over the years. It was not anti-Semitism that inspired them. It was sanctioned, state-sponsored piracy. It was not the first time they needed to replenish the depleted cash pots. When it came to the Jew, the church and the king saw eye to crooked eye. The Jew, as the occasion demanded, was invited, honored, consulted, then kicked and betrayed—the designated scarecrow for the masses.

Every year, as Passover approached, he looked forward to the moment they'd be eating again from the fine, gold-rimmed china. Their regular, everyday dishes were scrubbed and cleaned in boiling water, to wash away any traces of *hametz,* then hidden away and out of sight for eight days, the duration of the holiday.

The flat round plates, the soup plates, the cups and saucers, the large serving bowls, would appear one by one as his mother, barefoot on a kitchen stool, would reach up to the top cabinets and hand him the plates, one at a time, and he would place each plate, carefully, on the table, listening for the clear, sparkling ring as he put one plate on top of the other, each on its pile.

He sees the two of them working together: his mother, a slender woman of thirty-five, at this moment unusually quiet, a faraway look in her dark eyes; and he, understanding but not understanding, quiet as well.

He likes to think that he was born with the right instincts, if instinct is what it was, that guided him to appreciate not only the symbolic significance of this china set in his parents' lives, but also the delicate work and beauty of the porcelain itself, off-white in color, strewn with tiny yellow and red and blue blossoms. It occurs to him, too, that it must have been his parents' reverence that drew his attention to things of beauty.

Where is the set now? he tries to remember. It was stored for many years in a cabinet in his living room. Then his daughter took it, and now, he believes she told him, his granddaughter has it, still intact, no pieces chipped or missing.

He thinks, How anxious we are, throughout our lifetime, not to lose, not to break our precious possessions. But the day comes and we let go; all the treasures of the world no longer matter: we draw our last breath, we withdraw into ourselves and are gone forever.

He tries to imagine how it will feel, the drawing of the very, very last breath.

Like his mother on her hospital bed. His mother when she was still herself, though thin and frail, too weak to hold the mirror in one hand and apply lipstick with the other. So he holds the mirror in front of her face and watches how she, in slow practiced motions, pulls off the cap, turns the rotating bottom until the red, glistening tongue of lipstick emerges. He watches how she maneuvers the lipstick between her fingers so that the flat side faces her. She then slowly brings it close to her lips, trying, but not entirely succeeding, to open her mouth wide, stretch her lips flat against her gums for a smooth, easy application. Soon, though, she leaves it to him, to hold both the mirror and the lipstick, as he follows her instructions, his mother telling him he must cheat a little, go beyond the natural line on the left side where her upper lip droops and pulls her mouth downward. It's been an annoying problem, she tells him in secret, for many years now.

The old man raises his eyes to the ceiling; his nostrils and eyes sting with the threatening onset of tears. But he's caught himself in time: his eyes, just a bit moist with a thin layer, soon dry.

The salt and pepper holder! He almost bangs the desk. He must call his daughter later in the evening, make sure they still have it, perhaps even ask her to bring it when they next come to visit. Such a relic from the past, he must feast his eyes. He hasn't seen it in more than forty years, but he could draw it exactly: the shape, the colors, the way it glints in the light. Placed at the center of the table, it looks like a tiny boat, dainty and feminine, holding the curves of the figure eight; one receptacle for pepper, the other for salt. And in the center a sort of stem, or loop, by which to pick it up and pass it around. You dipped the tip of your knife in the salt, the pepper, and sprinkled it over your food. If less fussy or mannered, you might dip thumb and forefinger, pinch the grains of salt, careful not to lose any as your hand traveled from holder to plate. The absolute no-no was dipping a piece of radish or cucumber directly in the salt, because the moisture of the vegetable would crust the surface.

He sees the soup tureen and its matching lid and inhales the aroma of his mother's chicken soup. It may be a cliché to insist on it, but his mother's chicken soup—of the palest, purest yellow, streaked with the thinnest threads of gold—was the best and the clearest. And when soup was served, so were radishes, thinly sliced on a side dish. You put some salt on the edge of the dish, dipped the radish in the salt, took a bite and began to chew, spooning the soup.

Years ago, he told a friend that at his parents' table he had learned to eat like a Jew. A Jew, he explained, always clashes temperatures and tastes. The Jew needs contrast. He always eats something with something: soup with sliced radishes; *gefilte fish* with *hrein*—bright red horseradish; hot borscht with sour cream; a broiled, hot potato with cold borscht; *kugel* as dessert with fruit salad, or as a side dish; latkes with sour cream or apple sauce, or both.

Every Sunday for breakfast, his mother sliced the leftover challah, soaked each thick slice in a beaten egg, fried it in a pan until it browned on both sides, then served it to them, to him and his father, whereupon father and son immediately sprinkled sugar and cinnamon over their slices. In America, his parents discovered, it was called French toast, but in their home it was always *gebakene broyt,* fried bread.

Wherever a man goes, he carries his parents with him. If lucky, he carries his grandparents as well. He himself wasn't so lucky, he never got to know his grandparents, they had perished in a Nazi death camp, but he did see them in a few salvaged photographs, and they did hold him in their arms, and they did kiss his face, before his parents took him and fled. And so he does carry them in his heart, not as a memory but as a notion of deep love, or, something beyond love, beyond words, beyond history; something akin to the most primitive, the most precious element: blood.

Fifteen

He has guests in the living room. He is in his study, looking for a notebook. This time it is Assya who asked to hear it, the quote he'd mentioned. "If it's not too much trouble," Assya said. "No trouble at all," he said and, as he rose from his chair, glanced at Gina and saw her face darken. He thought she was going to stop him, but she didn't. It was Oscar who'd brought up the subject of the Holocaust, and it was Assya who'd asked to hear the quote.

He finds the notebook and returns to the living room. Gina has just finished telling a joke about a Jewish schlemiel, and they all crack up. She becomes so lively when I'm out of the room, Marcus muses. As he comes in, Oscar looks up and says, "Here he is. So eager. So nakedly out there, so earnest. Looking at him, I wish I were a bit more like him. I wish I were Jewish."

Again they laugh.

"Thy will be done," Marcus pronounces, making the sign of the cross. He opens his notebook, waits for them to quiet down, then says, "This is Bernard Malamud, in an interview: 'I for one believe that not enough has been made of the tragedy of the destruction of six million Jews. Somebody has to cry—even if it's a writer, twenty years later.'" He looks up at them. "I don't know if you know this, but up until the mid sixties, the Holocaust remained a nameless and not much talked about event. It's as if the world needed a period of adjustment, of realignment, before it could emerge from its stupor. But you will also find those who will tell you that the Jews needed twenty years to regroup, rethink their strategies, before they could launch another successful campaign, the Holocaust Fable Campaign."

"When I watch a documentary," says Oscar, "about the Holocaust, it occurs to me that the very images I watch with horror and revulsion, bring pleasure to others, to those who watch them gloatingly, those who think that not enough has been done to the Jews."

Everybody nods and, after a silence, Gina sighs. "Can we change the subject now?"

"But why?" Oscar turns to her. "I thought you liked it when Jews sit around discussing Jews."

"Assya is bored."

Assya, who's been leaning against Bernie, straightens up. "No, I'm not."

Pushing forward on the settee, Bernie says, "I wonder if Christians sit around discussing themselves."

"They don't have to," Oscar says. "They're not a minority."

Marcus says, "As Oscar said, there are those who'd say that the Holocaust, if it happened at all, is further proof that Hitler and his thugs had the right idea. Look at the Jew, they say. Even the massive German machine could not destroy him. And look at him today. Again he's too strong, too powerful, armed with a new tool, the cry of the Holocaust. He even has a homeland all to himself. The Jew, as you know, is the standby victim in history. Read Raul Hilberg. The Jew is made to order. He comes in fit-all varieties. You can make him out to be too meek, too aggressive, a filthy parasite or a wealthy exploiter—in either case, he sucks the blood of his Christian, goodhearted neighbors. He is mentally deficient, he is too smart. He is a great healer and doctor, he brings disease and contaminates the world. Take your pick. The Jew, an insidious fifth column, not only doesn't contribute to the community he lives in, he plots to destroy it. The Jew is too influential—he pollutes our waters and our culture. My mother once told me that the good old-fashioned European brand of anti-Semitism is merely a matter of preference, like the simple dislikes one acquires in childhood, like the instinctive dislike for cats or dogs. But what hurts me the most, what's absolutely incredible to me is the fact that often even the educated, thinking gentile also buys into these myths about the Jew, and I say to myself: How could it be? Why are people so hateful? So ungrateful?"

"As the token gentile in your midst," Oscar says and reaches for the plate of rugalach on the table, "let me tell you: some of us are grateful." He bites into the pastry, holding his napkin under his chin to catch the crumbs he'll then pick and put in his mouth. "Especially for Jewish cooking. But kidding aside, I'd be the first to admit that looking at history, at the great cultural centers of the past, the Jew was always right there, at the center. When the Jew was made to leave, those centers collapsed. If in ten, twenty, fifty years the Jews are expelled from New York, New York will collapse. But"—Oscar puts the last of the rugalach in his mouth and, chewing, raises his hand to indicate that they should wait, he'll resume in a minute—"but you, Jews, call us gentiles. I'm a goy, right? And our women are shiksas. Not that I mind, but we've allowed you to label us, to appropriate the term gentile and apply it to us. We've allowed you to infiltrate the language: our dictionaries are filled with Yiddish and Hebrew words. But the general truth about the Jews is this: they're so irritable, so intrinsically impatient. They have attitudes and feel compelled to display them; they can't keep those attitudes to themselves. The whole world has to know they disapprove of this or that. Take Marcus to the theater or the movies and you'll know what I mean. He is such a practiced theater or moviegoer, he can tell right away, from the very first minute, if it's going to be good, or awful. And he is such an altruist: not only does he know, he wants you, and all those unfortunates who sit around him and don't know better than to like what they're watching, he wants them all to know, too. I mean, in case he hates it, which is frequent. When he likes what he's watching, I'm willing to admit, he is quite normal, he behaves, but when he hates it, he shifts in his seat, shuffles his feet, makes a show of trying to tell the time on his watch in the dark. He crosses his legs, then uncrosses and recrosses them. He sighs. Loudly. Straight from the heart. His old suffering Jewish heart. Fatigued and disgusted, he bends forward and shades his forehead in his hand. A veritable tortured torturer."

They laugh and look at Marcus, nodding, recognizing.

"Not all Jews are like Marcus," Bernie says.

"Tell it to Marcus."

"That's why," Marcus says, "I prefer to go alone, so I can quietly leave the theater if I don't like it."

"But you wouldn't, see," Oscar rejoins. "You'd make it your point to stay to the bitter end, if only to prove you were right, and also to protect against the chance that the next day someone might come up to you and tell you the play got livelier the moment you left. To his credit, though," Oscar addresses the others, "he doesn't go much anymore."

"Never to the movies," Gina says. "Unless they're foreign."

"There's an old Jewish lady on my floor," Oscar says. "Mrs. Rivlin. A widow. In a funny sort of way she reminds me of Marcus. She must be around eighty, and some days, when I meet her in the hallway or at the mailbox, she seems so gray and disheveled, so out of it, I'm thinking to myself, That's it, it's touch and go. And already, in my heart, I begin to mourn her. But a few days later, I meet her again, and she's all decked out, her clothes match, her hair is done, she's on her way out or coming back, and she's as well as can be, and I say to myself, God bless her. The other night, coming out of my apartment, taking out the trash, I see her at the other end of the hallway, far beyond her door, beyond the elevators or the incinerator, and I'm thinking to myself, What is she doing out there? She must be lost, her mind is going. And as I approach the incinerator, and she comes toward me, and my mind is racing, thinking up some polite way of finding out what she's doing in the hallway at eleven o'clock at night, she smiles at me, sweetly, broadly, clasps her hands and says, It was so quiet and peaceful in the hallway, so I took a little walk. That's good, I say, encouragingly. Exercise is good. I thought that perhaps you were taking out the trash. That too, she says, making perfect sense. I came out to the incinerator, then took my little walk.

"Once, in the elevator, I heard her speak Yiddish with a friend, and I said something to her, about Yiddish sounding very juicy, and she said Yiddish was invented with two emphases in mind: endearments and curse words. She said Yiddish had the most wonderful endearments, and the cleanest, most convoluted curses. She told me a few." Oscar scratches his head. "Here is one. I'm not sure I'm telling it right, but it's close enough. 'May you live like a lamp. Stand on your feet all day and burn all night.'" They burst out laughing, and Oscar nods with obvious pride. He continues. "May you swallow an umbrella, and may it open in your gut." Again they laugh, and Oscar modestly says, "Of course, they sound much better, more twisted, in Yiddish."

"I knew some Yiddish when I was growing up," Bernie says. "I went to a cheder for a whole year, where they teach you both Yiddish and Hebrew before the age of five. Let me tell you, we're not called the People of the Book for nothing. And those Hasids don't waste time, they start you young, which, I think, makes for sharper minds. From day one, you're schooled in the art of memorizing. They teach you to repeat the various prayers and blessings: there's a different kind of blessing for different foods, beverages, fruit, even a glass of water. Nothing goes into your mouth before you say the blessing, and after each meal, there's yet another blessing. Even when he pees, the Jew blesses the Almighty, thanking Him for having made him with openings and cavities, or as they say it in Hebrew: *nekkavim nekkavim, haloulim haloulim.*"

"Quite the rabbi," Marcus says.

"You didn't know this about me, did you?" Bernie grins. "I'll tell you about the Jews," he says to Oscar. "One of our scholars, Ahad Ha'am, said that the Jews' unique spin on religion had been to invent a God who had given the people His commandments. This, instantly, made their teachings valid, authoritative, because the teachings and interdictions came from Him. But where I think the Jew really screwed up, his worst tactical blunder yet, was to invent the Messiah, opening the door for Jesus and Muhammad, and who knows who else is waiting in the offing. I once wrote a paper about the Jews and their foolhardy Messianic idea. I even considered, for a while, turning it into a book."

"Write a book about Jews," Assya says, "and Jews will buy it."

"I'd want non-Jews to buy it. I'd want them to repent."

"It's not their doing," Gina says. "It's the Church's."

"Let the Church buy it, then, and read it from the pulpit. But the most absurd concoction of all is the blood libel scheme." Bernie clears his throat. "To this day you'll find plenty of Christians and Muslims who believe that Jews need the blood of young children to bake their matzo. *The Protocols of the Elders of Zion* is in great demand in certain parts of the world. The blood libel is not only absurd, it's cynical. It takes for granted, and plays on, the ignorance of the masses, an ignorance the Church was never too eager to dispel. The fact of the matter is: the special laws the Jews decreed concerning *shehita,* the slaughter of the animal, have a double purpose: a swift, painless death for the animal, and the free flow of blood out of the veins and arteries. No bloody rare steak for the orthodox Jew. Whatever blood remains in the carcass will be drained by the observant housewife who will sprinkle meat and poultry with salt and let it stand a couple of hours, and then rinse the meat of any remaining traces of blood. And if she cracks an egg and sees a dark stain or a drop of blood, she won't use the egg, she'll toss it in the garbage . . ."

Listening, Marcus nods, learning; he tells himself to observe and listen carefully. Hopefully, sitting at his desk, he'll be able to recall the exact words, will be able to endow his characters with specific physical traits. Still, how can he become only ears and eyes that record for the future, while he, too, is a living person, a living participant who interacts in the moment? He must find the quote he copied from Jung, something about the artist being a duality: being both a man with a personal life, as well as an impersonal, creative process.

He looks at the people in his living room. They're so palpable, alive, and yet, he and they will only matter in the books that will be written about them, about their particular historical moment; what finally counts will be determined by future generations.

Maybe all that really matters now, at this very moment, is love and generosity, the mitzvah to share and belong.

"He is off again," he hears Gina say. "See, his eyes are getting cloudy."

"I'm right here."

"Then answer a simple question: Do you want more coffee?"

"No, thanks."

"What were you thinking about?" Bernie asks.

Marcus hesitates. "Love," he finally says. "I was thinking about love. About how absolutely vital it is for us to feel love. Love, our Sages said, is fiercer than death. The present feeds on love, or the hope for it."

They look at him a moment, contemplating, considering.

"So?" Bernie asks.

"Nothing," Marcus says. "That's all we have."

Sixteen

Marcus copies into his novel notebook:

Gina, in her own words: I'm in a car, in the back seat, my right arm on the armrest, and I'm looking out the window, tourist-like, at the passing scenery. The feeling is of comfort and leisure. We now arrive and pass through what appears to be the poor, desolate part of town. Remembering it now I think of it as a leper colony. An all-male leper colony. As if in slow motion, we (I don't know who is driving the car. I mean, it could be just a driver, or someone I know) drive by a fenced yard (I think there's a fence), where a few men are scattered around the yard. They're skin and bones, wearing rags; they look like inmates. These men—it slowly dawns on me—in trance-like motions, are screwing animals, domestic animals, from the rear. It is apparent to me that they don't do it out of lust, but out of despair, desperate for any kind of touch. One man in particular is so frail, he's more dead than alive. He holds the limp, lifeless carcass of a bird, a pigeon perhaps, or a chicken, and presses it to his groin, as he repeats the motions of copulation. He moves his hips, pounding the bird. I see so much in the man's face. I can see he's aware of how low he's stooped, but, at the same time, he is also beyond caring, and he is aware that he is beyond caring, which adds a dimension of self-loathing, of deep cynicism directed at his dispossessed self. Right now all he cares about is to continue fucking the bird, for, even though the pleasure he draws out of it is measly, at least he gets a satisfaction from knowing that he, too, is getting something for nothing, that he too, for once, is screwing the system.

Gina says, dream-like: "It's such a weird dream, don't you think?"

He nods. "Your dreams usually are."

"How come you never remember yours? Writers are supposed to remember their dreams."

"I don't know. Sometimes I do remember an image, or a phrase, but not the entire dream."

Marcus switches notebooks, and continues in his journal:

To write the ultimate female novel.

To penetrate the barriers of the physical word, live inside the meanings it houses.

Unhook the shackles of the plot.

Place yourself with Archimedes. A heavyset man, lowering his naked, hairy behind into the bath, slowly, so as not to shock the flesh.

Here he is, immersed in the water, absentmindedly peering over the edge of the tub to observe the overflow of water spill onto the floor. For a man preoccupied with questions of weights and measurements, the spilled water, for now, is just another nuisance of everyday life.

He soaks in the warm, velvety water. Somewhere in the room, a third element exists: the floating atom of discovery. He soaps his head, shoulders, armpits. And bingo! The question of weight, and the fact of spilled water on the floor, collide in the brain.

Imagine the joy, the unbelievable joy.

The author as God.

The author playing cat and mouse with the reader.

Yesterday afternoon I put on my coat, my gloves, and went downstairs for a walk. George, the doorman, gave me a funny look, which, at first, startled me, and then I thought: No, it's not George, it's me, I've been in all day, absorbed in my work, and now that I finally emerge, all seems a bit peculiar to me. But soon, as I walked outside, I discovered why George had looked at me the way he did. I was dressed for winter, but outside it was an unexpected spring day. Of course, it gave me a jolt, if only because I didn't immediately connect the picture I was seeing—people walking around in short sleeves—with the actual weather. But slowly it penetrated: the sun is out, it is hot. Only upstairs, in my novel, it is cold still.

Marcus picks a few scribbled notes, switches notebooks again, and copies out:

Samuel Johnson: "Every man may, by examining his own mind, guess what passes in the minds of others."

"Few moments are more pleasing than those in which the mind is concerting measures for a new undertaking."

"All knowledge is of itself of some value. There is nothing so minute or inconsiderable, that I should not rather know it than not."

André Gide: "I confess to you that I see each one of my characters as an orphan, an only son, unmarried, and childless."

Seventeen

The old man is tired. He has just switched off the lamp on his desk, but now switches the light back on, remembering that he has not looked for his word in the dictionary. So he begins his search, hoping it won't take very long.

He's in luck. He finds his word quickly, two actually, on the same page. First he falls on *verbicide,* then *verbigeration,* and copies them out:

> **verbicide** *n* [L *verbum* word + E-*cide*] (1858) 1: deliberate distortion of the sense of a word (as in punning) 2: one who distorts the sense of a word

> **verbigeration** *n* [ISV, fr. L *verbigeratus* pp. of *verbigerare* to talk, chat, fr. *verbum* word + *gerere* to carry, wield— more at word, cast] (ca. 1891): continual repetition of stereotyped phrases (as in some forms of mental illness)

As he copies these down, he realizes that what he enjoys in particular are the backslashes and brackets. His dictionary, he thinks, is a good friend, a good companion, always illuminating.

He switches off the desk lamp and stands up. And now, where to? The kitchen, naturally; it's time to eat.

In the kitchen, he measures a cup of rice into three cups of water and sets it to boil. He chops a small white onion and browns it in olive oil, then adds the package of ground meat he's defrosted overnight. With a wooden spoon, he mixes in the meat, delighting in the aromas reaching his nose. He then empties a can of pinto beans into the pot and adds black pepper, chili, and paprika. He's making chili con carne, a dish he discovered some sixty years ago in Paris, in a small jazz club off Montparnasse named Rosebud, where he and his friends sighted Sartre more than once. He checks the rice—it's almost ready. Now he looks forward to sitting down to his meal, watching the evening news. It's been years upon years, and still he draws contentment from his routine, from the deep silence around him, from the fact that he requires so little.

He turns from the stove and rinses a few leaves of lettuce. True, it happens that he'll be standing at the counter, slicing a tomato, and all at once he'll feel a weakening in his arms, a certain hollowness in his heart, and he, his mind blank, will become aware of the mechanical motion of his hands, of the fact that he, an organism, has tired of the need to feed itself. But such moments pass quickly, and soon he'll be carrying his tray into the living room, sit down at the coffee table, switch on the news.

He sits down to his dinner. The hot chili, deliciously spicy, burns in his mouth, almost making him swoon. This is good, he thinks. He sips from the glass of red wine, and again works his fork under the chili and rice, then the salad. Once in a while he glances at the TV, once in a while he catches himself not listening. The voice of the newscaster, young and energetic, drones on, providing a pleasant background noise.

In his mind the old man is back at his desk. He thinks of the work he's done today, of the work he has yet to do tomorrow. It's a bit sad, but also a bit comic, the way his days and nights roll one into the other, without much variety. But today, when he went down to get his mail, he did exchange a few words with a young woman who had just moved into the building. When he stepped into the elevator, he was startled to see her, a beautiful young thing with long legs and short dark hair. He nodded and said hello, and she pulled out her earplugs and smiled and said hey, and gave him her hand and said she'd just moved in, and when he told her he'd been living here for nearly forty years, her eyes opened wide and she said, Wow. She was going out for a quick jog around the block, but maybe one day soon they could have coffee together, and he said that yes, sure, it will please him enormously, all she need do is knock on his door, he's always in, or nearly always. What do you do? She asked, and he said, This and that, and she threw her head back and laughed, magnificently.

This and that, indeed, the old man thinks. It will be nice if she knocks on his door, but if she doesn't, he'll understand. He'll be content just meeting her in the elevator every once in a while, drink in the lively green eyes, the wide mouth, wait for her to throw back her head and laugh, carefree and sweet and so very young, so very much alive. As long as he can open his mouth and make sense, or better, make someone laugh, he has no reason to complain.

Eighteen

Spring is around the corner, and he feels a new excitement, a restlessness; he should be out, taking advantage of the mild weather. But he is at his desk, imagining Gina in bed, in her own bedroom; she is sick with the flu. Propped up against her dainty white pillows, she's enveloped in white: her white, wide-sleeved linen nightgown, her white, wonderfully fluffy duvet. Against such a white, shimmering background, and the pronounced paleness of her skin, her hair is very dark, and her eyes, under puffy lids, take on a purplish glaze. It becomes her to be sick, he reflects, smiling. She hasn't combed her hair, and it's tangled around her face in a way he finds alluring. In her slightly puffy lips, her puffy lids, and the strands of dark hair going every which way, she looks like a reluctant teenager, awakened from sleep. She holds her hands clasped on the duvet, while Assya, sitting on the bed at Gina's side, spoonfeeds Gina chicken soup she herself made.

Marcus, reclined on the other side of the bed, observes the black, narrow band of Assya's watch on her left wrist. The simplicity of the band moves him. It makes her look practical, straightforward and frank. Careful, motherly, she spoons the soup and brings it to Gina's mouth, her lips moving as if mouthing the spoon when Gina does. All at once he feels hungry. All at once he is made aware of the closeness of women, of their ethereal rapport. He feels superfluous. It occurs to him it is more natural for these two to love one another, rather than love him—the trespassing male.

Assya says she seems to remember from childhood that when she had high fever, her mother would wrap her chest with large swaths of cotton, soaked in Assya's own urine. "I mean," Assya says. "I can't remember for sure. It may have been just heated cooking oil. But I seem to remember it was urine, though I don't remember it having an odor."

"It makes perfect sense," Marcus says. "Your own urine carries antibodies and other goodies. Do you know that young suckling bears devour their mother's feces for nutrients?"

"Marcus," Gina groans, choking. "I'm eating."

"Sorry."

Marcus watches the hand that holds the spoon. It's a bit warm and stuffy in the room, but he doesn't mind; he won't even move to take off his jacket. Assya dips the spoon in the bowl and brings up a little bit of everything: a little bit of the clear liquid, a little bit of short, slippery noodles, the kind his mother used to make, a piece of carrot, celery, and a sliver of chicken meat. Only a woman, he reflects, would take such care when spooning soup. He recalls how, when a child, he fervently wished to be a patient in hospital and so be freed of his duties, freed of schoolwork. In hospital, he'd be lying in bed, reading books, receiving gifts and visitors.

How he longs now to be lying in bed, to be fed chicken soup. Why can't a man, again, be treated like a child?

He considers asking them, Why can't a man be treated like a child? But he knows the kind of look he'd get from Gina, the kind that says, Here he goes again, seeking attention.

With each spoonful of soup, Gina seems to gain in strength, and the mouth that closes on the spoon seems more eager, greedy.

"Is it good?" he asks Gina.

Gina eyes him, she nods. "Look at him," she says to Assya. "I bet he wants some of your soup."

"It's your soup," Assya says. "I made it for you."

"That's what I'm saying, you made it."

"No, no," he denies, "I don't want any soup. You eat it," he tells Gina, and looks at the bowl, "you need to get well."

Assya is doing her trick again, getting a little bit of everything on the spoon. "Here." She reaches toward him and he, leaning forward and half shutting his eyes, accepts the spoon in his mouth.

"He's such a baby," Gina says.

"Why not?" Assya says. "He's entitled."

Soon, the soup is finished. "I'm very proud of you," Assya tells Gina, peering in the now empty bowl. "Except for one spoonful we've donated to our friend Marcus, you finished it all." Assya smiles at Marcus and places the bowl on the night table. Gina wipes her mouth with a napkin, then, with a sigh, collapses back against the pillows, her face the image of contentment and gratitude. As she looks at them she seems to be thinking, I deserve such good friends as these.

In the afternoon, he feels ready to go out and conquer his neighborhood. Happy with the work he has done, he experiences a brief elation, as though his senses have joined hands and set out on a Matisse dance. He puts on his silk-lined jacket, puts a pad and a short pencil in his pocket, and prepares to leave, when the telephone rings. It's his cousin Becky. She calls to tell him she won't be having a Seder this year, she'll be going to California for Passover. Myra and Jack, Myra's new husband, will be there, as well as Rosina. A sort of family reunion. He and Gina must join them.

"I can't," Marcus says. "I'd love to but I can't. Frankly," he adds as Becky remains silent, "I don't think I'd be comfortable with Gina and Myra in the same room."

"But, that's childish, Marcus."

"I know. Besides, I can't leave my book."

"It sounds like a dog," Becky says. "Your book."

He laughs. "Yes, you're right, it is my dog."

"You know what I'm thinking?" Becky says. "I may decide to move to California. The truth of the matter is, Howard and I have reached a point of no return. I'm barely fifty. I can start my life over. What do you think?"

"Sure," he says slowly, "but—"

"I know, I know, it's tough out there, but at least I can try. Myra did all right, why can't I?"

"Remember Bernie?" he asks. "Myra's brother?"

"Of course I remember Bernie. I like Bernie. Myra tells me he's back."

"Yes," he says, then tells her how Gina has managed yet another marvel, and now Assya and Bernie are a couple.

"Good for them," Becky says, a shade of envy in her voice. "What will you do for Passover?"

"I don't know. We've always gone to your house. Now, I don't know. But it's no big deal. Yom Kippur is my holiday."

"I feel responsible for you and Gina. You must eat matzo."

"Of course we will."

"And no bread."

"Becky."

"I'll kiss Rosina for you."

"Yes, and call me when you get back."

Outside his building, he stands a moment. It's three o'clock in the afternoon. He'll go south, he decides. It's been a while. He'll go into one of those dainty establishments, their windows shaded with lace, where they press a lemon peel into one's espresso, and where they serve the fluffiest *croissant au chocolat*.

He walks down Broadway. Peddlers and shoppers crowd the pavement. He feels warm and unzips his sweater, taking pleasure in the punkish irreverence of the shop windows. He feels part of the scene, and yet looks at it with the eyes of an outsider, with what he thinks are the eyes of an outsider. For all he knows, all these people around him, the shoppers and peddlers, may be observing the scene, thinking to themselves that they are part of the scene and yet observe it with the eyes of an outsider. We may all be outsiders to our own experience. Not even the physical, the visible, is to be owned.

He turns west, his gait light, youthful. He'll take a small, round table in the corner, by the window. He'll have his espresso and croissant, his pad and pencil at the ready. The waitress, petite and energetic, in a white, starched shirt and black trousers with suspenders, will take his order. Briefly, fleetingly, as men and women inevitably do, they'll size each other up as remotely potential sexual partners, then resume their roles of waitress and patron.

The café is pretty much filled up, but he hardly notices those seated around him, for each bite of the warm and fluffy croissant, and each sip of the double espresso, engage all his senses. Every so often his eyes are drawn, involuntarily, to the door, responding to the ring of the bell above it, and he notes who's coming in, who's leaving.

He has finished the croissant, but still feels he hasn't had enough. Hungrily, enviously, he sneaks glances at the neighboring tables, at those who still have a whole, or half, croissant or pastry on their plate. He licks his lips, swallows his saliva, considering, reasoning. Of course, he could have another croissant, another espresso. The croissant is saturated in butter, but he doesn't do this very often. One more croissant won't kill him.

Now that he has decided, he signals the waitress and soon she places before him another croissant, another espresso. Ah, life! He bites and chews, eagerly, yet slowly, savoring. When he's finally done, he lets out a silent, controlled belch, rests a moment, then leans his elbow on the table, parts the lacy drapes, and peeks outside.

Across the street, near the entrance of a corner grocery store, two women—artists, he thinks—stand and chat. Apparently, a chance meeting in the neighborhood. One, the shorter one, has done her shopping, her stacked paper-in-plastic bag is at her feet; the other, tall and slender, her jeans stuffed into cowboy boots, holds a Labrador Retriever by the leash, while with her other hand, she adjusts the fedora on her head. She is so American, he thinks. So sure, so free.

Someone taps his shoulder. He turns and looks up at the smiling faces of Assya and Bernie.

They're so happy to have surprised him! They say nothing, just stand there, beaming like children who have outwitted their parent.

It takes him a minute to adjust. "What are you doing here?" he asks.

"We have to eat, too, you know." Bernie laughs, pulls chairs for Assya and himself. They sit down. "We, too, can appreciate a good French pastry, just as you do. But what"—Bernie leans across the table in mock conspiracy—"if we may ask, are you doing here? You're supposed to be working, on our behalf, on behalf of humanity, writing your book."

Marcus looks at Bernie, smiles to show that he appreciates the humor. "Not to worry," he says. "I'll return to it just as soon as I can. I'm allowed little breaks. Like you, I'm only human."

"Good," Bernie says. "That's good to hear, that you're human. You only need to learn to loosen up a bit. Loosen your grip."

Assya and Bernie exchange a small mischievous smile, then look at him with bright eyes.

He doesn't mean to say it, but it escapes his lips. "You two seem so happy."

They smile, they agree, but are surprised, all the same, to hear it from his lips. "Don't forget," he continues, "that I had a hand in getting you two together."

"Oh." Bernie laughs. "We're indebted to you forever. We give you credit at every opportunity."

"We do, I swear," Assya says, and the three of them nod and smile.

"Tonight," Bernie says and glances at his watch, "I'll try to get there around seven. Is that all right with you?"

"Get where?" Marcus asks.

"Hasn't Gina told you?" Bernie asks, then looks questioningly at Assya.

"Tell me what?"

"We have plans tonight."

"She tells me nothing. She counts on me being there, always, regardless."

"Here's the plan," Bernie says. "I come over around seven and keep you company until Gina and Assya get back."

"Back from where?"

"Who knows? But you and I will have a chance to sit and talk. Just the two of us for a change."

He leaves them in the café and walks back home. He's unmindful of his immediate surroundings, but he knows he's heading east, then north; soon, he'll be home. Now he finds himself in a small, quiet street. It is dusk, a sudden breeze cools his face. He notes the tall, narrow windows, the stark beauty of tree branches, when suddenly, through an open window on a second floor, the clear, sailing sound of Coltrane wraps itself around him, and his heart leaps up toward the window. He stands and listens. He can't see into the room—only the high ceiling is visible—but he imagines the owner of the music, of the apartment, a woman, he guesses, in a happy, exultant mood, preparing for the evening, a spring evening of leisure, perhaps with her lover, her husband. How he wishes he had their life, if only for a moment, the life of that couple. It's been so long since he took time out and just listened to music. Every once in a while he must remember to do that, put his books aside and listen to music.

In the evening, as he opens the door for Bernie, all at once he feels crammed, invaded; it's as if the proximity of Bernie's bulk, the sudden fact of Bernie, is too much for him. He leads Bernie into the living room, points him to a chair, and proceeds to the bar. But Bernie, instead of sitting down, follows behind, talking about an accident he witnessed coming over: two cabs collided on Sixth Avenue and Tenth, practically around the corner. Marcus could not imagine the destruction, the bloody mess, the ambulances and police cars. And the crowd, Bernie says. The crowd. How quickly they all gather around the smell of disaster. Of course he is not excluding himself; he, too, is repulsed and fascinated by the sight of blood.

"Real blood," Bernie cries. "Just imagine. It could have been me lying there on the pavement, with all the debris, in a pool of blood. A third car, in a last-minute attempt to avoid the collision, jumped the curb, hitting three people." He takes the drink from Marcus. "You're safe up here. You have no idea what goes on down there."

"I think I heard the sirens," Marcus says absentmindedly. He goes around Bernie and takes his chair. Bernie takes the couch. "What were you doing on Sixth and Tenth?" Marcus doesn't like the way he sounds. "It's out of your way."

"I like to walk," Bernie says, crossing his legs. "I walk everywhere. I like being around people. I like people, I like the streets. The idea of streets is a great one. The idea of sidewalks."

Marcus nods. He wants to be friendly but he feels blocked, trapped in fact. He considers that Gina should have told him beforehand about her plans for tonight, instead of assuming he'd be willing to play host to Bernie. He begins to develop a case against her, but all at once seems to recall, vaguely, that she did mention something the week before. He thinks he recalls her saying something about dinner plans. This punctures his ballooning argument, but idly he continues to run the scenario in his mind. In a strange way it's pleasurable, masochistically so. Besides, she could have reminded him in the morning that tonight . . . Next time, he tells her, she should consult him before committing his time. "But you like Bernie," she says. "What's got into you? I can't constantly be guessing your moods." "You don't have to guess my moods," he says, vehemently. "Just ask me." "All right, I'll ask you," she says, just as vehemently. "You yourself don't always consult me." "Are you kidding me?" he says, indignant. "I always do. Always. Especially when it involves others."

At the drop of a hat, he and Gina can become so hateful. So self-righteous and vengeful. Humans are so inflammable—they flare up in a matter of seconds. In point of fact, Gina has told him more than once that often, even when she is not angry with him, not consciously, she constructs in her mind dramatic scenes where the two of them fight, fight to the end, and she tells him to get lost, and he does, he walks out, and that's that. "Do you get us back together again?" he asks. "It depends," she says. "Sometimes I do, sometimes I don't." "What does it depend on?" he asks. "My mood," she says. Which, of course, wounds him. "How can you be so callous, so flippant, about our future?" he asks. "Our future together?" "I'm not." She laughs. "It's only a fantasy." "What do we say to each other during these fights?" he asks after a pause. "Well," she says, smiling. "I do most of the talking, you're too crushed to utter a word, you're so shocked and overwhelmed by guilt and remorse because you know you're in the wrong. I tell you that I'm tired of our routine, that I finally find you boring. You and your endless books, your coldness to everything that's human and alive. Your asociability. I tell you everything. Everything that I meant to tell you, and everything that I didn't. I tell you that I wish I didn't need you, that dependence is awful. Then you say something like: 'With all the animosity you feel toward me, it's a miracle we're still together,' and I say, triumphantly, 'Tell me about it.' Sometimes," Gina says, "I finish you off over the telephone. I tell you that lately I don't *hear* you listening to me. I don't hear you loving me. And you say, 'But I do, I love you.' And I tell you that you love me out of habit, that we might as well kick the habit, and you mournfully say, 'I thought you loved me,' and I laugh, derisively, and say, 'Love! Go ahead, tell me about love, I'm listening.'

"But eventually," Gina says, "we make up, and you say that women are enamored of antics and dramatics, and I say, 'What else is there? Conflict, you know, adds spice to a relationship.' And you say, very sweetly I might add, 'Ours is spicy enough.'"

"You seem restless," Bernie says. "Distracted. Is something the matter?"

"No, nothing." Marcus rubs his forehead.

"I know how it feels," Bernie says. "I call it the urban dead-end feeling, the urban cul-de-sac."

Marcus looks at him, surprised, and Bernie laughs. "You thought I was a dimwit, you couldn't do enough to get away from me, and suddenly I open my mouth and you like what you hear, you want to come nearer, all at once you're enchanted, even taken. Why deny it?"

"Well." Marcus smiles and shifts in his chair. "There's nothing to deny. You're so full of surprises, Bernie, and always direct. It's true, I do like what you said, yes. An urban dead-end. I like that."

"You can put it in your book."

"I can put it in my book."

"How is it coming?"

"Ah." Marcus waves his hand. "Depends. Sometimes I hate it, sometimes I like it. On the whole, I'm anxious. Each move I make may undermine me."

"It can't be that serious. You can always fix it, mold it as you please."

"Yes and no. It's not that simple."

"Nothing is simple. This is our life. We engage time. What gets us in the end is not the pull of gravity, but disillusionment; it's the hardest blow. But I am prepared, my expectations are kept at a minimum low. When I go, no one will miss me. Except my broker, maybe."

"And Assya," Marcus duly adds.

"No," Bernie says. "Not Assya. We go together. Where I go, she goes."

"Where to?" Marcus is alarmed. "I thought you meant death."

"Australia." Bernie smiles. "Remember Butch Cassidy and the Sundance Kid, bleeding to death in that cave, while a thousand Bolivian soldiers take position outside, aiming their bayoneted rifles, ready to shoot on sight? And Butch says, I've got a great idea, and the Kid says, I don't want to hear it. And Butch says, You'll change your mind when you hear it: Australia! They speak English in Australia. How are the banks? asks the Kid. Easy, says Butch. What a great ending for a movie."

"I feel a little faint." Marcus sits up and leans forward. "I think I may be hungry. Let's go into the kitchen."

In the kitchen Marcus prepares a ham and cheese sandwich. Bernie, who at first says he isn't hungry, becomes hungry watching Marcus prepare his sandwich, and is soon preparing his own.

"Why Australia?" Marcus asks. "What would Assya be doing in Australia?"

"Just kidding," Bernie says. "We're not going anywhere."

"Good," Marcus says, relieved. "How many friends does a man have in the world?"

Bernie nods his agreement. For a while they chew in silence, savoring their food, their thoughts.

"It's at moments like these," Bernie, his mouth full, says, "that I come to understand why our forefathers elected to exclude women from bars and clubs. It's so much calmer with just men around."

Marcus nods. He reflects that he actually likes women around; men, usually, bore him.

"Men, as you know," Bernie says, "are the greatest chefs. They have the patience and the stamina to turn a necessity into art. Most women, it seems, tend to do things by rote, following recipes in books, not trusting their own instincts, their own intelligence. They always seem to be in such a hurry, wanting to get this or that out of the way, to be done with this chore or that."

"I don't know," Marcus says. "My mother was a pretty good cook, and a marvelous baker."

"Sure," Bernie says. "Mine too. But those days are gone. Whole traditions have vanished."

"You're forgetting that ninety-nine percent of the male population wouldn't know what to do with a spatula. That includes you, I'm sure."

"No, you'd be surprised. I can whip together a meal or two."

They hear keys inserted in locks, then the front door bangs shut. They hear the sound of whispering and paper rustling coming from the hall, and a moment later Gina and Assya burst into the kitchen. "Look at them," Gina says, "they couldn't wait."

"Marcus was hungry," Bernie says.

"He's always hungry."

Gina and Assya lean over Marcus and Bernie; they exchange quick kisses.

"Have you eaten?" Marcus asks. "I can make you a couple of sandwiches."

"Later," Gina says. "Are you finished here? Let's go inside."

They go into the living room where a large, colorful flower arrangement sits on the coffee table, as well as three wrapped packages. "Surprise!" Gina cries, and Marcus stands there, uncomprehending, asking himself what it is he has forgotten this time. He turns to Gina to find out, but doesn't get a chance to open his mouth. "It's your birthday, dummy." She kisses him on the mouth.

His birthday? He thinks a moment. "My birthday," he says, exasperated, "is next week."

"Well, that's the point," Gina says and leads him to the wrapped gifts. "It won't be a surprise next week. And next week you and I will celebrate alone."

"I see."

Now Assya, earnestly, kisses his cheek, Bernie takes his hand and shakes it. Absurdly, in the brief commotion of handshaking, laughing, and congratulations, Marcus feels like an invalid.

"We've decided," Gina says, "that later, after we eat, we'll let you read to us from your quotes."

"From your dictionary," Assya says. "I'm very eager to hear what you've included."

"I can only read you a few samples. Unless"—he smiles—"you're willing to stay up all night."

"No, thanks." Assya laughs.

"All right." He begins to edge toward the kitchen. "I'll go make those sandwiches for you."

"Don't you want to open your gifts?"

"There's plenty of time."

Back in the kitchen, after a moment's reflection, he turns on the oven, deciding on hot sandwiches, his own version of *Croque Monsieur,* using seeded rye instead of French white bread. The French won't mind—he cracks a joke between himself and the walls.

On the counter, next to the cutting board, he places a large baking dish. What will he read to them? Perhaps he could start with a small introduction, trying to convey to them the elation, the appreciation, that the connoisseur of literature, the trained reader, draws from his reading. He may talk about those consumers who pursue "art" as if it were a civil, social duty, consumers who, in their gullibility and wholesale eagerness to be part of the scene, loud as it may be, unwittingly nurture and support a degenerate and cynical industry that feeds them schlock and mocks them in its heart, works their insecurities to the point of intimidation, while pocketing their money.

Here Gina may interrupt, saying something like, True to form. Our prophet is out again with his trumpet.

His ram's horn, Bernie will correct.

With a nod of the head he'll acknowledge their remarks, glance at Assya for courage and continue. He'll tell them a bit about the writer's fears. His agonies. He'll tell them the famous story about Flaubert—or was it Chekhov?—and the comma, and use the story to illustrate what an important and effective tool punctuation becomes in the hands of a master. He'll explain how the punctuation symbols sort of tug at the words, nudge them into place, suffuse them with intonations, direct them into lanes of intent and meaning.

Consider the ominous-looking period, the naughty comma. The question mark, the dash, the ellipsis . . . Read Nathalie Sarraute, see what miracles she works with the dots. The exclamation point, the colon, the semicolon—these instruments, or their absence, like magic, transform a text. One has to become an aware reader, a reader who regurgitates his response and, with the fine point of a surgical implement, separates out the components of his experience.

A reader does not come empty-handed. He fills in the gaps, paints the backdrop, builds on the foundation the author provides. The writer says: They sat in Marcus's kitchen, and the reader—knowing something about Marcus, knowing that he lives in New York City, in an apartment on Tenth Street between University and Fifth—brings forth his own idea of Marcus's kitchen, his own "generic" environments. The reader supplies the walls, the cabinets, the counters, the appliances. He supplies the common areas, such as the hallways, the elevators, the downstairs lobby, the doorman. You tell the reader it's an Irish bar, a dainty coffee house, you provide a few pertinent details, and the reader immediately, and busily, cooperates, adding the final touches.

The reader has an advantage. The reader reads a novel. His mind is engaged, focused, absorbing all the particulars: it is all new information. He reads and stores away all the clues. In most happy cases, it is easy going for him, his reading runs smoothly: the careful author has made sure that all the clues click: there are no discordant notes, no jarring deviations, no uncalculated contradictions. But if he finds an instance where the author eased his guard, the watchful reader, like a cat trapping an insect in its paws, pounces on the error, holds it up as a trophy: the writer, such a phony, has been found out! Such gleeful readers should be aware that unlike the reader, the writer, especially during the earlier stages, is so immersed in the minute buildup of his structure, he is bound to commit certain consistency errors, errors he hopes to catch later on, as he works on the second, third, fourth drafts.

What kind of consistency errors? Assya asks and the others nod; they, too, want to know.

Let's say, he replies, happy that they are interested, that you have a character who's been sitting on a chair for the past ten pages, and suddenly the author says that so and so sat down. Or, he may have the chair suddenly metamorphose into a couch, saying that so and so stood up from the couch. He may have a character stub out a cigarette he hasn't lit. He may give a character blue eyes, and later on in the novel give that same character green eyes. As a matter of fact, there's a famous debate about exactly such a problem, a debate that has entered the history of literature. I forget the names of the protagonists in this drama, but there's a raging polemic about what the author—was it Dreiser?—had in mind: did he mean to be ambiguous about the character's eyes? And if yes, why? Others speculate that her eyes changed color, depending on her mood, on the hour of the day. And yet another school claims it was a simple mistake, an oversight.

A writer, he'll tell them, likes to refer to himself as an old miser, a misanthrope of the worst sort, interminably bent over his desk, muttering under his nose; he's cantankerous, petty, always pecking, picking, worrying; he's garrulous, a ventriloquist of the first degree.

Now he'll pick up a notebook and leaf through it, confiding, in passing, how he, as a reader or spectator, always worries about the character's financial affairs, always worries that a character get what's coming to him, especially when the character is needy. If a character loses his wallet, he, Marcus, prays that someone should find it and bring it back. If he gets a parking ticket, Marcus's heart aches. And if a parcel is sent in the mail, he worries until the parcel indeed arrives at the proper address; if the parcel gets lost, he is devastated. He can't help himself, he explains. He has the character's interests at heart.

Assya laughs and confesses that she too worries about the characters, about their money situation. She hates it when they get cheated, or lose something that's lawfully and rightfully theirs.

He then tells them: It's simple, you know. Characters, just like you and me, need to be liked, appreciated, cuddled, cared for. They, too, have feelings, wants; they wish to appear strong, important, attractive. They share our petty and lofty aspirations. That is why, he says and points at the open notebook in his lap, one cannot resist a Mr. Palomar, a Mrs. Palomar, their lawn, even the blackbirds that frequent their garden. Here, for example, I want you to note the sure-footed, slow-advancing gait of Italo Calvino as he dissects the lawn of Mr. and Mrs. Palomar:

"Around Mr. Palomar's house there is a lawn. This is not a place where a lawn should exist naturally: so the lawn is an artificial object, composed from natural objects, namely grasses. The lawn's purpose is to represent nature, and this representation occurs as the substitution, for the nature proper to the area, of a nature in itself natural but artificial for this area. In other words, it costs money. The lawn requires expense and endless labor: to sow it, water it, fertilize it, weed it, mow it.

"The lawn is composed of dichondra, darnel, and clover. This mixture, in equal parts, was scattered over the ground at sowing time. The dichondra, dwarfed and creeping, promptly got the upper hand: its carpet of soft little round leaves spreads everywhere, pleasing to the foot and to the eye. But the lawn is given its thickness by the sharp spears of darnel, if they are not too sparse and if you do not allow them to grow too much before cutting them. The clover sprouts irregularly, some clumps here, nothing there, and farther on a whole sea of it; it grows exuberantly until it slumps, because the helix of the leaf becomes top-heavy and bends the tender stalk. The lawn mower attends with deafening shudder to the tonsure; a light odor of fresh hay intoxicates the air; the leveled grass finds again a bristling infancy; but the bite of the blades reveals unevenness, mangy clearings, yellow patches."

You see, he says. You may ask: What's in a lawn? Why would a Calvino even bother to shine his intelligence on something as mundane and boring as a lawn? Now picture him seated at his desk, distractedly gazing out of the window. The butt of a pencil sticks from his mouth, and he gently chews on it, when he suddenly notices something he's been looking at for years, but this morning, for some reason, it hits him: he notices his lawn, his own lawn, and a thought begins to form—a miracle! Or, he may be sitting outside, on a lawn chair, a blanket over his knees against the morning chill. He is reading a book, vaguely aware of his neighbor across the way mowing his lawn. As he continues reading, perhaps a bit annoyed at the noise, he may be reminded that he, too, should mow his lawn. If not today, then soon. Gradually he realizes that he's no longer concentrating on the book, but rather is thinking about his lawn, his neighbor's identical lawn, then lawns in general, their purpose. In no time at all, he's jotting down a note, then another. Or: Mr. Calvino considers installing a lawn in his front yard. He has asked for and received several promotional materials in the mail, and he sits in his den, going over the brochures. Reading about the various types and genera, he is amazed, as he often is, to discover that there are so many facets to life on earth, down to the tiniest blade, of which he knows nothing. He hurries to his desk.

Marcus turns a page. Here, he says, we're still with Palomar. Now he's in the garden, listening to the chatter of a pair of blackbirds and brooding about the meaning of language and silence.

"Mrs. Palomar is also in the garden, watering the veronicas. She says, 'There they are,' a pleonastic utterance (if it assumes that her husband is already looking at the blackbirds), or else (if he has not seen them) incomprehensible, but in any event intended to establish her own priority in the observation of the blackbirds (because, in fact, she was the first to discover them and to point out their habits to her husband) and to underline their unfailing appearance, which she has already reported many times.

" 'Sssh,' Mr. Palomar says, apparently to prevent his wife from frightening them by speaking in a loud voice (useless injunction, because the blackbirds, husband and wife, are by now accustomed to the presence and voices of the Palomars, husband and wife) but actually to contest the wife's precedence, displaying a consideration for the blackbirds far greater than hers."

And on and on they go, Marcus says, and shuts the notebook, reaching for another where he knows he'll find Flaubert and Nabokov.

It's very good, Assya says, and he, gratified, appropriates the credit to himself—as if on behalf of Calvino—yet tries hard not to let his pleasure show on his face; he wants to impress on her that he is one of those serious, committed men who take such comments as a straightforward evaluation, as a statement of fact, and not as a compliment. He wants her to know he is immune to easy self-congratulation, he's a man dedicated to his craft.

But where's the gesture? Bernie interjects.

Everywhere, he says. The whole exchange is gesture. It's there, in the text, between husband and wife. It's the imperceptible stuff that makes us human, set in vibrant motion here before our eyes.

Now. Are you ready for Nabokov? He glances up at them to see if they're still alert and interested. Yes, they do seem interested; they look at him, an expectant expression on their faces.

Again he reads to them, this time from Nabokov's *The Defense*. As he reads, he becomes aware of his voice swelling, filling up the room. "His mother with a mewing sound was about to reach out and arrange his cloak, but noticing the look in his eye she swiftly snatched her hand back and merely indicated with a twiddle of her fingers in mid-air: 'Close it up, close it tighter.' "

Here, he says, his voice trembling with excitement, you have the gesture, as well as the tenor of a whole relationship, conveyed in one sentence. You can also glean the character and insecurity of the mother vis-à-vis her son; and the son's unforgiving, uncompromising attitude toward her. And somehow you feel for both of them, for both of them are trapped in their characters, in their personalities.

And now, he concludes, one last passage and I'll set you free.

At this they laugh, appreciatively.

This is our friend, Flaubert: "At about four in the morning Charles, well wrapped up in his cloak, started out for Les Bertaux. He was still sleepy from the warmth of his bed, and let himself be lulled by his horse's gentle trot. When the animal stopped of its own accord at one of those holes, surrounded by thorn-bushes, that are dug beside the furrows, Charles woke with a start . . . The rain had stopped; it was beginning to grow light. In the leafless branches of the apple-trees birds sat motionless, their little feathers ruffling in the cold morning wind. The flat countryside stretched as far as the eye could see; clumps of trees round the farmhouses made patches of dark violet at distant intervals on that vast grey surface which merged at the horizon into the somber tones of the sky. From time to time Charles opened his eyes. But then, his senses growing weary and sleepiness automatically returning, he soon went off into a kind of doze, wherein recent sensations were mixed up with memories, and he saw himself as two selves, student and husband at once—lying in bed as he had been an hour ago, and going through a wardful of patients as in the old days. A warm smell of poultices mingled in his consciousness with the sharp tang of the dew . . ."

A funny sensation spreads in his chest and up his throat. All at once he feels dizzy, it feels as though his body is swaying at the counter. It's very warm in the kitchen, maybe he should turn off the oven. The bread knife feels heavy in his hand, he must let go of it.

Nineteen

They tell him they found him on the kitchen floor, the base of the knife sticking out from under him. "I thought for sure you fell on it," Gina recalls, "on the blade. Thank God for Assya and Bernie who were there to help. We called an ambulance right away."

Marcus is uncomfortable on the hospital bed. The top is raised in such an awkward angle, he's half-sitting half-lying, feeling helpless. He looks at Gina, he looks at Oscar, thinking that the bed alone would turn a healthy man into an invalid, a terminal patient.

They kept him overnight for observation; they took all sorts of tests, but found nothing. Emotional exertion, says the young doctor. Exhaustion, or an acute form of an anxiety attack. Perhaps even a very mild stroke. They want to take a few more tests, so he'll have to stay one more night. Oscar believes that Marcus just fainted, that his mental defense mechanism took over, fighting off emotional stress. Marcus shrugs and mutely notes that Oscar himself doesn't look too well.

"Whatever it is," Gina tells Marcus, "you need a vacation."

"That's the last thing I need," Marcus says, a bit sharply.

Surprised, hurt, she looks at him. "Suit yourself."

Now, he decides, he'll let her have it. Indeed, he is seething: too many things are suddenly unclear. "There was no need to bring me here, to put me in the hands of these engineers of health. Now that they've got me in their clutches, they demand that I stay another night."

"Marcus, stop," Oscar says.

Her voice trembling with contained anger, Gina says, "I thought you were having a heart attack. Better safe than sorry."

He says, "I thought you said it was the blade," hoping he sounds sarcastic, but it's suddenly so absurd, this back and forth bickering, that against their wills, their lips twitching with the futile effort to stop themselves from smiling, he and Gina finally break and allow that smile to show. It's a hard-won smile, not free of anger, and as Oscar begins to laugh, they join him, but each planning to press their point, at a more appropriate time, and show how the other behaved wrongly, rudely, abominably.

The following morning, after another sleepless night, the young doctor comes to see him off. Nothing conclusive in the tests, says the doctor, but his blood pressure is a bit high, Marcus should take it easy for the next few weeks, decrease his alcohol intake, and generally watch his diet. "My diet!" Marcus exclaims. "I eat like a saint." "Nevertheless," says the doctor, the final authority.

Going home in a cab, Marcus recalls the second croissant and the second double espresso he had on the day he fainted. And then the ham and cheese sandwich with Bernie. Maybe the doctor is right. Maybe he should watch his diet. As the cab approaches his building, he feels like one coming home after a long absence. Upon seeing him, George jumps to his feet and opens the door with such servile pomp, Marcus wants to laugh. George reaches for his handbag, but Marcus waves him off. In the elevator it dawns on him that they all must know what has happened, and his stomach turns as he imagines himself, presumably unconscious, on one of those horrible-looking stretchers, being wheeled out into the ambulance, while his worried, whispering neighbors stand and watch.

He puts the key in the lock and enters his apartment. There's a hushed, barren air of vacancy, as if no one has lived there in quite some time. He puts down his bag in the hall, steps into the kitchen, then goes from room to room, as if testing the feeling of this homecoming, testing the legitimacy of his invasion. He is a bit uncertain on his feet.

He peers into his study, then approaches his desk, taps it, moves his hand over his notebooks, over the pile of notes waiting to be copied.

He goes into the living room, draws aside the curtains to let in light. The three wrapped packages are still there, on the coffee table, waiting to be opened, but he doesn't feel like opening them. He takes the packages into his study and stacks them under his desk.

He goes into the kitchen. It's almost noon. Soon, he'll go down to Gristede's to buy a box of matzos. Tomorrow is the first night of Passover, and he will spend it alone. Gina has come up with a last-minute plan: join Assya and Bernie who will celebrate the Seder at a friend's home where they, Gina and Marcus, would be more than welcome. But this morning, when he called her from the hospital to say he was going home, he said he wasn't feeling sociable, that he wanted to stay home, but she must go to the Seder if she wants to. "This will be our first," Gina said. "Our first Seder apart." "Not to worry," he tried to joke. "We'll overcome." "Very funny," she said, waited a moment then hung up. Which didn't help his mood. Perhaps that's why he feels he's enveloped in a cloud of uncertainty and foreboding, a foreboding that tells him that nothing will ever go his way, that everything around him, all that constitutes his life, will slowly disintegrate and crumble. Maybe his collapse, right at the spot where he's now standing, signals the beginning of the end.

He chases the thought away, reminding himself that all his premonitions, so far, have yet to come true: he has yet to crash in an airplane, be swept into the ocean and drown, become paralyzed from the neck down after a car accident. He has yet to contract some awful, rare disease, he has yet to die of pneumonia, of cancer: the list is long, but he is still here, on his feet. Perhaps a bit shaken, but still standing. He got overly excited, preparing in his mind to read to them; and it was warm in the kitchen—he remembers sweating. And so, he fainted. The only unpleasant aftermath of this incident are a couple of images he has to carry with him, like the one of himself on the floor, an incapacitated, helpless heap of flesh and bones. He has to carry the thought that Gina, Assya, and Bernie stood around him and, if only for a moment, saw exactly that, a heap of flesh on the floor: lifeless, characterless, featureless.

He turns and leaves the kitchen. Tomorrow he'll start again, pick up where he left off, plunge himself into his work. Tomorrow night he'll have his own little Seder with matzo, the four glasses of wine (he'll only have one), the hard-boiled egg (only the egg white) that symbolizes the Jewish people—the longer you boil it, the harder it gets. He'll read the Haggadah and repeat all the blessings, sing all the songs, dip his finger in the wine while reciting the ten plagues. He'll leave the door open, place a glass of wine on the table for Elijah. As to the meal, he'll order Chinese: a wonton soup without the wontons, and some chicken dish. He must stick a note on the refrigerator to remind him that on the eve of the eighth day he is to light a Yahrzeit candle for his parents and for the six million; then, the morning after, he'll go to synagogue for the Yizkor service. Who was it that said that every time you turn, a Jew, somewhere, is lighting a candle?

He'll sing *Ma-Nishtana* from beginning to end; he'll sing the *Had-Gadia*, he'll sing, with a full-throated voice, *Ehad Mi Yodea, Ehad Ani Yodea*—his favorite holiday song since childhood: the slow climb upward from question one to question thirteen, then the quick, cascading answers, picking up speed in repetition.

The phone rings. He hesitates a moment, as if it is not he who lives in the apartment, then picks up the receiver. It's Assya. She is asking how he is, and he nods his head. He's fine, thank you. She asks him to reconsider, to please join them tomorrow night. No, no, he says, he prefers to stay home. But, she says, it's a holiday, people are meant to get together on holidays. Next year, he promises. But he'll be all alone, Assya throws in her last argument. He assures her that he prefers it, that whatever it is that happened to him the other night, he feels he needs to be alone. He needs to reassemble his broken parts, he says, and laughs to show her he hasn't lost his humor. He needs, he says, to rediscover his own company. "It could be," Assya says, "the stage you're at, writing your novel." "It could be," he agrees. "You're very astute." "It's our responsibility," Assya says, "to take care of each other." "Yes," he says, and to his horrified surprise, hot tears spring into his eyes. Why? Why? From where these tears? Feeling lost, he wishes he could shout. He is in mourning. In perpetual mourning. Yes, yes—he wipes his cheeks. He feels a little better already, he feels reassured. "We'll see you soon, then," Assya says, and he, although he wants her to remain a while longer on the line, says, "Yes, soon."

Twenty

It's my birthday today, is the first thought that comes to him upon waking. He rolls onto his back and, for a few moments, remains motionless. In spite of his premonition a couple of months ago, he's made it through yet another winter; a cold, harsh, New York City winter. His daughter and son-in-law have suggested many times that he move to San Diego and live near them, and he considered it, yes he did, but somehow could never bring himself to make the move. He's been living in this apartment nearly forty years—how could he possibly leave? How could he leave behind all the memories these walls contain? How could he leave his neighbors behind, some of whom have grown old with him, and when they meet in the elevator or out on the street, they exchange an impish smile, as if to say, Hey, we're still here, we're still alive.

It takes a lot of determination to remain alive, a passion and willpower.

He is eighty-one today, and if it were up to him, he'd be willing to go it for another hundred years. The truth be told, he'd be willing to go it forever, doing exactly what he does: reading, learning, writing, thinking. If he were to stay here another hundred years, he might be looking for a mate.

Except for a weariness in his limbs—a weariness he believes will dissolve in the warm summer sun—he feels all right. He gets around.

Young women on the street and old ladies in the park find him charming; they like his old-fashioned ways. They like the fact that he's always dressed up, that he always wears a hat. They find it amusing that he is both fussy and debonair. They love his walking stick, which, they think, he carries more for style than need. Some young persons hang on his words, waiting for him, the wise old man, to reveal to them some great, important message about life and the world. Years ago, in the dim afternoon light of a hospital room, he happened to overhear a dying man impart a message to his daughter, but it wasn't the kind of message one hopes to hear. He heard the man whisper, in a hoarse voice, It's all for naught. What's for naught? the man's daughter hung anxiously over the bed to better hear her father, thinking perhaps he was delirious. Life, the dying man replied. Clearly, lucidly. Life!

How awful he felt when he heard that. Awful for himself and for the daughter. How awful, he thought, to hear such blunt words and know them to be the final testimony of a dying man, especially when the dying man is your father. Words that confirm one's unvoiced thoughts, words one is unwilling to confront, or to be confronted with. He remembers feeling awful for the stranger, too, obviously a man of education and some standing, a man who had to die with the bitter, uncompromising conviction that his life, his struggle, had been in vain. And he was leaving behind a daughter who would have to live the rest of her life with her father's words reverberating in her heart. She'd have to live out her life remembering that at the last, after all was said and done, her father rejected life. She'd have to live her life knowing that her father left this world a dejected, discouraged man. She'd have to be thinking: What an awful way to leave this world, a world that for all its miseries did provide short moments of joy, a world in which her father lived, married, fathered her and her siblings.

If she had any siblings, the old man muses.

At the time he felt that the man would have been wiser to keep his harsh verdict to himself, and so spare his daughter. But later on he came to think that the dying man knew exactly what he was doing. What he said, in fact, to his daughter was that man was greater than life, that man's spirit, his power to reason, conquered death and placed him above the petty, messy matters of everyday existence. Man, in the end, could reject it all, he had the final word. It was a message of hope. And by conveying this message to his daughter, the proud man let her know that her father, till the end, was the same man she had known all her life; he let her know that he was not reduced to a sniveling old man, cowering before death. He let her know that he was not just another old fool, laid out on a white bed, resignedly accepting his fate. In the grandest gesture of spirit he invited her to participate in his last revolt, in the final declaration of mind and spirit over matter and decay.

Perhaps, the old man thinks, when he himself is on his deathbed, he too will have the strength of that stranger. But right now he'd happily sign up in Hobbes's camp and shout with him: "Seeing all delight, and appetite presupposeth a farther end, there can be no contentment but in proceeding."

Time to get up and out of bed. In a few hours the phone calls will begin, wishing him many happy returns. The sooner he gets to his desk, the more work will get done. Often, most days in fact, the only proof he has that a day has come and gone are the pages he is left with at the end of the day.

Later, weather permitting, he'll get his walking stick and go out for a walk. He'll pat the dogs, talk with their owners. Thank God, he'll never lack for dogs, and dog owners, in this neighborhood. He'll sit on a bench and marvel at the strong young thighs of the half-naked joggers.

No wonder he chose to remain in the city. Everywhere he turns he readily finds other people like himself, willing to stop a moment and exchange a few words; every inch of pavement, now warm and defrosted—just like the citizens who walk upon it—holds sights he'll never tire of watching: the ever-striking variety of men and women, boys and girls, babies and toddlers, living, perhaps, the most precious moments of their lives.

The old man pushes off the bed. His feet find his slippers, and soon he is up, making his way to the bathroom.

Twenty-One

He has a lot of work ahead of him, but he takes a moment to read what he has copied into his notebook:

Samuel Johnson: "No mind is much employed upon the present: recollection and anticipation fill up almost all our moments."

Erasmus: "Scarcely anywhere will you find two words so close in meaning that they do not differ in some respect."

"For things should not be written in such a way that everyone understands everything, but so that they are forced to investigate certain things, and learn."

"According to the proverb, Not every man has the luck to go to Corinth. Whence we see it befalls not a few mortals that they strive for this divine excellence diligently, indeed, but unsuccessfully, and fall into a kind of futile and amorphous loquacity, as with a multitude of inane thoughts and words thrown together without discrimination, they alike obscure the subject and burden the ears of their wretched hearers."

Schopenhauer: "In the most barbarous period of the Middle Ages—the times of Alfred the Great . . . the ability to read and write exempted a man from the penalty of death."

"It is only by life that a man reveals what he is, and it is only in so far as he reveals himself that he exists at all."

Jung: "Every creative person is a duality or a synthesis of contradictory impulses. On the one side he is a human being with a personal life, while on the other side he is an impersonal, creative process."

Browning: "All we have gained, then, by our unbelief / Is a life of doubt diversified by faith / For one of faith diversified by doubt."

Unamuno: "I believe in God as I believe in my friends, because I feel the breath of His affection, feel His invisible and intangible hand, drawing me, leading me, grasping me; because I possess an inner consciousness of a particular providence and of a universal mind that marks out for me the course of my own destiny."

He now switches to his novel notebook and continues:

At the very beginning, when he first began to think about his novel, things were pretty hazy in his mind, a haziness he likes to think of as the primordial chaos referred to in Genesis and in the science books; a haziness out of which characters, men and women, gradually emerged, bringing with them all that comes of man: stories, thoughts, ideas.

As he advances from the second to the third draft, from the third to the fourth, he feels a new strength, a new competence, having to do with the residue each draft, each word used and replaced, has left in him, and upon which he continues to build. He comes to trust himself that if he doesn't get it right the first time, he'll get it right the second, the third, the fourth. And if necessary the fifteenth, for it took William Faulkner fifteen drafts before he closed the book on *The Sound and the Fury.*

In other ways, too, he feels like God. It happens at times that while he works, he may suddenly stop and zoom ahead to a time when his novel will be completed, and he, like the Creator, will look over his work and see that it is good.

He talks to himself in his journals, and this talking soothes him, for it provides him a moment of quiet, of stilled suspension where his mind and heart seek to satisfy no one but himself. Often, indeed, he feels an overwhelming, and yet impotent, desire to break through the hard confines of his brain, emerge through bone and glide in a new sensation of freedom, of liberation, of absolute knowledge. Like the Talmudic embryo who, in his mother's womb, perceives the whole of the universe. It is not original sin man must contend with, but original knowledge, what was known and then forgotten.

Like the Talmudic embryo! Is he wishing for death? For rebirth? He still suffers flashes of his fall, of his shameful collapse to the floor. But he knows he must anchor himself, anchor himself in his work. At times his characters won't cooperate; they seem aloof, regarding him with a cold eye. Every so often, he needs to get up from his desk and pace in his rooms. In every room, he glimpses the piles of books he has yet to read, and he is filled with a vague, spreading apprehension, having to do, he imagines, with his a priori acknowledged frustration that no matter how much and how fast he reads, there will always be more, he'll never get to all of them. At the same time, he is also reminded of the pleasure yet awaiting him, the pleasure he feels when he starts a new book, and therefore concludes that his apprehension is in fact a form of anticipation, for he is eager to get to them, to all of them, embrace them in his arms and be contained in them.

Indeed, when he puts down a book he has just finished reading, he immediately picks up another (hour permitting) like a day laborer who must fill a quota with no time for breaks. And as he sits down with the new book (has he written somewhere, "a weighty promise"?), he pauses for a moment and stares into space, allowing time for a silent prayer, or a blessing, as one would before embarking on a new road, a new adventure. This short pause also serves to clear his head, to store away all images from the previous book, and so make room for the new one. A never-ending chain.

By now, it is obvious, he considers himself a book expert. He can tell, at a glance, whether or not the book he holds will satisfy his hunger and bring forth another—a deeper, richer hunger. A paragraph or two, and sometimes even a sentence, help him decide the fate of a book. And so it happens that when he browses through books in bookstores, he thinks himself a physician, checking the vital signs of his patients.

As Arnaldo Momigliano already said, reading is more important than writing.

Now he reads Elfriede Jelinek, amazed at, and admiring, the cold efficiency, the crystalline clarity of the writing. He reads many passages over and over again; going back, again and again, to the title page of the book, to note the name of the obviously excellent translator. He copies passages into his notebook. The one he has just copied delights him for its sheer elegance. It's from *The Piano Teacher*: "Erika orders Klemmer not to look at her like that. But Klemmer is as open as ever about his desires. The two of them are wrapped up like twin pupae in a cocoon. Their hulls, delicate as cobwebs, are made of ambition, ambition, ambition, and ambition, resting weightless, fragile, on the two skeletons of their bodily wishes and dreams."

When he questions his voraciousness, his fanatic devouring of books and authors, he reminds himself that Flaubert, while humorously deriding Bouvard and Pécuchet for their excessive (and seemingly useless) scholarship, had himself admitted to having read one thousand and five hundred books in order to write *Bouvard et Pécuchet.*

Marcus lays down his pen and rubs his wrist; he's had a productive day. He blesses his luck, quietly, cautiously, so as not to provoke the evil eye. He glances at his watch. It's five o'clock; he is done for the day, but remnants of thoughts, like meteors, still shoot across in his head. Things he needs to remember to include in his book, things he tells himself he must make sure he has already included. He has to make sure he does not repeat himself, unintentionally. He must insert somewhere that his narrator, for all his ambition to better the lives of people, will readily admit that he knows nothing about "people out there." When he watches a ballgame on TV, he is always astonished to discover anew that so many people seem to be leading full lives far from New York, far from the center of the world. These people marry, have children, hold down jobs, open a business. He is similarly astounded when he dials an 800 number, which for all he knows may be ringing in Omaha, and a bright, cheerful voice comes on the line to take his order or complaint, giving him occasion to silently marvel that people everywhere fill all sorts of jobs.

Marcus jots down a note and puts it in the file. There was something else he was thinking about, something to do with his narrator. What was it?

Oh, yes. For the sake of his narrator, he must sit down one day and catalogue his fears, his worries. He should also insert, where appropriate, that his narrator wishes for readers to be on their toes; he wishes his readers to turn the pages not only forward, but also backward, checking on him and on themselves. In his view, the role of the reader is to mutely beg the author: Don't betray your insecurities, the little faith you have in my intelligence.

The author, for his part, should aim to plough deeper, rather than onward.

Marcus makes another note. He must remember to describe his narrator being amazed when encountering in the elevator a neighbor he hasn't seen for quite a while, amazed that this neighbor is still alive, has been alive all this time, quietly going about the business of his life. Much in the way that he himself has, he reminds himself. And still he marvels at it, not because this particular neighbor is old, but simply because the very idea that this man, or woman, is still here, waking up every morning, brings home the fact that death, after all, and for all its reputation, is not as prevalent as all that; death, too, has its limits, it bides its time.

Marcus reflects: The deeper he advances into his novel, the more associations and ideas develop in his mind, ideas that he feels he must include. And so they accumulate, build themselves up, and often the new wants to swallow the old, push it aside and be positioned upfront and thus take precedence, become prominent. And in his mind's eye, his novel becomes a lump of dough in the hands of a baker, a lump pounded on the floured board, stretched out and refolded, piled onto itself.

Marcus stands up from his desk and goes into the living room to pour himself a drink. He considers going out for a walk, then decides to stay in. He'll read and wait for Gina and, over dinner, she'll tell him all about the Seder and the new people she met.

Deep in thought, he goes to the bar and pours himself a whisky. So, he didn't get to read to them, after all. But he will read to them. If not today, then tomorrow. And if not tomorrow, then the day after.

Twenty-Two

"Stop! Stop!" Gina yells, and his heart contracts, not because he is the target, but because it pains him to see her like this: pale, distraught, out of control, waving her arms like a madwoman. He wants to get up from his chair and go to her, to where she is standing, so helpless and trembling, in the doorway. But he's afraid to make a move. If he stands up to go to her, she might turn and leave. She has barely arrived five minutes ago, and hasn't even changed her clothes as she normally does, and he knows how she aches to get out of her clothes, relax, get ready for the evening. And he, he has been waiting for her, looking forward to a quiet dinner, expecting to talk about the Seder she went to, and when he heard her come in, he went to welcome her, but as soon as she entered and he saw the dark expression on her face, he knew something was wrong. He approached her anyway, but she warned him, "Don't come near me," and stormed into the bedroom, slamming the door. So, his heart heavy, he went back to his chair, picked up his book and sat down, waiting, and a moment later she is raging in the doorway. "What am I doing here?" she shouts. "Who are you? What are we doing together? What do we have in common?"

"If it's because of the Seder," he tries to calm her.

"Fuck the Seder, it's you I'm talking about. You. You." She paces in the room and then, as if realizing she's in the same square footage with him, she retreats back to the doorway. "Do you have a book in your lap? Good. If only you paid as much attention to Rosina, or to those around you, but no, no, you have loftier things on your extraordinary mind."

"What are you talking about?"

"I'm talking about the way you attacked me in the hospital. I'm talking about your indifference, your selfishness, your blindness."

"I'm sorry about the hospital, I wasn't myself."

"Oh yes you were, that's how you are, the minute you feel inconvenienced, everyone else is to blame."

"Look, it's true, I'm working on the novel, but—"

"I know you're working on the novel. Everybody knows you're working on the novel. But do you know what I do? What I go through? When is the last time you asked me how my work was going? My life? And, if you really need to know, then yes, it is the Seder, but not the way you imagine it. It has to do with me sitting there with Assya and Bernie, and this other couple, all of them good looking and happy together, normal together, and I'm thinking: Why can't I have normal? Why am I stuck here with you and your stupid books? I want out. I want a vacation. From you. I want to see what's out there. I want someone who's light on his feet, I want to go dancing, I want to see things, be involved with people."

"But we do go out. Besides, you like being alone. You like it when we stay in, just the two of us."

"But I also want variety. I want things, I want life, to happen to me."

"Okay, we'll do it, we'll go out, I promise. But please, Gina, can we talk about this tomorrow? I'm under a lot of strain, and the doctor said—"

And here she screams, "Stop! Stop!" and presses her hands over her ears. "It's always about you, isn't it? Well, enough, I don't want to hear it, not a word of it. I spoke to the doctor and he says it's all in your head, okay? You're under a lot of strain? Why, goddamn it? You're sitting here in your little room, nice and cozy at your shiny desk, and concoct all sorts of scenes to suit your fancy. But do your fingers get dirty? Do you know what's going on out there? You think you're superior, but let me tell you something: You're a lacking human being, you're incomplete."

Her words sting him, and he wants to ask, What's got into you tonight? Maybe she lost a client, or a large order. Better be gentle and defend himself, try to explain, and so maybe calm her down. "Whatever happens to my characters, Gina, happens to me, you know this."

"Great. A lot indeed happens in your little brain."

The mocking expression on her face and the sarcasm in her voice finally get to him. Now he, too, is upset. He feels his blood rising in protest, and for a moment considers letting go and joining in the shouting, in the waving of hands, but then he remembers his blood pressure and the doctor's warning. He'd better not add fuel to the fire. Later, when she's herself again, he'll tell her how incoherent and melodramatic her performance was. He'll ask her if perchance her period is due.

No, he remembers. With her it's not her period. With her, as she has proudly told him many times, it's the middle of her cycle, just around the time she's ovulating. That's when her tolerance level goes down to zero, and she feels vulnerable, useless, unwanted. She has said it is possibly a defense strategy her body has devised against childbearing, her temper and shoddy nerves making her inaccessible to males precisely when she is fertile. Now he tries to figure out in his mind if indeed it is the middle of her cycle, which would explain her irrational behavior.

"Is it—?" he begins, and she looks at him, leaning against the doorway, calmer now, but a scornful smile still lingers on her lips. He has paused to reconsider his approach, fearing that he might reignite her anger if he suggests belittling it by placing the blame on her eggs and hormones. But he continues all the same, unable to resist the temptation to offer a logical explanation for her behavior. "I thought perhaps it was the middle of the month for you?"

"The middle of the month?" Her eyes narrow, as if trying to make sense of his incongruent remark. "The middle of the month," she repeats, but now she gets it, he sees comprehension settle in her eyes. He nods his head encouragingly, encouraging her to see how absurd her attack on him is, encouraging her to end it soon so they could sit down to dinner, then make love, and if indeed she's ovulating she'll use her diaphragm, or he'll withdraw and come on her stomach. Whatever she wants; he'll do whatever she wants, because now as he looks at her he is reminded again that he is bound to her, that he loves her. After they make love, or while they're having dinner, they'll talk this over, he'll explain better the kind of pressure he's under. He'll inquire about her work, about her frustrations. He now sees in her eyes that she too is realizing this, realizing that she is bound to him, that she can't just get up and leave him. She might leave him for a day, two days, drag out a fight for an entire week, but eventually the two of them must come together. And once they make up, they will cuddle up, and she'll tell him in the dark all the thoughts that ran in her head, all the dreams she dreamt and had been dying to tell him, and he will stroke her hair and tell her how empty and heavy his heart felt, how he went through the motions of sitting down at his desk, of sitting down to dinner, lifelessly, joylessly, and she will admit she overreacted, and he will admit to being insensitive, inconsiderate, or whatever other accusation she hurled at him during the fight. He may even suggest they get married, and so close the lid on the possibility of one of them leaving because of a silly fight.

"The middle of the month, eh?" Gina says, and he looks for the twitch in her mouth that will tell him that she wants to laugh but tries to fight it, because this is usually the turning point of their fights when one of them manages to make the other laugh against his or her will, and the other, laughing although still angry, is made to see how ridiculous it is for them to fight. And once she laughs, it will be easy for him to go up to her, hug her, apologize.

But this time Gina controls it: she doesn't laugh, she doesn't let herself break into a smile. But he can tell she's close, she's on the verge, he only needs to nudge her. "Come on, Gina," he says, but she turns and goes into the bedroom, and a minute later he sees her walking resolutely toward the front door. "Wait," he says, jumps to his feet and goes to her. Gina, her hand on the knob, turns to look at him.

He says, trying to keep his voice even, "You know what will happen, don't you?"

"No," she says. "That's your department."

"If you go out the door, we'll both suffer two or three days of agony—why do it?"

"Because," she says, "I like to suffer."

He is not prepared for this response, and it must show on his face, for now she laughs, pointing a finger at him. Still, it is not the kind of laugh that will throw her, repenting and remorseful, into his arms, but, on the contrary, it's the kind of laugh she uses to distance herself from him, a laugh that tells him, and her, she is even more resolute and confirmed in her decision than she's been aware of.

"Tell me," she says. "Do your characters ever surprise you?"

Her laugh and her question envelop him in a cloud; still, quietly he says, "Yes, of course they do."

"Well, then," she says, "real people, you know, people like me, may surprise you, too. You may be right in assuming we'll make up in two or three days, but you may also be wrong. Time will tell." She opens the door and shuts it behind her.

It happens so fast, he stands there, staring at the door. He tells himself he must go after her, amuse her while she waits for the elevator, deliberately make a fool of himself, a clown, anything, until she cracks. But he cannot bring himself to move, he cannot go after her; if she wants to play games, he can play them, too. But then he's reminded of those movie scenes where he silently urges the character: Go after him. Go after her, stupid. If you don't, you'll never see each other again.

In a sudden determination he opens the door, but the hallway is empty, no one is waiting by the elevator. She took the stairs, he thinks. Anything to avoid him, anything but give him a chance to mollify her, to bring her back from this madness.

She is not there, but he walks out anyway, walks to the exit door, opens it and peers into the stairway. Nothing. He walks to the far end of the hallway, then back toward his door. He recalls Mrs. Rivlin, the old lady on Oscar's floor, who takes late night walks in the hallway. Oscar. It's been a while since they spoke, he should call him.

He enters his apartment, shuts the door, and goes into the living room. He sits down, then stands up again. He goes into the bedroom, into the bathroom, and stands gazing at the long counter, at Gina's creams and lotions, her hairbrush. He reaches for the brush, sniffs it to pick up her scent, then begins to move the brush across his scalp, observing himself in the mirror. It is good to massage your head like that, Gina always says. See, Gina? I'm following your instructions exactly. Maybe that's the problem. My obedience, my need to keep the peace. You once said it was because of the Holocaust, because of my parents. But your parents were survivors too, so what exactly do you mean by that? No need to drag the Holocaust into every issue, every argument. It is not the Holocaust, it is us. Alone, and together.

Twenty-Three

An April snowstorm. A book in his hands, the old man, propped in bed against his raised pillows, looks out the window. The snow comes down in dense, majestic droves, and the fact that mere glass stands between him and the raging forces outside, thrills him. He imagines the first man, open-mouthed, watching a storm from the mouth of a cave. All around him are members of his tribe, his family, murmuring their awe. Living in a cave, close to the ground, opens one to immediacy, neutralizing the hidden valve of inhibition. For he—now lying in bed, on the hard mattress that often makes him feel he is actually floating, suspended in the air—as much as he feels awed by what he sees, knows himself to be incapable of expressing it. If he opened his mouth, attempting to utter a murmur, a cry of awe, something in him would block the sound.

The old man opens his mouth and, like a man about to dive, draws in breath, feeling his diaphragm rise in his chest. He prepares to shout, let out a cry, but indeed is blocked, and now tries to locate the point, the exact moment when he stops himself from sounding his awe. So again, he draws in breath, feels the diaphragm rise in his chest, and again, just when he attempts to let out a cry, his stomach hardens, his muscles contract, constricting all sound.

What is it? he asks. Is he intimidated by the mute solemnity of his walls, white and observing? Or, is there another person living in him, someone who might ridicule him if he cries out?

He is his own man; the old man rebels and forces out a cry. His voice crackles in the room, hoarse, broken, inauthentic. He shrugs his shoulders. So what if his voice is hoarse, broken, inauthentic? Who knows what other forces operate on him, in him? He is not a machine, there's no known, complete blueprint of him. And even if he were a machine where one could trace the minutest component and its optimal function—even then one could not grasp the magic at the heart of the process, the essence that made it/him work as a whole.

The snow, like a lacy white curtain, has taken the slant of the wind, shrieking past his windows. How thrilling it would be to live alone in the entire universe. As Kate does in *Wittgenstein's Mistress*, the book he is holding in his hands. Have a world all to oneself. No pressure, no crowding, just living as the lone and final beneficiary of Western civilization. Living alone, one retreats ever more deeply into oneself, in tune with his own silence, his silence reverberating in circles against the greater silences around it. There's a new fluidity, a primordial fluidity where time constraints and other boundaries are suffused, merging into a new chaos. Ambition has been abolished: no need to compete, to prove yourself; it's finally the definitive abolition of self.

The old man shuts the book and switches off the light. He rearranges the pillows, pulls up the cover and rolls onto his side, facing the window. He watches the snow come down, and is filled with a mild sadness. Tomorrow, upon waking, he will . . .

Twenty-Four

Marcus copies into his novel notebook:

If it's not one thing it's another. It's been too long, too many mornings since he's looked in the mirror and seemed real to himself. Since she left, the reflection he confronts looks haggard, withdrawn; his features are frozen, etched in the glass, lacking depth or dimension. He tries, and fails, to form a relationship, a kinship, with the frosty likeness before him. And when he thinks, This is not me, this is not my face, he is reminded of those photographs where, in his own eyes, he appears as a collapsible cardboard ghost, a startled smile on its face, having been inserted, as if by mistake, among the healthy, vigorous living.

He needs comforting.

At his desk, he longs for the simplicity of sentences one would find in foreign language textbooks for beginners. Such as: The window is open. The book is on the table. Is Jimmy a boy? Yes, Jimmy is a boy.

He contemplates the charm of proverbs and idioms, the charm and fascination they've held for him since boyhood when adults, left and right, appropriated them for easy, quick use. Such ready tools, such neat and irrevocable eternal truths. "The apple falls not far from the tree." "Easier said than done." "First thing first." "If I can do it, you can do it." "All roads lead to Rome." "Actions speak louder than words."

The one he has always liked the best is the one with the camel; every time he heard or used it, he saw the camel's back break under the weight of the last straw.

Since his father, like Tevye the dairyman, liked to quote from the Sages and other sources, these quotes and injunctions, inevitably, shaped him, the son, in the shape of the father. The one that his father impressed on him in particular and which affected him for life, was: Do not shame the face of another in public. Therefore, to this day, when he believes that his retort might shame or embarrass another, he keeps his mouth shut.

In his youth, he avidly read the *Ethics of the Fathers,* and keeps a copy of it on his desk, taking pleasure in the succinctly short and precise epigrams that, in their wisdom, seem to touch on all pertinent aspects of man's life, man as a private and social animal. When he reads the *Ethics,* he can actually picture the rabbis' old faces, the long and flowing white beards, the vivacious gaze, the resplendent light shining from the wide foreheads.

In his mind's eye, he envisions a page from the Torah or the Talmud: at the center of the page, in a narrow column, a few verses in bold Hebrew print. And all around the column, in minuscule script, the texts of the various commentators. These commentators, he thinks, are the first deconstructionists, the first practitioners and arbiters of semiotics. Take Rashi, or Onkelos. Think about the dedication, the devoted scholarship. Watch them bend over their desks, quill in hand, the long beard getting in the way, as they sit and write in candlelight.

His novel, he thinks, just like his life, any person's life, is like a page from the Talmud: the thin column in the center is the plot, the thread that runs through a person's life and holds it together, and all around it is the commentary, all that happens to a person, all that needs to be put into words, the stuff the writer needs to dig into: the living substance, the trembling flesh, the ever-evolving density of a lived moment.

Some mornings he wakes up with a peculiar clarity of mind, a clarity that brings him to his desk with a tentative certainty that things will connect for him in a new way. On such mornings he doesn't worry about continuity. He has named such mornings "ruminating mornings" for he lets the dreamy and, on the face of it, incoherent part of his brain come to the fore, while he sits, his gaze focused on a point in space; he is concentrating, waiting. Words, phrases emerge, suggest themselves, then retreat, in the manner of pictures flashing in a mind, in the manner of figures anonymously waiting on the sidelines to suddenly step forward, approach, sometimes cross each other's path, and then retreat, unless he grabs them, holds them up for closer inspection.

The writer triumphs not in inventing, but in inventiveness.

The writer is to find that necessary and intimate distance from his work, an intimate distance that will allow him the perspective from which to judge it.

Some mornings, when his work goes well, he interrupts himself for a moment and plunges ahead into the future, and his book is completed, published, to general praise. Modestly, he answers questions, tells about the actual writing of his book. The interviewer has many questions, and he answers them all, opens new, unsuspected vistas for a new world of readers, viewers, listeners. He tours the country. The book is made into a movie. He's invited to Hollywood and, after much hesitation, agrees to go. Soon he's on stage, accepting an Oscar.

Other mornings he is not as sure about things. He oscillates between his wish to remain truthful to the drab, hard facts of life, and the inviting appeal in the larger-than-life conceit. He leans toward bravura at such moments, as when he suddenly sees a loved one do or say something, nothing in itself out of the ordinary, but something—it could be a gesture, a certain movement of the hand, an expression, facial or vocal—that sharply jolts him into the heart of the moment and awakens in him a great compassion, a sadness, grand and pathetic at once, for the mortality of humans, the temporality of flesh.

It is often rhythm that sways him in the direction of this one word rather than another.

He looks up Oscar in the dictionary, hoping to learn if the Oscar award, like the Nobel Prize, is named after a certain individual. But this time the dictionary is not much help, and all he learns is that Oscar is a trademark, used especially for golden statuettes.

Marcus pauses his pen. This again reminds him that he must call Oscar. Definitely later in the afternoon.

He continues with his novel notebook:

Awards. Words. And more words. A word in the hollow of the brain. A word, like a piano key, activating a certain chord, producing an effect it was meant to produce, causing a man to sweat, to tremble, to long, to fear. Words remembered for a lifetime, words forgotten as soon as they're heard or uttered. One aches at times to correct oneself, correct an impression his unfortunate words may have created, only to find out, years later, that the words were long forgotten, if at all retained for longer than the time it took to hear them.

Often he finds himself chasing after a thought that crossed his mind in a flash. For a split second, as it made its journey in his mind, he thought he had it, but now, for the life of him, he cannot bring it back.

It may also happen that when he looks at a prompter note he has jotted down a few days earlier, he either cannot remember what idea this note was meant to prompt, or what got him interested in the first place. No matter how long or hard he tries, he cannot recapture the meaning, the fascination that made him write it down only a few short days ago.

And so, some thoughts are lost forever. He may be sitting at his desk, or in his living room, with a solid thought firmly rooted in his mind—he only needs to reach for pen and paper. And because he is so confident that he is in possession of it and that he'll have no difficulty reclaiming it, he allows himself a moment of distraction, of thinking about something else while reaching for a pencil, a piece of paper. And then, with a painful shock, he suddenly realizes that he has lost it, he no longer possesses it. He'll sit there, disbelieving, cursing his carelessness, his cockiness: experience has taught him that thoughts are not to be trusted, that thoughts will vanish, desert him, at the turn of a head. And yet he, ignoring the wisdom of past experience, assumes an overly confident attitude as if to prove to himself that this time his confidence is well founded, and so he lets go of the thought, lets it loose to float somewhere behind his forehead, if indeed that's where thoughts float, only to lose it, probably forever, and there he is, sitting in his chair, immobile as a lizard, half waiting for the thought to return, half mourning its loss.

As he sits there waiting, pining and groping for the lost one, other thoughts present themselves. They may be thoughts he has already discarded in the past; they may be new ones, but not the one he is so stubbornly after. It occurs to him that these thoughts which now so readily offer themselves, are, in possible fact, precisely such thoughts as the one now lost; that precisely these thoughts he now rejects offhand, without giving them a second thought, they too, at one time or another, were lost ones he desperately tried to recapture.

But now he is no longer interested in them. He leans forward and racks his brain with a repeated question: What was I thinking about just before I reached for the pencil? And when this doesn't work, he tries another tactic: What was I thinking about just before this other thought, the lost one, came into my head? If one thing leads to another, then all I have to do is remember the first thought.

Sometimes he gets lucky, and the thought, almost coyly, reappears before him, as if teasing him, as if telling him it had to give him a fright, punish him for his momentary negligence when he foolishly, haughtily, assumed the thought was his for all time. He then quickly plucks it from between the singles and couples that stroll and parade the boardwalk of his brain, and this time commits it to paper.

But when he fails to retrieve it, or traces of it, even though the loss upsets him, he consoles himself with the thought that ultimately it doesn't matter, for important thoughts have a way of returning; that eventually, in one form or another (perhaps better) the thought will come back to its source, which is he. At that time, when the thought reappears, he'll either accept it as good and valid; or, he'll discard it as just another thought that has lost its luster and now loiters in his brain as ambient noise.

It also happens that as he chases in concentration after that one elusive thread, he may suddenly alight upon another, a new one altogether, a thought that grabs him and which he grabs with gratitude as compensation for the loss he's just suffered. And soon the old, lost thought is forgotten, and he busies himself with the new one, writing it down as a prompter note to be investigated further in the future.

He asks himself: Does a thought have a notion of itself as a thing lost? Since the thought did exist, ever so briefly, ever so fleetingly, in one's mind, does it mean that it got registered somewhere as a thing that was, as a possible meaning, as a possible illumination? Does the brain engage in a meticulous bookkeeping on itself?

He ponders: Since most people follow a daily routine, one may assume that most people most days have the same recurring thoughts, having to do with their jobs, their wives, their husbands, their immediate duties and concerns. Thinking, too, in fact, becomes a sort of routine, thoughts and worries that travel in pre-set, pre-established tracks.

At times, usually during the evening rush hour, he takes the bus or subway to observe his fellow citizens returning home from work. He tries to guess their professions, their financial situations, tries to determine if this or that person is happy, in general, with his life; if this or that person is aware of the fact that this is his one life. From observation he finds that women, often, seem more unhappy, and he asks himself if it is just because duress and age harden women's features more readily than men's, or is it because women expect more out of life, out of others, and are therefore victims of frequent disappointments?

He feels for them, especially for those women who seem so troubled, it is hard to imagine them laughing, smiling. Many of them just stare ahead, as if engaged in some never-ending internal monologue. They bite their lips, chew the lining of their cheeks. He wants to go up to them and say something, something in the vein of: You live only once. Don't let worry mar your life.

But of course he says nothing, just watches them get on and off at their regular stops.

Marcus lays down his pen and, with a sigh, leans in his chair, throws his arms behind his head and puts his feet on the desk. He is done for the day. Soon, he'll go out for a walk, but there's one note he wants to copy into his notebook, a passage he encountered the other night in Alfred Jarry's *The Supermale,* a passage, he thinks, that begs to be underlined and copied: "There is certainly no reason for men to build enduring works if they do not vaguely imagine that these works must wait for some additional beauty . . . which the future holds in store. Great works are not created great; they become so."

Twenty-Five

Every morning, as soon as he wakes, Marcus remembers Gina, their situation. No, it wasn't just a bad dream; their fight was real. She actually said those hurtful words, then walked out the door. A whole five days ago. A heaviness sets in his heart, not because he misses her—he's too angry for that—but because their relationship now hangs as a problem. Unresolved problems disrupt his life, putting everything on hold.

He raises himself from the bed and goes into the bathroom. First he pees. Then he examines his face in the mirror, moves his hand across his cheek. His skin, it seems, lacks the pale hue, the moisture it absorbs when he and Gina sleep together, breathing into each other's pores. But who cares? He can live without the benefits of skin luster.

He turns on the water in the shower, sets the temperature, and steps in. He has vowed not to call her, not to beg her to forgive him for a crime he is not even sure he has committed. That's what she's waiting for, but he's not going to do it. Not this time. Why not? Because. He's just not going to do it. For once, let her come to him. Let her beg his forgiveness. And he'll give it—willingly, generously. Whereas she, when he asks her forgiveness, she seizes it as an opportunity to draw out his guilt, weigh it, add a few, just thought-of, last minute accusations, then finally, finally, she grants him the word, his pardon.

And what is he being accused of this time, being punished for so cruelly, so disproportionately? He has trouble remembering how it all began, what he said before she stormed out. What did he say? All he remembers is Gina yelling, Stop! Stop!

Who needs this? he thinks. Useless complications. Of course, he could call her and say he was sorry, and so, by lying, regain his peace of mind.

She was yelling, Stop! Stop! when he tried to explain how he is pressed for time. And she wouldn't listen. Forget it, then. He is not going to call her. She is spoiled and selfish, has nothing on her mind but her immediate, physical needs. Her designs. Her clients.

He comes out of the shower, vigorously rubs himself dry with a towel. He rubs her out of his thoughts. Done, he lets the towel drop to the floor, reaches for the shaving cream. He shakes the can, sprays foam onto his hand and spreads it evenly over his cheeks, his throat. His mind blank, he begins to shave, his eyes following the movement of the razor. He pauses a moment, squeezes out a fart, then shakes his head at his own vulgarity. And yet, when it comes to our anatomy, he muses, to our bodily functions, there are no secrets. The Queen of England must part her legs for her pap smear. And when it comes to those fleeting, shame- or guilt-ridden thoughts, we share in those, too.

He rinses his face and goes into the kitchen, sets water to boil. Now he feels invigorated, ready for work.

As he sits down with his coffee, he remembers, in a flash, how their fight began, and again, instantly, forgives himself. He recalls distinctly that just before she arrived, he was looking forward to a quiet, loving evening with her. That day he'd done good work, giving no thought to his fall, to his hospital stay, to the unpleasant eventuality that he might have suffered a mini-stroke. What does he have to do to make her understand that what he is dealing with are matters of life and death?

This is a new thought for him too, he now realizes. That he holds in his hands, however subliminally, both life and death. Somehow, it sounds too pretentious, too extravagant. If he were to suggest such a thing to her—

The telephone rings and all at once his heart is racing. It must be her, he thinks, placing his hand on the receiver; he mustn't allow his voice to betray the sudden turmoil he feels. That she can generate so much joy, so much pain, so much expectancy in him, frightens and humbles him, fills him with gratitude.

He picks up the receiver, but it's Oscar, Oscar speaking in such a low voice, Marcus can hardly hear him.

"What's wrong?" Marcus asks, preparing for the worst. "I'd meant to call you yesterday, but it totally slipped my mind."

"Lottie," Oscar says. "Lottie has received her death sentence."

"What are you talking about?" Marcus shouts. "How come you haven't told me?"

"Cancer of the liver," Oscar continues. "We've just found out."

"Where are you? I'm coming over."

"No, no. You're not supposed to know. I'm not supposed to tell you or anybody else. She wants to keep it private."

Yes, Marcus thinks. I would, too. "Come over tonight, then," he says. "Or whenever. Come now."

"I will," Oscar says. "Maybe later."

Shaken, Marcus pushes his hands hard against the desk. No. Not Lottie. His entire being fills with emotion, and for a split second he can hear himself deciding not to keel over and bawl his heart out. He stares at his forearms. They're hairy, but not too hairy. The hairs display a pleasing blend of colors: brown, black, gray. He sees Lottie. Bright, lively, beautiful Lottie, reclining on the arm of John's chair, one hand resting on John's chest.

He picks up a pen and begins to doodle. Absently, he watches the tip of the pen drip ink onto the page. Before his own parents passed away, he could not envision surviving them. He'd observe friends whose parents had died, and he'd ask himself, How can they stand it, the loss, the pain: where do they hide it? Then his father died, and he survived, mainly because, so he thought, his mother was still alive. And for the four years that his mother survived his father, he would not even try to imagine her passing, convinced he would never be able to bear it. Nine months she bore him in her womb, gave substance to him, gave birth to him, cleaned and washed him, diapered him, fed and nourished him from her breast. But his mother, too, small and frail, passed away; and although he still mourns her and thinks of her, the stabbing pain and anguish are gone, to emerge only occasionally when, reminded of an instance when he could have been more patient, more understanding, he is filled with so much shame and remorse, he experiences her living and passing all over again.

He has crammed the page with doodling. What began as a few lines, as a small, uncertain island at the righthand corner at the bottom of the page, has spread upward in bold, confident strokes. It is amazing to him that his hand, and probably some part of his brain, combined together to create this shape—it looks like a spider, or an airplane—while his mind was absolutely taken with Lottie, Oscar, his own parents' passing.

Oscar and death. Marcus turns the page and begins a new drawing. Cancer of the liver—indeed, a death sentence. Whom should he grieve for first? For the dying? For the living? He can't think of all of them at once. He needs time to grieve for each. He wants to grieve for Lottie, for Oscar, for John. She is only seventy-five years old. Too young to die. His mother died even younger, at seventy-two. Lung cancer. How reluctant he had been to reveal the secret, tell acquaintances that his mother had cancer. He felt embarrassed for her, as if cancer, dying, was cause for shame.

Dying, he thinks, is a cause for shame. Especially when the dying person is not ready to go, when the dying person is still full of passion and plans. Is one ever ready to go? When one has lived into his nineties and has had what they call a good, full life, is he ready to go? He knows for sure that his mother wasn't ready. She told him as much, shyly, confiding that she had hoped to live five years more. He thought he detected resentment in her voice, resentment toward her Maker, for being so stingy, for cutting her life short, for conferring on her the dubious honor of being the first to go among her friends.

He now wonders if holding on to life has anything to do with man's natural competitiveness. As long as one is conscious and alert, one thinks, to the very end, that he could have gone a little longer. He himself, since his parents' death, has been keeping a jealous watch, a sort of vigil, on their and his behalf. Every time he learns that someone has passed away, be it an acquaintance, a stranger, or a celebrity on the news, he notes and compares the age of the deceased with that of his parents, feeling a certain relief when the numbers work in his parents' favor. It's as if he needs to be convinced, again and again, there was nothing he could have done to keep them longer in this world.

The dead and the dying cannot defend themselves; they become public property. It is up to their sons, their daughters, to protect them.

He now doodles with intent, intending away all thoughts and pain. He sees a round shape forming under his hand, and he goes after it, assertively, committing himself. Ink, easily, obediently, drools onto the page. His pen, he thinks, drools doodles. He himself is a doodle, an insignificant noodle. He now wishes tremendously for Oscar to show up, so they can sit and talk. Sit and talk. He wants so much to just sit and talk.

When Oscar arrives in the evening, Marcus pours him a drink, and they sit in the living room, each hunched over in an armchair. Marcus wants to tell Oscar the truth, namely, that Oscar looks awful, that he must take better care of himself, something he would normally tell him without hesitation, but not tonight. Instead, he asks if Lottie is in pain, and Oscar nods and says, Yes, a lot of pain. Marcus nods too, as if to himself, as if to say, As you know, I've gone through this with my own mother.

"It's so incongruous," Oscar says, "that one should receive such a blow in spring, that Lottie should learn the verdict when the sun is shining, and everybody is looking forward to summer. And she felt so good lately. She actually blossomed, she and John together."

"Yes," Marcus says. "They say that right before, a month or two before the tumor turns nasty, before you even know you are sick, you actually feel a sort of renewal, as if the rapid growth of cells fills you with a new energy, a new hope."

"She's collecting sleeping pills," Oscar says. "She's not going to wait." Oscar looks at his hands. "Where's Gina?" he asks.

"Home," Marcus says. "I haven't told her yet."

Oscar nods. "This is all so ridiculous. If God exists, He probably rots up there, in His own hell. And all by His lonesome self. Which makes perfect sense. He's so miserable, He must make us suffer, too. This is something they won't tell you in church."

Marcus lets out a short, involuntary laugh, but soon Oscar joins him, and they laugh heartily.

"As long as we can laugh," Marcus says. "When my father lay in intensive care, we sat in the waiting area and passed the time, telling morbid jokes."

"You Jews are sick," Oscar says, and again they laugh.

"Are you hungry? I myself could eat something. You stay right here. I'll be right back."

In the kitchen, on a tray, Marcus puts together a plate of cold cuts: turkey, ham, roast beef, and Genoa salami; a plate of fruit, and a box of matzos. He brings the tray into the living room and sets it before Oscar. "I'm sorry," he says, "I have no bread."

"I don't eat bread during Passover," Oscar says in all sincerity, and they're hysterical with laughter.

"Have mercy," Marcus begs, wiping his tears. "I'm beginning to think that deep down you're Jewish."

"*I* really think," Oscar counters, "that deep down everybody is Jewish. We all come from the same stock."

"True," Marcus says, and for a while they say nothing, just chew and sip.

"This is delicious," Oscar says, rearranging the pile of cold cuts on his matzo. "Matzo should be proclaimed the right—what do I want to say, staple?—for cold cuts. Imagine the whole of America reaching for matzo. Imagine delis and diners across America serving matzo sandwiches."

"There's only one drawback," Marcus says. "It makes you constipated."

"That's even better. We'll consume less."

"Not at the rate you're going."

"Me?" Oscar says. "I'm hungry. I haven't eaten in days."

Marcus thinks: He would like to see Lottie one more time, just one more time, but how could he stand to see a weak Lottie, see in her eyes that she wants to hide? "How does she look?" he asks. "I mean . . ."

"I know what you mean. She doesn't look good, but she doesn't look like someone who will be dead, gone, kaput, in a few weeks. She looks drained, as if with the flu."

"Why a few weeks?"

"That's what the doctors say. Besides, as I told you, she's not going to wait."

"But doctors, you know, could be wrong."

"They weren't wrong with your mother," Oscar says. "And, liver cancer is liver cancer. There's nothing they or the body can do. Her brain, though, is sharp as ever, maybe even sharper, and this is what makes it so difficult." Oscar's voice catches in his throat.

"I wish I could see her one last time," Marcus says after a silence, and Oscar shakes his head. "Tell her it isn't fair. Tell her I want to say goodbye."

"I can't tell her you want to say goodbye. I wasn't supposed to tell you in the first place."

"But tell her," Marcus persists. "Tell her abstractly. Tell her it isn't fair to her friends. Just tell her."

Oscar shrugs. Marcus fills their glasses.

"I wish," Marcus says, "I were again the carefree smoker. I'd kill for a cigarette now, so I could sit here with you, like in the old days, drinking, smoking, talking our heads off, living the moment, the real, actual moment. We've become so careful, so cautious. Our eyes are set on the future. We want to live longer. As if it mattered." Oscar nods. "But you'll talk to Lottie, won't you? Tell her I need to see her."

"I won't tell her you need to see her. I'll tell her like you said that it isn't fair to treat her friends this way."

"Right," Marcus says. "Have another matzo."

"No, I'm full."

"Have a fruit, then, an apple." ·

"Not now. Maybe later."

"I've been reading today," Marcus says, "from your favorite book."

"Yeah?" Oscar says. "Which one?"

"The Gemara," Marcus says, and again they explode, Oscar spraying the table with the whisky he has just sipped. He wipes himself with a handkerchief, and Marcus continues. "You know, we the Jews, so legend has it, were the only nation to say, We'll do, accepting God's word, the Torah, before going over the fine print."

"I'm surprised," Oscar says. "On second thought, back then you were not the real Jews yet, you were a work in progress."

"Right. We were not instructed in the Word. But that's why, so the legend goes, He chose us from all the nations. He went to them, too, with His word, but they, before committing themselves, demanded to know what it entailed. So He chose us, the trusting ones."

"Smart move, on your part," Oscar says. "You knew you could negotiate after the fact."

Marcus laughs. "True. The Jew bargains with his God."

"Is that," Oscar asks, "what the Gemara taught you today?"

"I read about knowledge," Marcus says. "The Gemara teaches us that all outside knowledge reaches our consciousness through the brain. It says: Even the heart receives from the brain."

"I could have told you this myself."

"Wait. Here's the good part. An embryo, in its mother's womb, perceives the universe from one end to the other, and is taught the whole of the Torah."

"Busy kid," Oscar says.

"He learns, mind you, not through the brain, the intellect, but through the spirit: this knowledge flows to the embryo directly from the source, bypassing the constraints and limitations of consciousness, of time and space. But here's the rub: as soon as the fetus emerges from its mother's womb, an angel slaps it across the mouth and makes it forget all it knows."

"That's not fair," Oscar says. "And wasteful."

"But there's a purpose behind it. The angel makes it forget all it knows so it can relearn, the hard way, this time through the intellect, through choice and hard work. Man has to choose to study the Torah. But, once in a rare while, our internal light breaks through and we're allowed a glimpse of what lies beyond, of what we knew in the womb, and then were made to forget."

"Now that I think of it, it does make sense, actually. Babies are born with this smug, knowing expression which soon disappears and is replaced, over the years, with the weary, wary expression you and I wear."

"Except," Marcus says. "There are some very learned rabbis who have the same primary light shine from their eyes."

"It's their white beards." Oscar laughs. "Reflected in their eyes."

"I'm serious," Marcus says. "They do seem to have an inner light the rest of us lack."

"Maybe," Oscar says. "But do you know what I want these days, what represents nirvana for me? I have this fantasy that I own a small grocery store, far away in France or Italy, in the countryside. I can picture it very clearly, I have all the details worked out. It's a small stone structure. I live in the back, I sell my wares up front. Do you want to hear the rest of it?" Oscar asks, for Marcus has begun to peel a banana.

"I'm with you," Marcus says.

"So," Oscar continues. "Imagine a small store in the countryside. There are hills and meadows, and it's lush and green everywhere you look. In the backyard I grow a vegetable garden. In the front of the house it's all flowers, simple, delicate flowers with multicolor petals and blossoms. Of course, they're fragrant. I sit in my store and read the paper, or a book, and drink my tea. A beautiful ray of hazy sunshine comes in through the window. A gray cat dozes off on the windowsill.

On a warm day I sit outside, on a wooden chair by the door. Once in a while, but not too often, a customer comes by, he buys a few items, and then we exchange a couple of stories, maybe complain about the government. On rainy days, I rearrange the stock on the shelves, the variety of cheeses on the counter, the baked goods in the woven baskets. And, of course, the fresh produce in the wooden bins. I may wipe to a shine the squash and zucchini, the bright red tomatoes, the heartwarming purple of the eggplant. There's a lot to keep you busy in a grocery store."

"I know exactly what you mean." Marcus sighs. "Peace and quiet. And busy with real, immediate things. I'm the customer who comes in for a chat."

"I knew you'd make yourself room in my fantasy."

"It doesn't cost you anything."

"No, it doesn't. Lately, you know, I've been waking up with strange phrases on my lips. This morning I woke up with: Paperclips have many duties. And the other morning I woke up with: Ears are crucial. Not that it's real or means anything."

"But it's poetic. In the end, nothing means anything, really. And nothing is real. Except that you and I are sitting here, flesh and blood. We're real. At least we seem real to each other. But who's to say? I wonder," he says, staring at the fruit, "if I should have another."

"Another?"

"Banana."

"Sure," Oscar says, expansively. "Go ahead, have another. Don't deprive yourself."

"I love bananas," Marcus says.

"Me too." Oscar also reaches for one. "Any candy around?"

Candy, Marcus tries to think. "No, no candy, I don't think. Gina forbids them."

"Gina," Oscar says. "Good old Gina. She's home you say?" Marcus nods. "Her night off?" Oscar says, and they laugh.

"As a matter of fact," Marcus begins, then stops. They hear the front door open and close. Marcus stands up, his heart numbed.

"Gina?" he calls, and she appears in the doorway, halts a moment when she notices Oscar. "Oscar," she says, effusively, as if relieved. "What a pleasant surprise." She comes into the room, brushes past Marcus and goes to Oscar, bends over, and kisses him on both cheeks.

"Speaking of the devil," Oscar says. "We were just saying that tonight is your night off."

"Yes." She laughs and straightens up, lets her bag drop to the floor, goes around the table and settles on the couch. "I'll have one, too." She points at the bottle.

Heart palpitating, Marcus says, "Of course," and goes to get a glass. He feels meek, and he likes it; he wants to wallow in meekness.

"So," Gina says. "Cold cuts."

"Have some," Oscar says. "It's delicious."

"Not with matzo, thank you. So"—she looks around her—"I've barged in on you."

"Yes, you have," Oscar says. "But just in time. We've begun to tire of one another."

"Speak for yourself," Marcus says, handing Gina her drink. "I like your company." He sits down and glances at Gina. She seems to have a tan. "You look good," he says.

"Why shouldn't she look good?" Oscar asks.

"You've been in the sun?" Marcus asks.

Gina smiles. "As a matter of fact, I have."

Marcus nods. "Where?"

"What's the matter with you two?" Oscar asks. "You speak like two strangers."

"That's our specialty," Marcus says. "Where?" he asks Gina, and she purses her lips, considering. "Saint Martin," she finally concedes.

"Just like that?" Marcus asks, and Gina nods.

"I think I get it," Oscar says slowly. "You two aren't speaking. You're having a fight."

"We're speaking," Marcus says. "We're speaking."

After Oscar leaves, Gina gets up and goes into the bathroom. He hears the faucet run, and soon realizes that Gina, quite naturally, is preparing to go to bed as if nothing has happened. He stands up and takes the tray to the kitchen, puts away the leftover meat and matzo and returns to the living room. He tells himself he should go into the bedroom, get into the bed, but something stops him. He suddenly feels wounded, he wants to be cajoled. He wants to hear about this unscheduled, unannounced trip to Saint Martin!

Gina, naked, materializes in the doorway. "Come to bed," she says, smiling. Her nipples are erect.

"Saint Martin," he says, getting up. "Just like that. Without a word. While I wallow in misery, you bake in the sun."

Gina laughs, merrily. "Saint Martin my foot. You'll believe anything, won't you?" She brushes her lips against his, and he's suddenly aroused by the mere promise of her lips, her breath. "Come," she says and takes him by the hand, leads him into the bedroom. She takes the length of the bed, props herself on her elbow, and watches him undress. "Did you miss me?" she asks.

"You know I did," he says, again feeling meek.

"Then why didn't you call?"

"Because," he says, "I wanted you to call me."

"Well, here I am," she says, and he crawls into the bed. She reaches for him. "My great redeemer," she says. "He's so reliable, dependable. Unlike you, he never disappoints me. You're lucky to have him on your team."

Marcus laughs, stretching his body alongside hers, seeking her mouth. Lottie's image flashes in his mind, then Oscar's. He thinks: I have yet to tell Gina.

Twenty-Six

For the benefit of his narrator, he catalogues his fears, his recurrent doubts:

1. He fears that Erasmus talked about him when he said that not every man has the luck to go to Corinth.

2. He considers the possibility that the quotes he wishes to use are in fact trite, that his readers will not be eternally grateful, as he hopes them to be, but will, on the contrary, become annoyed and impatient. Too often, indeed, it happens to him that he loses patience with an author for using a reference that he, as reader, has seen before and that the author should have known has been overused.

3. He fears that his life, his way of thinking, is too rational. Everywhere around him, men and women behave irrationally. He tells himself to take this into account and complicate the lives of his characters.

4. Some mornings he faces, heroically he believes, the fear that he won't advance beyond a certain point, that the deeper he gets into the telling, the more entangled he'll become, and that the slightest move in the wrong direction will compromise his advance.

(But, he notes in an aside, the minute he gets immersed in the lives of his men, his women, his anxieties vanish. He himself vanishes.)

5. Often, looking over his work, he crosses out whole pages, even chapters, filled with anger and contempt for having written such dribble. When he feels especially masochistic, he reads the offensive passages out loud, as if to flagellate himself with his own words for the crime of his mediocrity.

6. At very dark moments, he no longer just suspects it, but becomes absolutely convinced that his brain is of average caliber, not fit for the task his misguided ambition has led him to.

7. When comparing his writing to that of writers he admires, he worries that his diction lacks the density, the necessary texture that weaves through a text like cartilage, bracing that mysterious tension that exists in the spaces between words.

And yet, as if to counter his fears, occasionally, briefly, he feels like a god, sitting on a high throne, mindful of the whole.

Twenty-Seven

Now that he is nearing the end of the draft, he tells himself he must slow down, he mustn't rush through to the end. He rereads what he has written, reminding himself to read slowly—not hurriedly, anxiously, as one fearing for his life, or as one wishing to avoid problems, even the hint of a problem. So he follows his own counsel and tries to read as one who has never seen the material before, as one who has no stake in the thing at all. But he soon realizes that in his attempt to distance himself from the text, the words on the page don't reach him, and so he gives himself a new instruction: bring down a notch his imposed distance. A reader, after all, does have a stake in the text; a reader is not stripped of expectations, wants.

Just read it, he tells himself, just read it. Write down your response in the margins, as one having a dialogue. Cross out what's absolutely awful.

As he reads through the chapters, the various scenes, he remembers writing them, and often, as he crosses out a section, he comes across a sentence over which he labored, endlessly it seemed, to get it right. He hesitates a moment, thinks of ways to somehow fit it in and so salvage the sentence, which had taken so much out of him, but usually finds he must leave it out.

At one point, he painfully decides he must do without the old man: he must take him out, make as if he has never existed.

But as soon as he thinks this, something stabs at his heart in revolt. He suddenly feels diminished, empty, deflated. Who is he to make such decisions? What right does he have? He sees the old man, propped up on his pillows, reading in bed. He holds a book in his hands, but is now looking straight at him, his dark brown eyes hard, uncompromising.

Quickly he repents, saying he didn't quite mean it, it was just a thought, an errant thought.

Now the old man on his bed rearranges his pillows and resumes reading, and Marcus, relieved, leans back in his chair. He thinks of Michael Krüger, chopping away at his novel in *The End of the Novel*. He thinks of the thrilling sense of power, control, such strokes of the pen give the author. The author, he thinks, must not let himself get carried away.

Marcus rests his pen and gets up. He is done for the day. Soon Gina will arrive. Gina. Ever since she came back, they've been enjoying a mini-renaissance. It's the weather, Gina says. It's nice and warm. It's easy to love when it's nice and warm. No, he says, it's not the weather. It's us. It's me. I love you more and you respond to me. She jerks her head and looks at him. More than when? she asks. I don't know, he says. Just more. I feel it right here—in circular motions he moves his hand over his chest. I love you more, too, Gina says, even though you're still a jerk.

She tells him the dreams she had when they were apart, and he records them in his notebook. One of them has to do with murder, a murder that he has committed. The two of them are on campus, outside in the square. A man pursues them, and they enter a building, run up the stairs. But the man still pursues them, so Marcus kills him, right there on the staircase, plunging a knife into the man's stomach. He and Gina stuff the corpse in a plastic bag filled with shredded newspapers. A few days later, Gina and a few of her classmates are on their way to class. As they enter the building and begin to go up the stairs, Gina suddenly remembers the body, but it's too late to turn back without calling attention to herself. She goes up the stairs with her friends, and the body is found. The police are interrogating Gina. The investigator, a tall, gaunt man with a long narrow face, flirts with her, and she allows herself to be seduced, hoping to divert him from the real killer, namely, Marcus. Do you make out with him? Marcus asks. Sort of, Gina says, unable to suppress a coquettish smile. I'm not in the least attracted to him, I do it to save you, but when he sucks my nipple I do get aroused, to my great surprise. So I try to fight it, my arousal, but then I say to myself: Why fight it?

In another dream, Gina takes a shower, then dresses to go out to her drawing class. When she steps outside into the bright sun and begins to walk toward her car, she moves her hand over the back of her head and realizes that she still has soapsuds in her curls. But she's late as it is, so she must continue on her way. She has long, thick hair, elaborately done up in drooping "bottle" curls, eighteenth-century style. She arrives at class where she and other women, her classmates, have come to collect their self-portraits. They stand in line, as the instructor, also a female, hands each student her canvas. The woman in line behind Gina is the haughty type: she makes snide remarks about Gina's hairdo, about Gina's self-portrait, which, the woman says, is sure to be dull. Gina tries to ignore the woman. But she, too, is secretly worried that indeed her self-portrait, from the artistic point of view, is not up to par. But when the instructor reaches Gina and hands her the canvas, Gina sees that it is quite good, not at all corny and true to life, but abstract, suggestive, with yellowish, reddish hues in the background. And the instructor, too, praises it, and the snotty woman behind Gina peers over Gina's shoulder and now voices her admiration.

All at once, Gina realizes that the face she is holding in her hands activates the sound system in the class: a constant hum emanates from the radio-speaker on the wall. She tells the instructor she cannot imagine having the portrait at home; she cannot imagine living with this constant noise. The instructor tells her she can adjust the volume, and Gina, at first, brightens at this simple solution. But the portrait in her hand feels and looks like a small, a doll-like baby girl: she coos, makes baby noises. Frustrated, Gina turns to the instructor: But how can I frame a live thing? I'd first have to kill it.

This is what Gina dreams. When she finishes telling them, she looks at him and smiles, waiting to be praised for the originality of her nightlife away from him. She sits cross-legged on the couch, her bare, bony toes, like flippers, stick out from under her thighs.

"Very interesting," he says, pours more wine into her glass. "How come you remember every small detail?"

"I don't even tell you the half of it. I'm giving you the shorthand version. Emotionally there's much more, but it's impossible to convey the intensity. In some dreams, I'm aware of myself as an active dreamer directing the action."

"It's amazing," Marcus says, "that you remember them in such detail. I remember only fragments . . . bits and pieces. Don't you make them up as you go along? They seem so neat, connected."

"I make nothing up," Gina says. "If anything, I omit stuff, to make them shorter and easier to tell."

Marcus observes the strong lines of her throat, the delicate, flaring nostrils. When she talks, her throat fills up, firms up with the strain of speech. She leans a bit forward, her straight back stretched in a slant. She's wearing a white, sleeveless T-shirt, white panties, and socks. Her hair is pulled back in a tiny ponytail—the frivolity of a few dark strands, too short to make it to the elastic band, makes her look French.

"You look," he says, "like Anouk Aimée.

"And you," she says, "you look like Marcus."

Twenty-Eight

Assya and Bernie got married. Over the weekend. In the Berkshires. Assya wants a child, Bernie tells Marcus in the kitchen where they cut up fruit salad for dessert.

"At her age . . ." Marcus begins. "It could be risky."

"I know. But that's what she wants. How old is Gina? I mean, she never wanted kids?"

"She's forty-five. She says she either missed the boat, or wasn't meant to have babies."

"Well," Bernie says. "We'll have one for you."

"Thanks," Marcus says.

When they go back to the living room, Gina and Assya are on the couch, whispering, giggling.

As he watches them, Marcus recalls Bernie saying that it's truly amazing that women allow men to come near them.

Indeed, Marcus thinks. Women are too trusting.

"By the way," Bernie says. "We've rented a summer house in the Berkshires. You're welcome to it anytime you like."

"Forget him," Gina says, pointing at Marcus. "He is finishing his book, he is going nowhere."

"Oh, your book," Bernie says. "How's it going, old man?"

Momentarily startled by the "old man," Marcus says, "Pretty well, pretty well."

"I was going to say, you seem more relaxed."

"It's his fall in the kitchen," Gina says. "Ever since his fall"—she looks at him, to see how he reacts—"he's become more humble. I think." She taps the back of her head. "He got knocked in a delicate spot."

Marcus laughs, and they laugh with him.

"You know," Marcus says to Bernie. "Just now, when you asked me about my novel, you called me old man, and there's a character in my novel, an old man, and for a moment I thought you were addressing him."

"Well now," Bernie says, "that's pretty convoluted."

"I'm very glad for you," Assya tells Marcus. "It's quite ambitious to pursue something from beginning to end."

Marcus nods, unsure how to interpret "ambitious." Assya seems to radiate a new light. She seems to have gained a few pounds. Is she pregnant already? Is that what she and Gina were whispering about?

"What's it called?" Bernie asks.

"*The Reverse Turn of the Heart,*" Marcus replies.

"Sounds interesting. What does it mean?"

"You'll have to read the book." Marcus smiles.

"Oh, that's how it works," Bernie says. "He hasn't finished writing it, and is already selling copies."

"It has a nice ring to it. It's sort of gentle. I like it, Marcus," Gina says, and he feels his heart open to her.

"But how do you know when to end it?" Assya asks. "I mean, what's to stop you from going on forever, making up new scenes, new dialogues, creating another conflict?"

"It's true," Marcus says, suddenly recalling his tears when speaking with her on the telephone. "As you reach the end, you wish to prolong it a while longer, extend its life. Since you're almost there, you're no longer in a hurry to get there. You feel a sort of leisure and luxury, you feel generous. I could, in theory, go on forever."

"Please don't," Gina says, and they laugh.

"There's a great book"—Marcus smiles as he speaks—"I'm sure you've read. Malamud's *The Tenants?* The entire book is a writer's tormented struggle to find a good ending; then Malamud himself gives you a killer ending: two writers, like two apocalyptic titans, stand to destroy one another, each feeling the anguish of the other."

Bernie asks, "What will you do once you've finished it?"

"I'm not there yet. I did begin to imagine a novel written in the future tense. But right now I look forward to beginning the second draft of this one. I feel myself getting better, more secure, every day, word by word. It's quite exciting." As he speaks, he becomes aware of himself, of his voice rising. "From revision to revision you actually see how your book evolves, how it is transformed. And the same happens to you, you become transformed. The writing becomes tighter. Every word you have replaced is still there, in the necessary layers upon which your new words exist. Your technical intuition, intuitiveness, is sharper, it's become second nature."

Gina laughs. "What's come over you all of a sudden?"

"Sorry." He smiles. "I forgot myself. I became my character, my narrator."

"A modern-day dybbuk," Bernie says.

"How is he?" Assya asks. "Your narrator? Is he nice?"

"He's all right," Marcus says.

"Let's go out," Gina, in a sudden burst of energy, suggests. "It's so nice out. Why stay indoors?"

They walk north, toward Gramercy Park. Marcus and Bernie fall behind Gina and Assya, who walk arm in arm. Assya wears a long, flowing skirt; Gina wears her cotton pantaloons, her Indian sandals laced around her ankles.

She must be pregnant, Marcus reflects, watching Assya's skirt swell in the light breeze.

At his side, Bernie says, "A perfect June night."

Marcus nods.

"On a day like this, watching people all around me, strolling, laughing, it's hard to imagine that there's war in the world. On the other hand." Bernie looks up; Marcus looks up, too. "At any moment," Bernie continues, "something lethal may drop from above. From the sky, from a roof, or from someone's window."

Marcus nods, again focused on Assya's skirt. The fabric, gauze-like, is almost sheer, although it isn't.

"I mean, you're shut up in your room all day. You don't get to see much life," Bernie says, sounding urgent.

"But I do," Marcus says. "I see plenty. They're very attractive together."

"Who?"

Marcus motions ahead. "Assya and Gina. The way they walk, *engagé*. You'd say, twins."

Bernie smiles broadly. "Indeed."

"Remember you once said it was a wonder that women let us near them?"

"I said that? I don't remember."

"Well, anyway. I was thinking about this, and I thought, Yes, compared to them, we're brutes."

"Brutes? I don't know. We've come a long way, to use their coinage."

"Not really. Outwardly we're tame, but we're still violent, all we need is a spark. Imagine the very first man and woman—that she trusted him enough to let him come near her."

"Simple," Bernie says. "She was horny. And she probably seduced him."

"Still," Marcus says, "I think it's remarkable."

"If you insist, but why dwell on it? That's what I mean about being shut up in your room. Here we are, on a perfect June night, it's almost nine o'clock and it's still light out. The sky is blue, the air is fragrant, we're taking a stroll: how more perfect than this can it get? But you, instead of looking at the sky, these majestic trees, their elegant trunks, not to mention the people going past, you worry your head about the first man who ever lived."

Marcus laughs. "You're absolutely right."

After a silence, Bernie says, "I hesitate to ask, but, are you still on their case? Are you still thinking about the first man and woman?"

"No," Marcus says. "I'm thinking about how a character makes his exit, how he exits a book. The lines we last hear him say. I think it's sad if he doesn't get to have his moment, and even if he does get to have it, it's still sad, the fact that he has to depart. I'm thinking about his last appearance. His last appearance, ever."

Bernie shakes his head, then says, conclusively, "You know what I think your problem is? You've forgotten how to empty your head, how to live the moment."

"I live," Marcus says, "every moment of my life. Twice. Sometimes three, four, or five times."

"Three, four, five times! How do you ever catch up?"

Marcus thinks a moment. "I guess I don't. I never catch up."

Bernie gets hold of Marcus's arm. "You're hopeless. Let's catch up with our girls."

Later, in bed, he tells Gina about his conversation with Bernie, about how miraculous it is that women allow men come near them, and Gina laughs, bites his lip and says, "Stop talking, you brute, and kiss me."

Twenty-Nine

He consults his thesaurus and proceeds to copy out all the equivalents he can find to "he said"—the two words that are rarely in quotes— including all verbs that convey the action of a verbal utterance:

he affirmed; he asserted; he averred; he declared; she spoke up; she spoke out; he stated; he expressed; he professed; he pronounced; he proclaimed; she maintained; she contended; she argued; she insisted; he held; she submitted; he answered; she answered back; he countered; she replied; he responded; she retorted; he rejoined; she riposted; she shot back; he rebutted; he refuted; she piped up; she put in; she uttered; he imparted; he disclosed; she related; he recited; she quoted; he remarked; she commented; he observed; she noted; he mentioned; she let drop; he let fall; she referred; he alluded; she called; he called out; she mused; he opined; she interjected; he blurted; she exclaimed; he cried; she cried out; he yelled; she shouted; he chirped; she cackled; he crowed; she barked; he yelped; she yapped; he growled; she snapped; he snarled; she hissed; he sibilated; he grunted; he snorted; she roared; he bellowed; he blared; she trumpeted; he brayed; he bawled; he thundered; she rumbled; he boomed; she screamed; he screeched; she shrieked; he squealed; she squawked; he yawped; she squalled; he whined; she railed; he told; she babbled; he blabbered; she drawled; he twanged; she addressed; he begged; he appealed; he pleaded; she invoked; he ascertained; he adumbrated; he postulated; he conjectured; she cursed; he swore; she fulminated; he adjured; she commanded; he urged; she condemned; he ad-libbed; she preached; he bitched; she gushed; he erupted; she howled; he blamed; she criticized; he accused; she indicated; he calmed; she soothed; he promised; he placated; she concluded; he continued; she added; he carped; she muttered; he mumbled; she grumbled; he scolded; she cooed; he corrected; she praised; she extolled; he explained; she admitted; he hinted; he menaced; she threatened; he suggested; she divulged; he revealed; she agreed; he acknowledged; she proposed; he reproved; she admonished; he cautioned; she rebuked; he pointed out; she denied; he warned; he flattered; he joked; he abused; she scorned; she ridiculed; she taunted; she scoffed; she jeered; she jabbed; she jabbered; she mocked; she gibed; he cheered; she sneered; he ululated; he prayed; she chattered; she interfered; he interposed; she griped; she tempted; she sang; she singsonged; she seduced; he asked; she enticed; he requested; she granted; he demanded; he implored; he supplicated; she intimated; she chided; he relayed; he advanced; he advocated; she complained; she derided; he emphasized; he advised; he reminded; he instructed; he insinuated; he insulted; he kidded; he intoned; he informed; he defined; she forbade; she interdicted; he claimed; he insisted; he bragged; he boasted; she deprecated; he apologized; she articulated; she flirted; she enunciated; he bantered; he deplored; he denounced; she announced; he termed; he elaborated; he belabored; she stammered; she persuaded; she duped; she lamented; he cajoled; he convinced; she concurred; he confirmed; she compared; he hollered; she snitched; he interrupted; she whispered; she murmured; he repeated; she enthused; he reasoned; she lied; he castigated; she deceived; she fabricated; she kibitzed; he attacked; he protested; she negated; he expounded; she confided; she confessed; he extrapolated; he enumerated; she chatted; he sanctioned; she assented; she greeted; she welcomed; he conspired; she voiced; he alleged; he justified; he persisted; he chimed; he touted; she questioned; he chafed; she inflamed; he flared; she spurted; he spewed; she lashed out; he teased; she adulated; he aggrandized; she implied; he reported; she instigated; he defended; he vocalized; he equated; she blasted; he consoled; he comforted; she clamored; she screeched;

she contested; she challenged; he stressed; she trilled; she shrilled; he promulgated; he modulated; she whimpered; she rambled; he moderated; she charged; she bawled; he predicted; she speculated; she exalted; he theorized; he recalled; she introduced; he guaranteed; he repudiated; she incited; he joshed; she refused; he inquired; he interrogated; he demonstrated; he specified; she inferred; he rejected; she embellished; he entreated; she approved; she formulated; she cited; she deliberated; he dismissed; he faulted; he canceled; he decreed; she depicted; he clipped; she conversed; he coached; she coaxed; he worded; he indicted; she crooned; he judged; she panted; he evaluated; he berated; she echoed; he pontificated; he summarized; she besought; she contradicted; he remonstrated; she clarified; she elucidated; she assuaged; he estimated; she sounded; he assured; he assuaged; she translated; he punned; she solicited; he pursued; she pounced on; she heckled; she hectored; he ruled; she interposed; he stipulated; she appeased; he interpreted; she distorted; she schemed; he bargained; she recounted; he described; she chanted; he bet; she pledged; he corroborated; she spelled out; he counseled; he rebuffed; he proceeded; she parodied; she offered; he proffered; she mimicked; he enunciated; she rhymed; he plotted; she slandered; he emoted; he badgered; she reiterated; he conspired; he colluded; she soliloquized; he monologued; she vowed; he queried; she testified; he bluffed; she attested; she evidenced; he ordered; she proved; he disproved; she objected; he vilified; she snickered; he quibbled; she gloated; he exaggerated; he lambasted; he altercated; she wrangled; she reproached; he recriminated; she declaimed; he mythologized; she apprised; she appraised; she probed; he blessed; she fussed; he rasped; he expatiated; she amplified; she rested her case.

Again and again he goes over the list, until all he sees are semicolons. And yet, he keeps at it, making sure he hasn't repeated the same verb twice, making sure he has exhausted the list.

Thirty

Gina is away in the Berkshires with Assya and Bernie. At moments, when he walks through his apartment, Marcus feels a bit left out, a bit left behind. Still, he can smell Gina, he feels her presence in each room. In the evenings he talks to her, tells her this and that, if not on the phone, then in his head.

And his work goes well. He advances, albeit with trepidation, like a soldier who must cross a minefield.

Now, more than ever, he lives the life of a monk. Left alone, he cherishes the quiet, the peace of mind. At his desk, he is under a spell: nothing moves, nothing happens around him. Whatever happens, happens in his head. Slowly things coalesce. Even without looking at his notes, all, or at least most, of the ideas he wished to incorporate in the telling but wasn't sure where and how he could fit them in, now, toward the end, they miraculously, effortlessly, find their way into the novel, find their intended places, as if all the threads, of their own accord, have decided to gather into a tight, neat knot. And the farther he advances, the clearer it is that the guidance he has sought in books by novelists writing about the novel, has become meaningful only after he himself has experienced the challenge firsthand.

It is past midnight, and he prepares to go to bed. He is a bit disgusted with himself for he has just watched the Mets lose a doubleheader to the Dodgers. He switches off the TV, vowing to never again waste time on the Mets. As he stands up, he is gripped by a pain that contracts his stomach and makes him hold onto the back of the chair. He stands there a moment, stock-still, afraid to make a move. It feels as though mountains move in his stomach, mountains of gas. Hunched as he is, he tries to remember what he's had for lunch, for dinner. When the worst of the attack is over, he makes his way to the bathroom and slowly lowers himself onto the toilet. He rests his elbows on his thighs and sits still, attentive. His stomach churns and again gases move in his bowels. It amazes him that mere gases can create such havoc. And pain. It could be, he thinks, the bacon hamburger he had for dinner. Or the beans he had for lunch. He feels another wave coming and knows that now is the time to push, hard. And he does, anticipating the relief that will soon come, as soon as his lower intestines are emptied, released of their burden. He remembers Gina telling him that when she takes antibiotics she becomes constipated and shits pellets.

Here it comes, in a long and protracted thick chunk; Gina would be proud. Release. The most welcome relief, shared by all. Now he is happy, smiling as one who has come through an ordeal. He flushes the water and leans back, remains seated on the bowl. Staring at him from the small wastebasket under the sink is one of Gina's pink, narrow pads. He reaches over and pushes the pad deeper, buries it in tissue paper. His housekeeper is due tomorrow; she doesn't need to be confronted with vaginal pads. How is it, he wonders, that Gina is careless about such intimate matters? After all, a few times a day she adheres these pads to the crotch of her panties to absorb her secretions. One would think she'd be more conscientious about where and how she disposes of them. If he, for instance, were to use such pads, he wouldn't just toss them and leave them exposed like this for all to see. But he is he, as Gina often says, and she is she. Case closed. Mind your business. To each his own. Take care of yours, I'll handle mine.

Perhaps, he thinks, women desire to turn men into full partners in their anatomy, in the evolving miracle of their biology. Perhaps they sense that the more they reveal, the more mystified men become.

And, the more mystified, the more obedient and docile. Indeed, men throughout the ages have felt responsible for women, for their well-being.

And yet, in other ways, Gina is secretive. When she goes into the bathroom she flushes the water so he won't hear her pee. Of course, he's only guessing, she's never told him this, but by now he knows, his senses know, her routine. He will be lying in bed and she'll go into the bathroom and close the door, sit down on the bowl, and the minute she's ready, she'll flush the water. Soon after, when the last trickle of water has been drained from the tank, silence descends, but Gina remains in there for another good ten minutes. And as he lies in bed, reading and waiting, part of his mind is in the bathroom with her, following her like a phantom. He reads, but his being, now a laser beam, is trained on the closed door, trying to pick up a familiar sound which will tell him what she's doing. Women are so finicky, so fussy about the smallest irregularities in their body, the tiniest dot or blemish on their skin. He imagines the secret uses she puts her tweezers to, her various lotions and creams. If Gina is felt in all his rooms, she permeates the bathroom; she loves bathrooms. When they go traveling, the first thing she does upon entering their hotel room is get her cosmetic bag and go into the bathroom to establish her territory and arrange things the way she is accustomed to having them at home. She usually takes the right side of the counter, leaving him the left corner. In bed, too, she takes the right side. But in his bathroom, for some reason, she's taken the left side of the counter, perhaps because it borders the wall—she likes enclosures—and has left him the right side, but only a small section of it, for her cosmetic products overtake the length of the counter. He wonders why she needs such a great variety of products, but he has to admit that he, too, feels seduced by the appealing design of the containers and bottles. It is all in the packaging, he reflects, and women, born with a severe case of aesthetic awareness, can't resist them. He particularly likes the dark, opaque look of the small bottle that contains miracle cryogenic drops to be massaged onto strategic spots. He also likes the pale elegance of emulsifiers in their small, round bottles, opaque and clear at the same time, which seem to blend with the white, fluid cream inside.

He also likes the foundations, varying in shade and tint, tending—so she tells him—to the beige in winter, to the tan in summer. These foundations, Gina reiterates, serve a double purpose: to give the face a smooth, even finish, and to protect the skin from the elements, such as dust and other particles, which would otherwise clog and enlarge the pores. "What's wrong with large pores?" he asks, and she inclines her head, regards him a moment with disbelief. "This only shows how clueless you are," she says. "You don't want to notice the pores when you look at a face. You want to see a firm, even layer of skin, like the smooth texture of linen, of a superbly woven Egyptian cotton. Got it?" she asks. "Got it," he says. "But what about my pores?" he asks. "Your pores are fine," she says. "You have good skin."

But as he looks over her collection, which also includes tubes and tubes of lipsticks, mascaras, eye shadows, it all seems to him like a lot of waste, considering that she has more of the same in her own home. Not to count the bowlful of samples happy saleswomen in stores shower on her. "Still," he insists. "Why do you need so many different creams? I mean, do you have a system? Do you even know what you have? It seems to me that two or three lotions should do the trick." "No," she says. "Each cream is different. For example: there are night creams, and there are day creams. Night creams, of necessity, are richer. And then there are days when the skin feels drier, requiring a more potent cream, especially in winter. On other days, the humidity in the air requires a light cream, namely, water-based." "Water-based?" he asks. "Yes, water-based. As opposed to oil-based."

When it comes to shampoos and conditioners, Gina is outright promiscuous.

Sometimes, when he's in bed and she's in the bathroom, he calls out to her, "Are you coming, Gina? What's taking you so long?" And she answers, haltingly, her voice somewhat muffled as one who's been interrupted, "I'll be right there," and indeed she soon appears in the door, tall and slim and perfect. "You know," he says, "I'd love to be in there with you, just once, to see what you're doing before coming to me." "Sure you would," she says, laughing, and gets into the bed. "Why do you have to know everything?" "I don't know," he says. "Believe me, I'm asking myself the same question. But then"—he continues—"don't you want to know everything you possibly can?" In the dark, Gina shrugs. "No," she says, "I don't think so." "Well," he says, "there's this writer—I forget his name—who said that there was nothing in this world that was of too little importance for him to want to know about." "You and your quotes," Gina says. "You know what you remind me of? You know those midget robots that glide across shiny floors? You've seen them in the movies. They seem so smug and content, cute, really. That's what you remind me of, a midget robot, gliding across the floor, spewing quotes." She laughs, and he laughs with her, their mouths touching. They lie on their sides, facing each other, and she reaches for him. "At least," she says, "he is an original. He doesn't need to borrow quotes." "Well, you see," he counters. "With him it's simple. He knows only two happy states, he has no questions, everything is clear-cut in his head." Gina laughs, then sighs. "What a blissful existence. Let's you and I exist like this for a while." "Yes, let's," he says, and the picture of a resort appears before his eyes, people sprawled in the sun on white plastic chairs. Even though the blue ocean is a few steps away, they stay by the pool, in various positions of abandon. "Did you ever consider," he asks, "why people require so much rest? I'm thinking about those millions who after a night's sleep come out to the beach or the pool and sleep some more, bake their sorrows in the sun." Gina laughs. "You're such a snob. It's a pleasure to lie in the sun, feel its warmth on your body, feel the breeze, close your eyes and let your mind drift. It has to do with pleasure, not rest." "Still," Marcus says. "You have to admit it's a waste of time: you've slept all night and then you sleep some more. In the sun. Which, they say, is harmful." "That's why, dear boy, we have what we call sunblock lotions, and once in a while, when the sun is real strong, we stay in the shade under an umbrella, or we don a hat. See?" "Yes," he says, "but why won't you go in for a swim? Or read a book?" "Some of us do, some of us don't." "You know," he says, "I have to confess. When I watch those people sprawled on their chairs, I think to myself, with a pinch of envy, that even in sleep they seem greedy for life; they exhibit this thirst, this hunger, for all corporeal pleasures, a kind of insatiability that repels but also attracts me." "So let's go somewhere," Gina says. "Ever since your novel, we haven't gone anywhere." "We will, I promise, as soon as I'm finished. It'll be good for me to get away."

They make love, and he watches her come, then come again. He tells her he's just found a new definition for JAP—Juicy American Pussy, and she laughs, happy, grateful. Later, as he moves his hand up and down her arm, along her back, he says, "God, I wish I knew, really knew, what love is. I know that I love you, but I want to be able to touch it, take a bite, know the essence of our love, the everyday things we say to each other and instantly forget. The way you order me around, in the kitchen and in bed. I want to touch that which keeps us together. I want to know what keeps us going. This kind of stuff." "Yes," Gina says, but from her voice he can tell he is losing her. "You're falling asleep," he says. "I'm not," she says. "I like to hear you talk. Go on, don't stop." "You know," he says, "what Saint-Exupéry thought of love?" "No," she says. "Tell me." "Well, observing the body of a young man who had just committed suicide because his girl had left him, he shook his head with contempt and remarked that, unfortunately, all that the young man had in his head was the image of one silly girl, while there were so many other silly girls, just like her." "He was right," Gina says, "your Saint-Exupéry. I'll tell you what keeps us going," she says, and turns her back to him. "Hug me," she commands. "Yes, like this." She sighs with contentment. "What keeps us going?" he nudges her. "The mere fact of our existing," Gina says. "The pleasure we take in our physicality, in our own flesh."

Marcus wipes himself, flushes the water again and goes into the bedroom. He gets out of his clothes and climbs onto the bed, anticipating, with gratitude, the comfort of his covers, his pillows. He's done his day's work, he's earned his rest. He's entitled to this pleasure of lying down, reading for a while until his eyes, absolutely, demand sleep; and he, resisting, wishing to squeeze in another page, another paragraph, will shut his eyes for just a moment, only to be suddenly startled out of sleep, just in time to put life into his hands to re-grip the book he is holding.

Tonight, a new author waits for him, and Marcus opens the book, a collection of short stories by Robert Walser, with great anticipation. He first reads the introduction, about the author's life, and his heart goes out to Walser. He begins with the first story, "Response to a Request," and soon reaches for a pencil, marks a paragraph for copying, then reads again: "Remember what I told you before; namely—and you'll know it still, I hope—that it is possible for one eye alone, open or closed, to achieve an effect of terror, beauty, grief, or love, or what have you. It doesn't take much to show love, but at some time or another in your, praise God, disastrous life you must have felt, honestly and simply, what love is and how love likes to behave. It is the same, naturally, with anger also, and with feelings of speechless grief; briefly, with every human feeling. Incidentally, I advise you to perform athletic exercises often in your room, to go for walks in the forest, to fortify the wings of your lungs, to practice sports, but only select and balanced sports, to go to the circus and observe the behavior of the clowns, and then seriously to consider by which rapid movements of your body you can best render a spasm of the soul. The stage is the open, sensual throat of poetry, and, dear sir, it is your legs that can strikingly manifest quite definite states of the soul, not to mention your face and its thousand mimings. You must take possession of your hair, if, in order to manifest fright, it is to stand on end, so that the spectators, who are bankers and grocers, will gaze at you in horror."

Marcus rests the book against his chest and gazes at the windows. It's so quiet, he thinks he can hear the distant hum of the streets. It has a rhythm to it, it vibrates; just the thought of it accelerates his heartbeat, and a feeling akin to anxiety overtakes him. He thinks such anxiety must be embedded in our DNA, in the memory of our blood, as the ancient response to the grand pulse of life, to all that is out there and beyond, to all that's open and waiting.

He takes a deep breath, and lets his eyes shut. In a moment, he thinks, he'll resume reading.

Thirty-One

In the morning, the old man sits up in bed. He feels out of sorts, disconcerted, disoriented. His heartbeat is irregular, his breathing uneven. He feels a terrible need to weep, shout, give in, release his hold. What's the point? Why is he struggling so hard to hold on?

Because! Another, more resolute voice, booms at him. Get out of bed, you whining old fool. The sun is out. What's the matter with you?

Yes, yes, he says, carefully brings his feet down to the floor. A flicker of a thought, an image, taunts him, and he wants to take a moment to concentrate, remember what it was. Oh yes, he now remembers. He had a nightmare, a terrible nightmare. A man, a stranger, chases him down the street, an ax in his hand. The streets are dark, and he, running, no longer knows where he is. The stranger is very near, and soon he'll have to succumb, there's no strength left in him. But then, something unexpected happens. Right at the moment when the stranger catches up with him, the stranger hesitates. He raises his ax, intently focused on him, and then seems to have a change of heart.

And that's where, thankfully, he woke up. Was it his own consciousness that woke him up and so prevented the act, or was it indeed the stranger who, for some reason, decided not to complete the act?

The old man puts his feet into his slippers and shuffles his way to the bathroom. His stomach is growling, and as he brushes his teeth he begins to plan his breakfast. He feels like having an egg, maybe an omelet—he hasn't had one in a while—and toast and salad, some cottage cheese and anchovies and, of course, coffee. A real feast, as befits the fact of a new day. He is now fully awake. He is alive and kicking, and if he needs any proof, all he has to do is look in the mirror, watch himself spread shaving cream on his face. Yes. And his sudden appetite. There's something to be said for appetite.

He purses his lips and begins to whistle a tune he makes up on the spot. He hasn't whistled in years, and the sound he produces is more like puffs of air forced through his lips than a real whistle. He actually feels like singing and resolves to turn on the radio and listen to music when he takes his breakfast. And later, for sure, perhaps in the afternoon, he'll go out for a walk, have dinner in one of the chic restaurants in the neighborhood, sip some exotic cocktail from a tall glass, perhaps even indulge and puff on a cigar. But first, a whole day of work stretches before him. It might zoom by, it might be slow-moving. Time often tricks him, especially in the morning, when he opens one eye to see what time it is, and it's eight o'clock, it's time for him to rise, and he shuts his eye for just another moment, and then wakes up with a start, certain he has slept for three hours more, but is amazed, and relieved, to see that only five minutes have passed. He then thanks whoever is responsible for this tiny gift, and rolls over on his back for a short while longer.

And now it's time to rinse his face and go into the kitchen. He'll take a shower in the evening, before dressing and setting out.

Later, after eight hours at his desk, he looks for his word in the dictionary. *Sopite* pleases him, and he copies out the definition:

> **sopite** *vt* sopited; sopiting [L *sopitus*, pp. of *sopire* to put
> to sleep, fr. *Spoor* (1542)] **1:** *archaic*: to put to sleep: lull
> **2:** *archaic*: to put an end to (as a claim): settle

Thirty-Two

You can't be too negative, he tells himself. If you are to continue, you must remain committed, hold onto your faith. Time is not running out, no one's breathing down your neck.

The trees in the yard bristle with new leaves, taut and shiny. As he watches, he becomes convinced that the leaves themselves delight in their moist, squeaky-clean newness, offering their small bellies to the breeze. Youth, he reflects, in all species, exhibits the same vigor, the same exuberance.

Marcus takes off his glasses and rubs his nose. With thumb and forefinger he presses against his shut lids, massages the hard balls of his eyes. He sees the pulsating pit of a simmering volcano; he sees his characters, in living flesh, toss and turn in the thick waves of lava. They flail and fling their arms—how tiny they seem—as they try to hold on to something. He watches them curiously, almost coldly, like a scientist observing an experiment. He wonders how it is that he feels no compassion for their obviously futile thrashing in the lava.

He opens his eyes. Still holding his glasses in one hand, he reaches for his coffee with the other, and, before he realizes what he is doing, brings the cup up to his eyes and pours cold coffee down his face. He leaps to his feet and, bending forward over the desk, grabs a sheet of paper and holds it under his dripping chin, and so leads himself to the bathroom sink. He rinses his face, then looks in the mirror, shaking his head in reproach and disbelief, but not without affection. He returns to his desk, but doesn't sit down. It feels as if his mind is in transition—he needs to get it in gear. He goes into the living room, parts the curtains and gazes at the traffic streaming down Fifth Avenue. For the most part, the cars remain within the lanes, and the long, straight lines of moving cars have a soothing, mesmerizing effect on him. His mind is still, very still. The dominant color is bright yellow, the yellow of cabs. Then, as if from nowhere, a blue police cruiser appears, and even from above it looks menacing, predatory, sneaking up behind the other, unsuspecting cars. This morning he called Gina to tell her he missed her, and Gina laughed, saying it had been a while since he told her he missed her. He tells her that his sleep is restless, that he wakes up a few times during the night, tossing and turning. Bits of phrases, like banners, shoot back and forth behind his lids. "What kind of phrases?" she asks, and he says that he recognizes some of the phrases as snippets from his novel, and he grabs hold of them, turns them over in his head, like a mechanic checking for flaws, for defects. And when he identifies a serious flaw and thinks of a way to fix it, he switches on the light, if reluctantly, and, his eyes squinting, jots down a few quick words and turns off the light. Then a new thought comes into his mind, and again he turns over, switches on the light, and so on and so on a few times during the night. "What a life." Gina sighs on the other side. "When are you coming home, back to your Marcus? I miss your mouth, your lips, your sweet breath." "Soon, darling," Gina says. "This is my vacation. Like you, I need to get away." "Like me?" he says. "I haven't gone anywhere." "But you have, Marling," she says, "you do, every day at your desk, you go away. But time flies, you know. I'll be back before you know it." "How are Assya and Bernie?" he asks. "Just fine," she says. "We gossip about you." "What do you say?" "Oh, Marling, only good things. How's Oscar?" "So-so. It doesn't look good. And Lottie won't see people, so . . ." "Maybe it's for the better, Marcus. She wants her privacy." "Yes, I guess you're right."

When they hang up, he feels such a tenderness toward her, he goes into the bathroom and rearranges her things on the counter, her creams and lotions, her combs and brushes.

Marcus turns from the window and goes back to his desk. Maybe he should call Oscar again. But Oscar, just like Lottie, wants time to himself, time with Lottie. "Sorry, Marcus," he said the last time they spoke, two days ago. "I don't feel like talking. I'll call you." "All right," Marcus said. "I'm here if you need me."

At his desk, seeking comfort, he flips through the pages of his notebook and finds Shklovsky, Einstein, and Proust.

Viktor Shklovsky: "Birds hold fast to a branch even when they sleep. People should hold fast to each other that way."

Albert Einstein: "My passionate interest in social justice and social responsibility has always stood in curious contrast to a marked lack of desire for direct association with men and women . . . the wish to withdraw into myself increases with the years . . . I lose something by it, but I am compensated for it in being rendered independent of the customs, opinions and prejudices of others."

Marcel Proust: "Those who have created for themselves an enveloping inner life, pay little heed to the importance of current events. What alters profoundly the course of their thinking is much more something which seems to be of no importance in itself and yet which reverses the order of time for them, making them live over again an earlier period of their life."

His book, he thinks, will be a copyright nightmare.

He goes out for a walk. He locks his door and takes slow, deliberate steps to the elevator, as one who's been let out after long months in solitary confinement. He feels old and young at the same time. He feels his spirit, what he thinks is his spirit, agitating upward in his chest, very close to the surface, very close to the depression in his throat. It's as if his inner wings are flapping, seeking an opening—when he steps outside, he'll see everything with new eyes. On the ninth floor the elevator stops, and a young woman and her dog join him. Both he and the woman observe the dog. He feels that perhaps he should say something, if only to hear himself talk. He looks up. The young woman looks up, too. They smile.

He says, "Dogs are such funny creatures. What breed is it?"

"Pekingese," says the woman.

He nods. "Of course," hoping to cover up his ignorance.

As they reach the second floor, the dog inches closer to the door and excitedly sniffs the ground.

"It's amazing," he offers, "how they know we're reaching ground level."

"Yeah," the woman agrees. "They're smart."

The door opens, and they step out into the lobby. The woman and her dog go outside, he goes to check his mail. He sifts through the envelopes. Nothing urgent. A statement from his broker, a museum postcard from his daughter. The rest is junk and he dumps it in the tall receptacle. When he comes out to the foyer, he signals Ivan, the new doorman, not to bother, and pulls the door himself. The door is quite heavy, heavier than he remembers, and for a moment, due to the effort, he feels a bit dizzy. His eyes, although open, register nothing but blankness. Not wishing Ivan to notice, he steps outside, blindly, trusting his instincts to take over until he is able to refocus. On the street, he stands a moment, then turns left, toward University Place.

He breathes deeply, recollects his senses. He feels as though his senses have been switched around to assume new roles. It feels as though he both sees and smells through his nose, hears and breathes through his ears, sees and tastes with his eyes. He feels like sticking out his tongue to lap the air. Like a dog. When he reaches the corner, he turns right, going south. All bones and stiffness in his body become fluid. He lifts his face to the sun and appoints himself the summer ambassador, the ambassador of good omen, of prosperity and goodwill. At the corner of Eighth Street, two of his neighbors, women in their fifties, stand and chat. He greets them, they greet him. They wear fashionable, ironed white shorts, white T-shirts, and dark sunglasses under their baseball caps. There's something in their demeanor, in their smile, that makes him think they're eternal: they've always stood there, and always will.

It's five o'clock in the afternoon, the sun is still quite strong, but a gentle breeze feels pleasant on his cheeks, sneaks up his back under his old Hawaiian shirt. He likes the fact that most of his clothes have been with him for years. When he opens the doors to his closets and looks at his trousers, his jackets, his suits and ties, his laundered shirts, his sweaters, his socks and shoes, he wonders why in heaven he ever bought all this stuff, most of which he rarely wears anymore, most of which they'll find in his closets once he's gone. His daughter will come, go through everything, keep one or two sweaters as souvenirs, perhaps a silk scarf, a tie, then call in the truck of the Salvation Army.

But he has no plans for departing very soon, not in this fragrant summer, this just-right breeze. He shouldn't be thinking about death, although you never know. You could be run over by a speeding bicycle, just like the one zooming past his nose as he crosses the street. When he reaches Waverly Place, he decides to turn back and walk north on the east side of the street.

Two young girls in tight mini-dresses come toward him. They swing their hips in a manner he thinks insouciant, European, as they chew on chunks of baguette they tear out of a paper bag. He smiles at them, almost working up the nerve to ask for a piece of their crusty baguette. But they go past him, he doesn't ask for a piece, but considers that maybe he'll stop at the gourmet shop and buy a baguette, one of those very thin and crispy ones. Or, he may eat out, at the bistro around the corner.

Two more chapters, he thinks. Perhaps three. Unless something he hasn't foreseen happens. He spots a beggar and fishes in his pockets for change. The beggar has spotted him, too, his good intentions, and extends his arm farther out. But he is still fishing in his pockets, a bit embarrassed now as he stands there, facing the beggar's hand. Not enough coins. He takes out his wallet and puts a dollar in the open palm.

From the bottom of his heart, the beggar says, "God bless you," and Marcus nods in thanks and continues walking, his heart rising in his chest. This has happened to him more than once, that a beggar's thanks or blessing moved and touched him; something is altered in the voice when the "thank you" or "bless you" come in response to a real need having been met. No one else in his life has ever thanked or blessed him as beggars do. Except for his father and mother. When they blessed him or wished him well, he felt it.

A couple of uptown buses are at the station, and he, on impulse, climbs onto one of them. His mind works well on a bus. Perhaps because of the elevated seats. Or the constant motion, a motion over which he has no control, and which requires nothing of him. He doesn't have enough change, but a woman sells him a token, and he lurches forward, halts, then advances to the rear, his balance attuned to the acceleration of the bus. He takes the center seat on the long bench all the way in the back—the worst in the summer because of the heat generated by the motor—from where he can survey the entire bus.

He's the only one in the back; the other passengers, only a few of them, are clustered upfront. But soon, he knows from experience, once they cross Fourteenth Street the bus will fill up.

He's a man on vacation. He crosses his legs and rests his arms on the backs of the adjoining seats. He looks out the windows at the passing scenery: trees at regular intervals, street signs, shop fronts, restaurants, a Laundromat, a barbershop. On the pavement, people, either singly or in groups, walk, stand, point, talk. Often—it's a habit he's acquired since the distant days of Paris—he perceives his own city as if through the eyes of a novice, a first-time tourist, hoping the visitor appreciates, is duly impressed, by the specialness of the city, its conveniences, its people.

The bus stops. People get on, and each person waits his turn, drops the fare in the slot, then advances into the bus. Through the back door, two people, a man and a woman, get off; such orderly conduct is very pleasing to watch.

A woman advances toward the back. She must be, he thinks, a Russian, or Polish, immigrant: she's stout, looks older than her years. Her skirt and her short-sleeved shirt are nondescript, except for the fact that their colors clash in a strange blend of purples, reds, and greens. Another woman, this one young and pretty, also advances toward him, toward the rear. She notices him, and he senses her hesitation: the fact of his sitting there with his arms outstretched, watching her, alters her step, makes her self-conscious; she'll hurriedly pick a seat so as not to appear fastidious about such a trivial matter as a favored bus seat.

He watches the Russian woman. She has taken the seat facing the backdoor and from her large, black plastic bag she brings out a small nylon bag. Soon, she's knitting: one needle jabs across the other, into one loop, then another. He listens for the soft click when the two needles meet, a sound he remembers from childhood. He builds a life around her: he sees her kids, her husband, her kitchen. Every so often she stops the knitting, stretches the tiny loops across the needle and pulls at the knitted, would-be sweater. Why is she knitting a wool sweater in the summer? Is she expecting a grandchild in the winter?

The bus is filling up. Even the less popular seats are taken, those that face in, their backs to the windows. Only he still reigns alone on the long bench. The bus turns into Madison Avenue. Someone rings the bell, and on the panel above the driver a red sign lights up: Stop Requested. An elderly woman, compactly dressed in a skirt and a tight-fitting jacket, has just boarded the bus. Gracefully, she advances on her high heels, takes a seat next to the Russian woman and clasps her hands on her small black handbag. He admires her rings, her erect posture, her still shapely knees and calves. Her hair, silvery gray, is pulled back in a chignon. Just like Lottie, he thinks, and his heart contracts. Lottie, who will soon leave this world.

The woman, he thinks, must be in her seventies. She seems frail and yet durable, a woman of the city—unsentimental, tough, and vulnerable.

A click of bracelets. She has unlatched her purse and it opens like the mouth of a fish. Her red-polished fingers disappear in the purse, moving things, looking for something. He looks on with greedy eyes. He's always coveted the feeling of busy-ness women manage to convey with their hands, their ringed fingers, as they look for something in their bags, as they gather things and move them about, like sheets of paper, books, paperclips. He thinks women must revel in it themselves, this feeling of busy-ness. Often it seems that they prolong the action, the gesture their hands are engaged in, delaying its completion. Women, of

course, have a special relationship with hands, theirs and other persons',
for the hands' role is to hold, contain, soothe, set things aright.

Her hands are still busy, moving objects he cannot see. He
watches her thin, tan wrists, and visualizes the contents of her purse,
inhaling the perfumed scent of its lining.

She finds what she's been looking for: a small mirror in a silver
frame. She looks at herself, sideways, and, with her other hand, pats
the chignon, as if checking its firmness. She must be, he thinks, on
her way to a concert, or the ballet. When he gets home, he'll sit
down and describe her. Before or after he eats his dinner? Before,
he decides. It is suddenly urgent. He wants to do her right. And the
immigrant woman. She is still knitting. Has she noticed the elegant
American at her side?

They are crossing Forty-second Street, and he stands up, presses
the yellow strip to activate the bell. He pulls his shirt away from his
back and shakes out his legs, discreetly smoothing out the seat of his
pants. At the door, he glances one last time at the two women. Only
the elderly lady acknowledges him. She looks up at him and smiles.
Her smile is warm and friendly. He smiles back—it is that kind of
day—and gets off the bus.

Thirty-Three

Lottie passed. She swallowed her pills and faded away, with John and Oscar holding her hands. She was frightened, yes, Oscar says, but she was ready to go. He held her hand, astonished how small it felt, so thin and soft. Then slowly life withdrew from the hand. "It didn't feel like much, you know," Oscar says. "Maybe because her hand retained its warmth for a while longer. Unless it was my own."

Oscar tells him this over the telephone, and Marcus tries to picture it, these last minutes together; and as he listens to Oscar, he's amazed that Oscar's voice doesn't break, doesn't falter. Perhaps, he thinks, Oscar is in shock, just as he was those first days after letting go of his mother's breath.

"John," Oscar says, "has flown to Arizona to be with his daughter." "Do you want me to come over?" Marcus asks. "No," Oscar says. "My place is a mess." "Then you come over here. Tonight. Or whenever. I'll make dinner. Or we'll go out, if you prefer." "We'll see," Oscar says.

He calls Gina in the Berkshires; she sounds so happy, so free of worry, he hesitates a moment, thinks perhaps he shouldn't tell her. But he knows it won't do, so he tells her about Lottie, about Oscar, John, and Gina begins to cry, so he stops talking and listens to her cry. She wants to come home, to be with Oscar, to see Lottie one more time. She'll take the train right away. Lottie has been cremated, he tells her. "How awful," she says. "How awful. I hate cremations, they're morbid.

It's as if you never existed." "That's the way she wanted it," he says. "Do Jews cremate?" she asks. "No," he says. "I don't think so." "I don't want ever to be cremated, you hear me?" "Of course not," he says. "Stop talking like that. And, you don't need to come home. Stay till the end of the week and drive back with Assya and Bernie." "Are you sure?" she asks. "Yes," he says, and smiles as he pictures her, curled in an armchair, the receiver pressed to her shoulder. He knows she hates trains and loves cars. She's been gone almost a month, and every so often he's been aching for her, but now that her return is imminent, the pressure, the urgency, is lessened. "Kiss Oscar for me," she says. "I will," he says, and they hang up.

"Strange things are happening to me," Oscar says when he arrives in the evening. His eyes, Marcus notes, are glassy, and he's unstable on his feet.

"What things?" Marcus asks.

"Things." Oscar waves his arm.

They enter the living room and Oscar heads for the bar.

Marcus says, "We need to get some food into you. You've been drinking."

"Drinking? Oh, *drinking*." Oscar pours himself a drink and takes the bottle with him to the couch. "In case you haven't heard, alcohol is medicinal, a medicinal blessing. Think about the very first time a human got a buzz. Imagine just picking a leaf of some hallucinogenic herb, and puff, you're gone on a tour. A freebie. Did you ever wonder how it is that the mouth never tires? We talk and talk, we talk so much, but these muscles here, they never tire. We could go on all night, all day, and our mouths won't tire."

"That's a sobering thought," Marcus says. "Let's go out and grab something to eat."

"Out? Hell, no. The streets are too crowded. Have I told you that?"

"Told me what?"

"That the streets are too crowded. In olden times they were smart, they had walls and gates to keep outsiders out, to keep a lid on the number of people in one crowded city. This is just a tiny island, you know. If we don't control the growth, our weight alone will drag us down. We'll sink in the ocean, buildings and all. The earth can take only so much abuse."

"I'll make a couple of sandwiches, all right?" Marcus says and turns to leave the room.

"No. Wait for me," Oscar says, picks up his glass, the bottle of Scotch, and follows Marcus into the kitchen.

"There isn't much, I'm afraid," Marcus says, pensively, as he pushes things around on the refrigerator shelves. "Unless we order in. Maybe sushi? Chinese?"

"Not appealing," Oscar says, rocking back and forth in his chair.

"Well, how about a can of beans? I've been having beans lately . . ."

"Good idea. Beans."

"You just sit there and relax. Stop moving so much. Here's some cold water, it will do you good." Marcus sets the glass in front of Oscar and stands watch, waiting for Oscar to drink it down.

"It's too cold," Oscar says, touching the glass.

"Drink it. It will clear your head."

"My head is clear, but for the sake of friendship." He takes the glass and sips slowly, cringing and grimacing. "It shoots straight into your brain. The cold. The ice. It goes up your nostrils and breaks your skull. What a waste. The good alcohol I poured into myself."

"Not to worry. You'll get more after you eat."

"Yes, mommy," Oscar says, and they look at each other as if waiting for something to happen. Oscar shrugs, twists his mouth in a smile. "It's all right to mention her. She is only dead. Besides, with me she's alive. It's all right for us to talk about her."

"Absolutely." At the sink, Marcus washes out a head of Boston lettuce. The soft, pale green of the leaves stirs something in him, and he turns to Oscar, extending a dripping leaf. "Look at this exquisite shade of green."

"You're wetting the floor," Oscar says. He takes the leaf, nods his head, then returns the leaf to Marcus. "Wash it again. My hands are not clean."

"You're such a pedant."

"I can't help it."

Marcus shakes the water out and breaks the leaves over a glass bowl. His novel comes to his mind, the three hundred or so pages of it. Soon, he'll have to go back to the beginning, start all over again.

"How do you Jews mourn?" Oscar calls out. "Oh, you have your famous Shiva and you light those candles."

"Yahrzeit candles, yes."

"What is Yahrzeit? Sounds German to me."

"It is," Marcus says. "It means, literally, time of the year, the anniversary of someone's death."

"And what does it do? I mean, it burns, obviously, just like any regular candle, like the ones we light in church."

"They burn," Marcus says, "for twenty-four hours. And when you light them, you ask God to pay special attention to the souls of your dead. You light them five times a year."

"Five times a year! How much do they cost?"

"Fifty cents, I think." Marcus laughs.

"But why five times? You said on the anniversary . . ."

"The anniversary, and also on Yom Kippur, and during the three holidays that commemorate our pilgrimage to the temple in Jerusalem. That's when you remember your dead, you light the candle, you go to Yizkor service in temple. It's quite moving, you know, the Yizkor service. You should come with me one day."

"Maybe I'll light a Yahrzeit, it can't hurt."

"Here." Marcus pulls open a cabinet and hands Oscar a Yahrzeit candle. "I'm well stocked. I buy them by the case."

"You'll make a Jew out of me yet."

"I wouldn't do that to my worst enemy."

Oscar chuckles. "But why would you use a German word for something as personal as a parent's death?"

"I don't know, actually. Maybe it's Yiddish."

The beans are ready, and Marcus, his hand in a thick glove, removes the pan from the stove. He pours the beans into a bowl and sets it on the table, as well as bread and salad.

"You're quite handy in the kitchen," Oscar says.

"I'm a good disciple—Gina's. By the way, I meant to tell you. She sends her love. I had to talk her out of cutting her vacation short and coming home."

"When is she coming back?"

"This weekend."

They eat in silence, Oscar alternately gobbling his food and fanning his mouth. "This is delicious. I've decided: I'm moving in with you."

"Sure." They laugh.

"How's your novel?"

Marcus sighs. "I have my good and bad moments. Sometimes I think I'm wasting my time. But then there are moments when I think that someone up there is guiding me, guarding my steps, making sure my novel gets written. Anyway, I'm almost done with the first draft. But then, of course, it starts all over again."

"I have to hand it to you, Marcus." Oscar points his fork. "Sticking with it and all. The discipline involved. The second draft should be easier, I think?"

"Easier, no, but hopefully better. By now, I know my characters a little better, but we have yet a long way, a long future together. I think the fifth or sixth draft might be easier. That's what's good about our work: we bring to the beginning the acumen of the end."

"Not bad." Oscar takes a deep breath and looks down at his plate. "You were right. I feel much better. Clearer in the head." He resumes eating. "You say you know your characters a little better. What are you going to do for them?"

Marcus thinks. "Well, it's like . . . No, what you try for is this. You want to give them the spotlight. You want to give them a chance to have their say, reveal themselves, show their worst and best sides. That's a chance they missed in life, in what we call real life. In real life, you're snatched from yourself. You're not allowed the freedoms, the attentions you crave. So in the novel you cheat a little. You let your characters take center stage. You let them have the last word."

They've finished eating, and Oscar leans in his chair, resting his hands on his stomach. "You know," he says, looking straight at Marcus. "Sometimes I think that I come very close to loving you. Sometimes you just do it, you say these things."

Marcus laughs, a deep, contented laugh. "I love you, too, actually, now that you've mentioned it."

"Well." Oscar reaches for the bottle and stands up. "I've been very good, you have to admit, drinking your water. I think this calls for a glass of something."

"In a minute. You go ahead. I'll clean up here."

Later, in the living room, sipping brandy, Oscar says, "You know, in the books I read, men don't talk the way we do, the way you and I talk. I'm sure I've never read one man saying to another, unless they're lovers, or father and son, I love you."

"Maybe. I myself can't recall offhand, so let it be a first, if it is a first."

"You're not going to put us in your book," Oscar says.

"I don't know. Why not?"

"I don't know."

"So."

Oscar tips his glass. "To Lottie, then."

"To Lottie."

"Life is so cheap. When I think of her now, of the void she's left behind, I mean, the space she occupied, the space that's now empty, not in my mind, but in the physical world, I think of those figures, those cardboard figures in amusement parks you shoot at for a prize. Once your bullet hits them, they drop out of sight, and you're left staring at a blank, at a black hole of nothing, of darkness. And, as if to compensate you—after all, it's an amusement park—they send you away with a teddy bear."

Marcus nods. He likes what Oscar says, and he locks it somewhere in his brain to make sure he remembers it.

"But she occupies a space in us," he says. "Are we going to have a memorial service?"

"No. She was very clear and adamant: no funeral, no idiotic memorials. John has her ashes, and that's that. When he passes, the ashes come to me. End of story."

"Tough till the end, our Lottie. We could, of course, sit Shiva."

"Let's consider this our Shiva. To Lottie."

"To Lottie." Again, they raise their glasses.

"You know," Oscar continues. "Last night I had a most fantastic dream. Short and fantastic." Oscar pauses—dramatically, it seems to Marcus.

"Well," Marcus finally says. "Are you going to tell it?"

Oscar laughs. "Look at you. I wish you could see your face. You're so eager."

"Of course I'm eager, anybody would be. You begin to tell me something, and then you stop."

"Once I tell it, you'll wish it were yours."

"Fine. Just tell it."

"I dreamt," Oscar says, "that me and my brain are engaged in a leisurely conversation—you might say like the one you and I are having—and my brain says to me, Let me show you what I can do."

"And—?"

"That's it. That's the whole dream."

Marcus nods again. Indeed, he likes this kind of dream. This, too, he resolves, he must remember. He's thinking about his tape recorder at the bottom of his closet. "You're right," he says. "I like it. I think I should tape you—you're overflowing tonight."

Oscar laughs. "I can see your mind working, plotting, thinking."

"Right now," Marcus says, "in my mind, I'm not plotting or scheming, I'm merely remembering that you've left your Yahrzeit candle in the kitchen. You have to light it when you get home."

"I will. Thanks for reminding me. You're good with things like that."

"What things?" Marcus asks, although he dimly guesses the answer.

"Little things. Things nobody worries about. But. Talking of Yahrzeit. We goyim, or at least this goy, have a funny feeling about your customs. It's a funny feeling mixed with the uncomfortable suspicion that your rituals are the more valid ones, and that Christianity is child's play compared to Judaism. And that's what makes us so . . . I don't know. Unlike the Jews, we gentiles, including our brethren the Muslims, have a rich and bloody history in the art of propaganda and proselytizing."

"Yes," Marcus agrees. "Hence your great numbers."

"In a way, you Jews are a constant reminder of our plagiarism. Therefore we must persecute you—eradicate our guilt. But, enough about the Jews. Although"—a new thought strikes him—"if we were all Jews, the world wouldn't be in such a mess."

"Who knows? One way or another we were meant to suffer. Suffer, and tell stories about it. Kill and destroy then build again. Maybe we learn something in the process. Maybe there's a purpose. As for me personally, I sometimes think I've missed the real point of living, of what it means. But when I remember that cynicism and corruption are the law of the fittest and the land, I know I don't wish to participate. Let me read you something." Marcus stands up and goes into his bedroom, then comes back with Walser. "This is relevant to what we've been discussing. Listen. 'Often I walked in the neighboring forest of fir and pine, whose beauties, wonderful winter solitudes, seemed to protect me from the onset of despair. Ineffably kind voices spoke down to me from the trees: You must not come to the dark conclusion that everything in the world is hard, false, and wicked.'" Marcus looks up at Oscar. "And a little bit further. 'Into society, that is, where the big world foregathers, I never went. I had no business there, because I had no success. People who have no success with people have no business with people.'"

Marcus shuts the book and looks at Oscar.

Oscar nods. "You're really serious about this stuff, aren't you?" By now, Oscar, again, appears to be losing it. His eyes are watery and he is slurring his speech.

"What do you mean, serious?"

"Just that, serious. I'm gaining new respect for you," Oscar says, reaching for the bottle.

"It's about time," Marcus says, thinking he should remove the bottle from the table.

"About time?"

"That you showed some respect." Marcus smiles.

"Yeah." Oscar fills his glass. "Better late than never. Never. What a difficult word. If I may have a say, life in this world invites us to feel rejected, to want to cry out against injustice, it is not just the privilege of writers. I mean, I understand what your author there says." Oscar hiccups. "But, but, in this great city of ours, you feel slighted when a cabbie passes you by and picks up some other slob, even though you were the first to spot and hail him. And only too often we're mortally intimidated by waiters and store clerks. There's no way out. But, that's life, we say, and drink up. To Life!" He raises his glass. "I forget who said it, but whoever said it, could have joined this table. He said he drinks to drown his sorrows, but the damn things have learned to swim."

The two of them explode, banging the table with their fists. "Hee-hee-hee. Have learned to swim . . . Have learned to swim . . . Stop. I can't laugh anymore . . ."

At last they calm down. Marcus goes into the kitchen to get some more ice water.

"They say," Oscar says, taking the glass, "that ice is not good for you. I need to pee."

"Go ahead. You know the way."

Marcus leans in his chair and rests his head. The beginning of a headache, of what he thinks might turn into a headache, begins to pound in his head. Aspirin, he thinks. We'd better take some aspirin. This is some night. Tomorrow is shot.

Oscar is back in the room, taking the couch. Marcus says, "We need to take aspirin."

"What for? I'm perfectly fine."

"Tomorrow you'll wake up with a headache, a hangover."

"I never think about tomorrow when I drink. I never get hangovers."

"Lucky you."

"Do you get them?"

"Occasionally, yes."

"Then go ahead, take an aspirin."

"Maybe later. I don't feel like moving."

"Me neither."

After a silence, Marcus asks, "What are you thinking about?"

"Something I heard today."

"Yeah? What was it?"

"The art critic S.C. Hall—you wouldn't know him, I don't think, he is not in your field—once remarked that while French nudes, in sculpture, look as if they had just taken off their clothes, Greek nudes look as if they had never put them on. Good, no?"

"I'm filled with admiration. I should get my tape recorder."

"You can't move."

"Right."

"Maybe I am the true writer between us."

"Possibly."

"No," Oscar says. "I leave the field to you. So long as, in moments of solitude and quiet, you remember me, your good friend Oscar."

Again they laugh, bang the table, hold their sides. Marcus wipes his tears with a napkin. "What a night," he says.

"Now you." Oscar blows his nose. "You give me a good one."

"The night is yours, Oscar."

"Come on, think of something." Oscar puts a hand to his chest and hiccups.

Marcus thinks. His memory lights up. "As a matter of fact, I do have something for you. Today, sharpening my pencils, I suddenly got a whiff of the graphite, and the scent, instantly, transported me to the room, the wooden bench, I occupied as a first grader. Remember our notebooks? We were allowed only pencils then. And we labored so hard, doggedly, as only children can, pressing the pencil onto the page, wanting to get it right, the shapes of letters, the spelling, the numbers from one to ten. Looking back, I often wonder how I knew to do the things the way I did them."

"You just did them," Oscar says laboriously, his head bobbing.

"I think," Marcus says, "I'd better get you to bed. You can stay here if you like."

"No, I'm fine. It is just my tongue, it feels huge in my mouth. That's our life, see, slapstick. We improvise. Here and there we find trail markers others have posted. But it's all slapstick, my friend, from beginning to end. We constantly bump into the hard wall of our consciousness, clash with what we perceive to be reality. Go on, talk to me, it's soothing."

"Do you want ice cream?"

"Ice cream," Oscar says. "That's a thought."

Between them they split a container of chocolate ice cream and proceed to devour it.

"Remind me," Oscar says. "Did we finish talking about your novel?"

"I don't remember. I think we did."

"Hmmm," Oscar says.

"What are you hmmming about?"

"This is good ice cream."

Marcus laughs. "I thought you were hmmming about my novel."

"No. I only hmmm about things I know. I know ice cream and this ice cream is good. How about if you wrote a novel going backward? I don't mean plotwise, like flashbacks, but I mean from the point of view of development, a sort of thinning out. You begin with the sum total right upfront, you deliver it at the outset, and then you go backward, retreating to the smallest, most insignificant detail, so that by the end of the book the characters, and I guess the writer, step out of the book and vanish. That's what you should try in your next novel."

Marcus laughs. "In the next one, maybe. Right now I'm trapped between the pages of this one. I really think I should put you to bed."

"No, no, not yet, I'm feeling good. I don't want this to end. Everything ends. I don't want this to end."

"All right."

"Aren't you having a good time?"

"I'm having a great time."

"That's fine, then. As long as we're having a good time."

Marcus laughs. "You're great when you're drunk. How come I haven't known this about you?"

"I'm getting better all the time."

"Like wine."

"Oh, wine, I don't know. I don't like wine. It puts me to sleep."

"Yeah, me too."

"Maybe a glass with a meal."

"Exactly."

"You see, I told you, our mouths never tire, never tire. That's why you see people talking all the time. They say talk is cheap, but it isn't. I appreciate talk."

"Me too."

"As long as you keep your novel simple. Readers recognize beauty and beauty is simple. Like the pure exquisite lines in a beautiful face. You can taste it without touching it. Readers appreciate simplicity."

"You're right."

"Although stupidity, too, has its place. I think I got this one from one of your quotes: Nothing is as mysterious as stupidity. I mean, it could be stupendously amazing. Write a novel about a stupid man. About his clinging to life. About his bewilderment, his small desires. Write about me, if you like. Permission granted."

"I'll use it, thanks."

"Write about ambition, pride, vanity. Write about our fear of letting go. Write about these things and even I will read you."

They laugh.

"Tell me," Oscar continues. "After a night like tonight, what remains? A vague memory? A still life?"

"More than that, I think." Marcus watches as Oscar lets his head drop back against the couch. "There's a residue, like the affection one carries for one's friend."

"Watch out, don't go overboard," Oscar says. His eyes droop

shut. "You're beginning to sound like a writer. And how does it end, your novel?"

"I guess I'll bring it to a point from where you can say, And they lived happily ever after."

"And if you could have a wish, one wish, and a writer were to grant it, carte blanche, what would it be?"

"Good question," Marcus says and takes a moment. "I wish," he says slowly. "I wish I knew every word in the dictionary. Every one of them, down to the last one, the last, absolute word."

Oscar has fallen asleep. Marcus goes into the bedroom and returns with two pillows and a blanket. He takes off Oscar's jacket, then swings him around, bringing his feet up on the couch. He takes off Oscar's shoes, his socks, unbuckles the belt and slowly pulls it off, loop by loop. To his surprise, Oscar's odor, although heavy and rancid with alcohol, doesn't repulse him. On the contrary, he feels very protective of his friend, loving in fact. He carefully places the pillows under Oscar's head, covers Oscar with the blanket, and stands there a moment, watching over him. He then switches off the light and goes into the bedroom.

Thirty-Four

September already! He has begun the second draft, magically, with renewed energy, consulting the pages of the first draft only when in trouble and needing a crutch.

It is all in his head. His imagination, Gina says, but he, so he tells her, prefers to say "in his head" because the word *imagination* has confounded him since early youth. "I understand it as a word," he explains, "a word we use lightly in everyday speech, like when we say, 'Oh, you've got no imagination.' I even understand it as a philosophical shortcut, but when applied to writers it doesn't feel exact. It feels to me like an unnecessary mystification. Obfuscation," he adds a moment later. "A better, more exact term to explain the writer's work would be: concentration." "If you say so." Gina smiles. She is knitting baby socks because Assya is pregnant. In fact, Gina has become motherly: she walks and speaks at a slower, gentler pace as if she were the one pregnant. And even though she is terrified of giving birth—all that pain, all that blood, all that *water!*—she asks him one night, biting the hard nail of her thumb, what he thought of . . . well . . . what would he think if she got pregnant? "Oh," he says, "I'd love it." "Really?" she asks. "Really," he says. "Assya tells me," Gina says, "there's a woman at the doctor's office who's forty-nine and pregnant." "See? We can do it," he says, and she nods thoughtfully.

The two of them, as a matter of fact, seem to have acquired a new mildness. When she came home from the Berkshires he whispered in her ear, "Let's nidificate." "Let's what?" she asked. "Nidificate." "It sounds," she said, "like fornicate." "Well," he said, "it's close. Nidificate—let's build a nest." "Is this a proposal?" she asked. "You say the word," he said.

He asks her, "What is the imagination? Where is it?" "In the dictionary." She laughs. "Look it up," she says, and resumes her knitting. "I won't find it there," he says, "it's not a matter of definition." "You're the expert," she says. "I never argue with experts." "Very funny," he says. "Very funny."

Now, at his desk, he picks up his pocket calendar. Soon the holidays will be here, he reflects as he flips through the mostly empty pages. He thinks of telling Oscar not to bother anymore. So little happens during the year, so little that he needs to record in a calendar. But Oscar is a creature of habit; he'll continue buying one for him, every year, every Christmas.

So little happens during the year, and yet so much is crammed into it: all the thoughts, the emotions, the gestures. All the talk. Interactions. The pain. The deaths. The births. The errands. The worries. The conflicts. The disagreements. The inevitable clashes.

Rosh Hashana. The Ten Days of Awe. Yom Kippur. A holiday he reveres. Although he doesn't consider himself a true believer, he fasts on Yom Kippur, more for his parents and their memory. He attends the Kol Nidre service on the eve of Yom Kippur, and the Yizkor service the following day. He feels a bit self-conscious when he wraps the tallith around his shoulders, feeling somewhat like an impostor, and wonders if the others feel like him. His temple is Conservative, and most of the assembled congregation, he thinks, must be like him: High Holidays Jews. The women and men are well dressed; some of them wear sneakers or canvas flats, as is the custom on Yom Kippur, but most of them wear their everyday leather shoes, and the women wear makeup and jewelry, which, in the old days, and in the more orthodox temples, would be frowned upon.

Gina, too, feels awkward in synagogue, but she comes along, only to please him, and often he fears she may start giggling at the most inappropriate moment, which, she'd later explain, was a nervous reaction to the overwhelming solemnity around her. But when he glances at her, her gaze is fixed on the bima, on the rabbi, on the cantor, and she seems as solemn as everybody else.

So he wraps himself in the tallith and stands facing the ark, pressing the prayer book to his chest, and soon his discomfort dissipates, and he looks around him, looks over the congregation, the men and women, the children who run around, the babies who sometimes begin to wail, and he is filled with pride, with joy, with a kind of exaltation. These are all Jews, he thinks. Jews who want to be Jews. These are everyday, rational, practical people, and here they are, in synagogue, from morning to evening, wrapped in a tallith, a yarmulke on their heads, fasting, praying, swaying and singing. Outside the walls of the synagogue, it may be just another Monday, just another Tuesday, with the usual traffic, the usual transactions. But within these walls the day is transformed, sanctified; he wants to say, *holified.*

When he stands there, looking at his neighbors, he feels privileged to be among them, listening to the rabbi, listening to the cantor's beautiful voice, to the pounding power of singing when the entire congregation joins in. He wants to call out to the world, to the non-Jews. He wishes to invite them all in, show them that Jews are not fiends, nor magicians. If need be he'll shake them; shake the realization into them that Jews are simply Jews, their rituals as elevating as anyone's, their traditions as rich and meaningful as anyone else's.

He joins in the singing; he knows most of the lyrics, most of the tunes. And toward evening, when it is time to sing *Avinu Malkenu,* a song he believes to be everybody's favorite, he and all the others sing it from the bottom of their hearts; sing it with feeling, with love and pleading, each aware of the sound of his own voice, of how it joins with the others, deep and powerful and all-embracing.

When they bring out the Torah scrolls, wrapped in their gilded, embroidered robes, he is filled with reverence for history, for tradition, for ritualistic symbols. In his childhood, when he didn't think in terms of history or tradition, he revered the Almighty, if begrudgingly: he envied Him His eternity, His freedom from worries of death and money. God could have whatever God wanted. God, up there in heaven, did not suffer from colds, didn't go to school, while he, down below, suffered through them.

Some years, he may skip the Kol Nidre service, but he'll never skip Yizkor, for that's when he recites the Kaddish for his parents and for the six million. Often, he has to take a deep breath and look up at the ceiling, pushing back tears, especially when the six million are mentioned.

After Yizkor he feels cleansed, somehow elevated. He and Gina go home, then go back to temple for the afternoon service, for Nehila, the closing of the gates, for the sound of the shofar, the last cry of the congregation for God's judgment and mercy. There's such excitement when the three or four men get on the bima with their shofars, and fathers lift their young ones up in their arms so they can glimpse the stage; and the men put the shofars to their mouths, and the old, primitive sound emerges, long and wailing and piercing, and the men blow the ram's horn for as long as their breaths last, and then it's over, the fast is over: the shaking of hands, children distributing candy, and the slow filing out, toward home, a hot tea, then soup and light foods, so as not to overburden the stomach.

It occurs to him that God, in His mercy, gives man credit: the Jewish New Year opens in festivities and joy, for sinners and tzaddiks alike. It's only ten days later that the Day of Atonement, of settling accounts, arrives. During the Ten Days of Awe, the gates are open and God listens to His people, to their pleas. It is good, Marcus thinks, that man, arrogant in nature, should enter the New Year humbled by the knowledge of his failings. He is given ten days to ask forgiveness from his neighbors, from all those he has hurt during the year, and he, too, is to forgive those who seek his forgiveness. No debts of bitterness and animosity are to remain open.

Earlier, leaving his dentist's office and walking home down Fifth Avenue, he notices an older man, a beatific expression on his face, standing near the door of a department store. He's holding a violin in one hand and in the other, a dollar bill. He is smiling his toothless smile at the bill, like a child who has just, unexpectedly, been given a gift, and he marvels at it, turning the bill in his hand as if making sure it is real. Marcus shifts his gaze and sees the elderly woman who is walking away from the man and his violin, the woman who has just given him the money. Marcus walks behind her, notes her low, gold-rimmed heels, her trendy raincoat, the black bow above her white-blond ponytail. Another Lottie, he thinks, and in his heart congratulates her: Good for you, lady. You've made someone very happy. It's our supreme duty, he thinks further. Bring happiness to others.

He looks around him, at the many people going every which way. In mid-step, they seem preoccupied, engaged. It is fall weather all over again; people begin to lose their summer tans, begin to bundle up, apprehensive about another winter ahead. He feels his heart expand in his chest. Most of them are in a hurry, carrying the moment to wherever they're headed. They run across the street, across the avenue, to catch the last seconds of pedestrian right-of-way, before the light turns green for the oncoming traffic. They don't give it much thought, but they're alive. Relatively speaking, they're well. This year. This day. This hour. He wants to open his arms wide and embrace them all, embrace their poignantly familiar anonymity. He wants to open his arms and take them all in.

Thirty-Five

They all huddle in him. His characters. The whole of humanity huddles in him.

Is he to leave his characters in limbo? Stranded in the desert of their lives, alone in the open, exposed to any hazard? If he has rooted them firmly in their present, in their past, they should be able to make it into the future.

These thoughts invade his mind as he leafs through the pages of his journal. And so, he stops leafing and gazes out of the window, leaving the door open for these and other thoughts to come in and join. But they don't. So he resumes leafing, and his eye catches a quote he has copied from Job: "One dieth in his full strength, being wholly at ease and quiet. . . . And another dieth in the bitterness of his soul and never eateth with pleasure. They shall lie down alike in the dust, and the worm shall cover them."

The worm shall cover them. In a strange way, the words of others, even at their bleakest, comfort him. Reading them, he feels embraced; in the seclusion of his room he feels included. Often he smiles, he nods, as if in company.

It is similar, he thinks, to the feeling he had the night before. He was watching the World Series on TV, and suddenly this commercial came on and filled him with light, with wonder. He no longer recalls what they were advertising, but what filled him with light was the handsome couple on the screen. Young and healthy, robust, and all-American: she, blond hair blowing in the wind, full lips, honest eyebrows, smiling, looking forward; he, short brown hair, clean face, looking at her. Together they presented the image of ideal humanity: good, generous, and vibrant.

Thank God, he thought, that I'm still touched by images. Watching the couple on the screen, he felt a strong stirring of kinship, was reminded of the image of the almost primitive-looking prototypes, male and female, their arms raised in greeting, catapulted into space in spacecrafts. He thinks there's something very moving in this mute, hopeful appeal, in the buoyant and friendly picture the human race wishes to project through these benevolent messengers, who are meant to portray human presence on earth; human presence as courageous, valiant, and peace-loving. The image is moving, and naive, for it is naive to be so hopeful, to want to believe there's something, someone, out there, someone who could help and love humanity.

The thought crosses his mind that some day, in the very far future, these mute prototypes may be all that's left of man's endeavors.

No, no, he rejects the thought. A thousand times, No! Not even in a million years.

The old man flips through the pages, laden with words. Unlike blank, virgin pages that fall in clumps, as if timidly aware of their nakedness, these ink-filled pages fall individually, with a swishing sound that's very pleasing to the ear. It also pleases him to see the straight lines of the pointed, accentuated, tight script. When he writes in his journal, he pays special attention to his handwriting, as if the stuff that really matters is being engraved there.

Samuel Johnson catches his eyes: "The natural flights of the human mind are not from pleasure to pleasure, but from hope to hope."

Hope to hope.

Deep in thought, he sticks a paperclip in his mouth and leans back in his chair. The paperclip feels cold and smooth on his tongue. He has a distant, yet definite, memory of himself, or someone else, saying, Paperclips have many duties. And indeed they do. A paperclip, when unhooked, serves him as a toothpick, or as a handy tool when he needs to rub an itch in his ear. Of course he does so with the utmost care, mindful of his doctor's dictum, years and years ago, that nothing smaller than one's elbow should be inserted in one's ear.

Memories fill his head. Not in orderly compartments, but in a friendly, hazy mass. They are all there. Will they all go to waste when he is gone?

Lately he's been a bit absentminded. This morning, drawing up his pants, he suddenly realized he hadn't put on his underwear. He had to pull down his pants, put on his underwear, and then draw up his pants again. Such occurrences annoy him, for they take up time; but later, as he remembers them, they fill him with affection, for himself and for the occurrence itself, as a thing that happened, and was then remembered.

He now notices the pigeon perched on the outer ledge of his window. A gentle wind ruffles the white-gray down of her feathers, but she stands, unperturbed, in profile. As he contemplates her, he gets the distinct feeling that she contemplates him back. Her head cocked sideways, she eyes him, quizzically it seems, her small, perfectly round black eye fixed on him like the blank eye of a camera lens.

Such a tiny head, he reflects. And no face to speak of. No lashes, no lids, just a button of an eye tacked on either side of a narrow profile.

Nothing lasts. Not the good, not the bad. He has no regrets. He lives his life in the only way he can; in the way only he can live it. Too bad it, too, will have to end.

About the Author

Tsipi Keller was born in Prague, raised in Israel, and has been living in the United States since 1974. The author of eight books, she is the recipient of several literary prizes, including a National Endowment for the Arts Translation Fellowship, and a New York Foundation for the Arts Fiction Award. Her novels include *Retelling* and *Jackpot,* and her most recent translation collections are: *Poets on the Edge: An Anthology of Contemporary Hebrew Poetry* and *The Hymns of Job & Other Poems.*